Ignited
in
Iceland

Victoria Walker

For anyone who has been to Iceland…
and anyone yet to discover it.

x

1

Iris Bellingham reclined in her camping chair, the canvas shade above her doing nothing to diminish the heat of the mid-afternoon Hawaiian sun. With her eyes closed and the sun baking her from the outside in, she found it easy to imagine that she was on a beach somewhere else on the archipelago, rather than at work. It wasn't that Iris didn't love her job. She loved it so much that it didn't feel like a job at all, but after a few weeks of crunching data in a research lab that was so nondescript it could be anywhere in the world, she was craving the outdoors.

Iris worked as a volcanologist and was well aware of how lucky she was to earn a living doing something so niche but so rewarding. All the data she helped to collect and analyse delivered predictability to some of the most volatile places on earth. The fact was that the better she and her colleagues were at forecasting, the safer it made these places for the people who lived there. People relied on her and she was good at what she did.

Today, Mount Kilauea wasn't causing Iris any problems. It had been emitting steam and gases for a few weeks, but the level of activity had been reducing steadily and they had concluded that there was a low probability of anything else happening in the near future. The lack of activity had made her restless and unable to resist the call of the outdoors any longer, so she had suggested a field trip to her younger colleague, Dylan. With the imminent danger of an eruption well and truly off the cards, she wanted to show him where the data they spent all day looking at came from. And so they had spent most of the day watching the instruments that were installed around the caldera of the volcano from the safety of their laptop screens in a small clearing. The canvas sails strung between the spindly trees sheltered them from the sun or the rain, depending on the day. There hadn't been many rainy days in the few weeks she'd been on The Big Island, but when it rained, it really rained.

'Shall we call it a day? If we go now, we can catch the tide.' Dylan had recently started studying at the Hawaiian Volcano Observatory and had been Iris's sidekick for the duration of her visit.

'Dylan, it's almost as if you're not interested in watching the seismometer any more.' She'd been hoping that they might feel some minor tremors, a common occurrence around active volcanos, so that he could get a sense of the magnitude of what they had been looking at for all these weeks on their computer screens. As it was, it had been a very quiet day on that score and he was bored.

'Iris, the waves are calling to me.' He was from land-locked Minnesota and had signed up for surfing lessons the minute he arrived in Hawaii. Iris loved the water so had been happy to tag along with him a few times to nearby Kahaluu beach, where there was a surf school. The water was fierce compared with what she was used to. The beaches she'd holidayed on in the UK had waves which were far more subdued unless there was a storm. Here, she'd been astounded at the size of the breakers, but Dylan didn't seem to be deterred. Perhaps because he had nothing to compare it to. Surfing here was far too intense, but at the end of a day in the lab, a dip in the shallows had been most welcome. Then she'd wait on the beach with a good book.

'Okay,' she said, good-naturedly. 'I think we can safely say nothing's going to happen while we're away.'

'I don't think anything's going to happen, period,' Dylan said. He was fresh out of graduate school and hadn't been in the field long enough to notice the nuances of the data. Today, he was probably right, but Iris had seen his impatience flare over the past few weeks and knew that meant he would likely miss something important. But that was what she was there for, and why he was with her: to learn from her.

'Not today. That's all we're saying.'

'Yeah, okay, Iris. I hear you,' he said with a lazy smile, that if she'd been fifteen, maybe ten years younger, she'd have had trouble resisting.

'Let's pack up then.'

They collected up their small amount of equipment, putting it into foam-lined cases that made it easy and safe to transport, folded up their chairs and took a last look around before they hiked back the short distance to the truck.

'You going to try surfing today?' He was teasing. He thought it was funny that she was wary of the waves and asked her every time they went to the beach.

'Nope, I'm happy watching,' she said with a grin. 'Not you, obviously. The really good surfers.'

'Ouch,' he said, hitting his hand on his chest. 'It kills me that you're not impressed by my skills.'

Iris threw back her head and laughed. 'You're in the wrong place if you're looking to be the best surfer out there.'

'Don't I know it,' he said ruefully.

'Anyway, this might be my last surf trip. I'm probably going to move on now that Kilauea's calmed down.'

'Ah, Iris. Man, I'll miss you.'

3

It warmed her heart that they'd struck up a friendship that mattered to him as much as it did to her. He was the little brother she'd never had.

They loaded their equipment into the truck and Dylan got into the driver's seat, as had become their habit. Iris didn't enjoy driving on the narrow tracks around the caldera, or the wrong side of the road for that matter.

'I'll be back if she so much as rumbles again, but I can't stay when there's nothing happening.'

'There's nothing happening anywhere, except maybe Indonesia and that's the back of beyond.'

'It's beautiful, but it's not the same,' Iris admitted. There were so many places she'd visited that were miles, sometimes days away from civilisation, and most of the volcanoes in Indonesia that showed any sign of activity tended to be those ones. Dylan was right. It wasn't often she could enjoy what any of these places offered because typically the volcano was all there was. 'We can't all be lucky enough to be monitoring a volcano one minute and lounging on the beach the next.'

'Okay, you've just reminded me I live in the most amazing place on earth,' Dylan said with a grin, throwing a huge dust cloud up as he brought the truck to a screeching halt in the car park at Kahaluu beach. It was a perfect afternoon. The sun was glinting off the waves and even though the waves were huge, the water looked inviting.

'With the best job in the world,' Iris added.

'It's different for you. You get to see all the action. I haven't even seen an eruption yet.'

'Stay here long enough and you will. Kilauea is one of the reliable ones. Don't get impatient and leave. The key to seeing an eruption is patience.'

Dylan looked at her sullenly.

'Come on,' she said, jumping out of the truck and then reaching behind her seat for her bag.

'I'm the only volcanologist in the world who hasn't seen an eruption,' he said.

'Oh, come on. There are plenty of you. And can you really call yourself a volcanologist yet?' she teased.

He laughed, his eyebrows lifted in surprise and glee. 'You're brutal!'

'You know I'm right,' Iris said, nudging into him as they walked side by side along the beach towards the surf hire shop. 'Want me to tell you the story of my first eruption?'

'Again?' he asked, nudging her back and grinning.

'Oh, shut up. I might be old and boring, but I'm right.'

'You're not boring.'

'Thanks.'

Iris waited outside the shop while Dylan went in and hired a surfboard, then they dumped their stuff in a pile on the sand and walked down towards the shoreline.

'I might be tempted in for a dip,' Iris said, letting the shallows wash over her bare feet. 'It might be the last time.'

Dylan groaned. 'You're killing me, Iris. Yes, get in here.'

'You go ahead. I need to change.'

He ran into the surf with his board while Iris went back to where they'd left their things and wrangled with her swimming costume while she tried to preserve her dignity under a towel. After the exertion of that, she sat on the sand for a couple of minutes, watching Dylan. He'd improved quite a lot even in the few weeks she'd been coming to the beach with him. When she'd first arrived, he'd still been at the stage of it being hit and miss whether he'd be able to stand up or not, whereas now, he was standing up almost as soon as he caught a wave and for a good few seconds every time.

Before she headed down into the water, Iris took her phone out to check her messages. The local time was ten hours behind the UK, so she and her family were like ships in the

5

night most of the time. They kept in touch with each other through WhatsApp. She and her parents and her older twin brothers had a family chat and messaged every day with news, or in the case of her brother Felix, endless links to random things on TikTok. He was a secondary school teacher, well-versed in all the latest social media trends, and spent far too much time on TikTok as far as the rest of the family were concerned. Finn was the quieter of the brothers and rarely shared anything about his life voluntarily, but he was the brother Iris spoke to more often on a one-to-one basis. He was a brilliant listener, whereas Felix was immediately uncomfortable if anyone shared anything too personal with him. He liked to keep things light.

There were eight unread messages in the family chat, as well as fourteen on a group chat she had with some of the other volcanologists she worked with regularly. Scrolling through, she saw that there were high levels of volcanic activity in south-west Iceland. She clicked on a link from one of her colleagues that took her to the Icelandic Met Office, where she found more of the technical information behind the headline.

'I thought you were coming in?' Dylan stuck the end of his surfboard into the sand next to her. Had she been sitting here that long? It was easy to get distracted once she started looking at data.

'Where's that?' he asked, looking over her shoulder and dripping all over her at the same time.

'Hey!' She swatted him away. 'It's in Iceland. I don't think it's a volcano. It sounds like something else.'

'Could be anything in that part of the world. The place is one giant rift.' He lay down, using one forearm as a pillow and the other to shade his eyes from the sun.

'Mmm.'

He lifted his arm up enough to look at her. 'That's where

you're going next, isn't it?'

'It's tempting. It could be huge. People live there. It's one of the most populated parts of Iceland. It's where all the tourism is centred. I don't remember an Icelandic event being this close to a populated area before.'

Iris's phone rang. She glanced at the screen and answered before it could ring twice.

'Jay.' She was aiming for detached, but it was difficult to keep the excitement out of her voice.

'Hey, Iris,' he said lazily.

'You're calling about Iceland?' The best she could hope for was to take some of the wind out of his sails.

'Oh.' It had worked. 'You've already heard?'

'There's not much point being the world expert in predictive seismic data if I'm not across these things, is there?' She was making herself cringe. Not that any of it wasn't true, but she didn't make a habit of blowing her own trumpet. Jay's constant one-upmanship forced her into making an exception to that rule. Technically, he was her boss, although he was not as qualified as her. He just happened to be in an administrative position of power. They'd been at university together when they were both studying for their Master's degrees and had had an unfortunate — from Iris's perspective at least — kiss which, amongst other things, had led to an unfortunate few weeks of Iris having to avoid him, followed by an unfortunate rest of the year while he constantly undermined Iris to make himself shine. She knew it was because she'd rejected him, but it still surprised her how much of an arse he could be. And the most unfortunate thing of all was that now he was her boss, he thought he'd won the battle for supremacy that had been going on between them for over ten years.

'Right. So you're heading to Iceland, then?'

'Of course. I'm on the next plane to LA.' It was a white lie.

She'd aim to be on the very next plane she could be, but the important thing was for Jay not to realise she was only a couple of minutes ahead of him with the whole situation. If it wasn't her dream job, she'd have been out of his research facility by now, but volcanology was a small world and even if she got a job at a different place, she'd no doubt still come across Jay at some point.

'I assume you've already booked hotels and transport in Iceland?' he asked.

She hadn't and it would be tricky to once she was on the move, but somehow it seemed like an admission of weakness to ask him for any kind of help. 'Yes, thanks.'

'Okay. Well, give me a call when you get there. Let me know how things are looking and I can organise whatever else you need.'

'Thanks.' She rang off before he could say anything else.

'Who was that poor sucker?' Dylan asked.

'My boss.'

'You talk to your boss like that?' His eyes were wide. 'I've never heard you talk to anyone like that. Man, your boss!'

'Well, we were at uni together so he might be my boss, but he's not interested enough in the science to have bothered pursuing a career in the field. He's my boss in as much as he runs the facility where I'm based in the UK.'

'Sounded more like you were telling him what was what, not the other way around.'

'We go back a long way,' was all she was prepared to say on the subject. 'We were never friends, though.'

'Don't worry, I worked that much out,' Dylan said with a grin. 'Makes me feel like a lucky son-of-a-gun to be buddies with you.'

'Oh, shut up.' Iris laughed and roughed his hair, which was full of salt and sand.

'Want a ride to the airport?'

'Yes, please.' She was going to miss Dylan with his easy banter, but they'd cross paths again, she was sure.

'You got it. I'll take my board back and we can go get your stuff packed up.'

While Dylan jogged back to the surf shop with his board, Iris stood and faced the sea, committing the magnificence of it to memory. Hawaii was incredible, and she was going to miss it. Going from the almost guaranteed sunshine to the cold wilderness of an Icelandic spring was going to be a shock.

2

Siggi Ólafsson was lying in bed. He had to go to work, but he had no motivation to. Instead, he was swiping through the photos on his phone from the trip he'd taken to Thailand over Christmas. Now, in March, it seemed like a distant memory and he knew the only way to shake the despondency that had settled on him was to plan his next getaway. He'd been almost everywhere that he'd ever wanted to go. Places he'd heard of as a child and longed to visit, and places he'd discovered on the way. He was a nomad at heart and couldn't settle back at home in Iceland for long. It was beyond him why Iceland was such a popular tourist destination. It was cold, dark and bleak for at least half of the year and that was when most of the tourists came. Why?

He sighed and threw off the covers. He'd be late if he wasn't careful and although his boss, Jonas, was easygoing, he was a stickler for punctuality. Siggi liked and respected Jonas and was grateful that his friend was willing to let him work whenever he wanted to. It helped that Jonas didn't mind too much when Siggi took off for his next adventure with next to no notice.

Yawning, he stepped into the shower and stood under the hot water, enjoying it sluicing over his body, then washed before he switched it to cold with barely a gasp since he was so used to it. Now he was awake. He dried off, grinning at himself in the bathroom mirror as he caught his reflection, before dressing in several layers of clothing. He ate a simple breakfast of overnight oats which he warmed through on the stove, because it was no good going out into the cold without something warm inside you, and drank a large mug of black coffee.

Sighing as he added yet more layers in the form of a fleece jacket, down-filled coat and hat and gloves, he laced his boots, locked the door to his flat and ran down the three flights of stairs to the ground floor. The building overlooked the main road that ran along the sea-front. It was the opposite end of the town to the harbour, where he would have enjoyed a much more interesting view. He was stuck with a grey sea that churned across the road from his third-floor flat, but he wasn't living there enough to need anything more than a bolt-hole and a bolt-hole didn't need a good view.

Siggi shoved his hands in his pockets and began walking briskly along the sea-front towards the middle of the old town where Iceland Adventures, Jonas's company, had their office. Today, Siggi would man the office. He preferred being out on excursions but he'd not long been back from a trip himself and had yet to be allocated those jobs on the rota. In the meantime, answering calls and emails in the office saved Jonas or one of the others from having to fit the admin in as well as leading tours. Jonas's wife, Rachel, sometimes helped in the office too. She ran excursions to artists and craftspeople who opened their studios for tourists, so she was happy to help but was glad to have Siggi back to give her a break.

He unlocked the office and turned the lights on as he went in. Before he did anything else, he turned the coffee machine on, popped a pod in and left it pouring while he took off his coat, fleece and hat. The phone had been diverted to the on-call mobile phone overnight, so Siggi cancelled the divert and fired up the computer. He sipped his coffee while he checked the emails for anything urgent that might relate to today's excursions. It wasn't uncommon for people to have missed a flight or something else that derailed their plans at the last minute. He sent a couple of texts to let his friend Olafur know he would be two people down on his glacier walking trip and another to Brun who was doing an airport collection later on in the morning because an additional four people had booked overnight.

'Hey, Siggi,' Jonas said with his usual grin as he came into the office, clapping his hands together to warm them before he took his coat off.

'Jonas, I thought you were having the morning off.'

'You know how it is,' he said, shrugging.

Siggi knew. Jonas loved showing Iceland to anyone and everyone. He hardly ever had a day off, even in the quieter months. But his love for his country and his business shone through, making it one of the most popular tour companies in Iceland. It helped that most people who worked for him had been friends forever. It made the entire company feel like a family, and the people who went on tours with them ended up feeling they were part of it too. In fact, Jonas had met his wife when he'd collected her from the airport. And Brun had been the tour guide for his girlfriend, Fliss, when she'd visited Iceland for a book tour.

'I'd have had a lie-in,' Siggi said, with a rueful grin.

Jonas laughed. 'You never change. You still live the life of a teenager.'

It was true. Of all his friends, Siggi was the only one who hadn't settled down. He hadn't wanted to, but it had been hard for the last few years, as his friendship group turned from a group of guys hanging out at the pool or the bar to a group of couples. They still went to the bar, less often to the pool, but it wasn't the same and now he felt like an outsider. The fact that he travelled for weeks at a time also meant that he missed out on a lot of what went on in his friends' lives.

'It is getting harder to live "on the road",' Siggi said, making air quotes with his fingers. 'I have started to miss a comfortable bed and hot showers. I think it is a sign I am getting old.'

'Hey, we're all getting older. Once you settle down with someone, I expect travelling will seem less appealing.'

Of course, Jonas saw everything through the lens of his own experience, as did the rest of his friends. As if there was a universal guide to life and happiness, and that eventually Siggi would cotton on and start following the same plan as they all had. Siggi had stopped pointing out that maybe he didn't want to settle down in Reykjavik for the rest of his life. Meeting someone and making a home here didn't appeal to him at all. But he didn't know what he wanted to do instead. That was the problem. The travelling that he had always loved only seemed to emphasise the fact that he had grown out of the typical backpacker lifestyle. Often surrounded by people in their early-twenties who had no worries and their whole life ahead of them, the age-gap more recently felt cavernous. He had nothing in common with them but nothing in common with anyone else in his life either.

'Did you see the IMO report on Reykjanes?' Siggi asked, keen to change the subject. The Icelandic Met Office, the IMO, constantly monitored all the natural hazards in Iceland. For somewhere that expected seventy or so earthquakes every day, the institution was a part of everyday life.

'No.' Jonas frowned and pulled out his phone. 'What's going on?'

'There have been some minor earthquakes north of Hraunvik.'

'That is not good news.' Jonas read the report while Siggi

searched for more information on the computer. 'Seems relatively stable still. We'll keep an eye on things.'

It wasn't unusual to hear reports like this. Iceland existed because the tectonic plates that form the continents of America and Europe were so volatile. The rift between the plates caused constant volcanic activity and earthquakes, and Icelanders were used to living with the geological uncertainty. In return, they harnessed the heat from beneath the earth's surface, and that gave the island cheap heat and power and the ever popular hot springs.

But for Siggi, the news from Hraunvik was close to home. He had family in the town. Family he wasn't close to; a decision he'd made fourteen years ago and regretted ever since. The threat to the town had started him dwelling on what might have been.

'You are thinking of Arna?' Jonas said quietly.

Siggi nodded. 'But what can be done?'

Jonas shook his head. It was a conversation they'd had many times, and there was nothing new to say.

'I have an email here that is strangely related,' said Siggi, peering at the screen.

'Related how?'

'Some woman claiming to be a volcanologist asking if someone can accompany her to the Reykjanes peninsula to set up some equipment. I think she's British.'

'That sounds like a tourist who is hoping to get a front seat for the next eruption or something.'

It wasn't unusual for them to get requests from people wanting a private tour to an eruption. It was something they could do, depending on the situation. They were always guided by the authorities, who were well-versed in dealing with the public wanting to view a lava flow. But these things were so unpredictable that they never agreed to anything outside of these parameters, however much someone was willing to pay. The safety of their clients was paramount.

'I don't understand why they're not working with the IMO or the University? Don't they usually set up equipment themselves?'

Jonas shrugged. 'No one's ever asked before, so I guess so.'

'I will politely reject that request.'

'That is fine with me. Okay, I'm going to the unit to get the kayaks down and check them over.'

Now that it was getting warmer, by Icelandic standards at least, it was time for the company to introduce activities that didn't revolve around snow and ice. It was fun, giving them all more variety in the schedule and the opportunity to get more work. That was why Siggi always made sure he was around at this time of year. It was the best time to build up his savings, ready for his next adventure.

He responded to the email, saying in a much more polite way that they weren't in the business of aiding and abetting amateur volcano hunters. Then he made himself another coffee.

Around an hour later, the door opened and a figure wearing too many layers for him to have any indication of gender or even whether it might be someone he knew, bundled inside, dragging a large leather holdall and a battered suitcase.

'*Halló, get ég hjálpað þér?*'

The person, a woman, Siggi could see once she'd pulled her hood down and taken off her hat, looked at him blankly, but with something in her eyes that Siggi thought, unfortunately, might be anger.

'Do you speak English?'

'Yes, of course. Can I help you?' He smiled in what he hoped was a charming, flirty way that would disarm her.

'I emailed you earlier asking about a guide and driver to take me to the Reykjanes peninsula.'

'Yes. I am very sorry —'

'Look, I'm not some idiot who doesn't know what they're dealing with. If the only reason you've said no is because you think I'm a volcano chaser, I'd appreciate it if you could review my request. You can see I'm genuine.'

Siggi managed to stop a laugh rumbling out of him. Because this woman, her eyes flashing angrily at him, was the complete opposite of what he knew most volcanologists to look like. She was slightly over five feet tall, slim with curly hair that sat above her shoulders and was brown with sun kissed golden streaks in it, much like his own. She had an elfin face which, if he wasn't witnessing the rage behind her eyes, he wouldn't have imagined could look cross.

'With respect, I do not know you are a volcanologist by how you look,' he began.

She tipped her head to one side, thoughtfully, but Siggi could tell from her expression that she was waiting for him to make a comment about gender. And he wasn't going to do that.

'I have met many volcanologists and they rarely work alone. Where is your team? And you are not Icelandic, so why are you not with someone from the Icelandic Met Office, the IMO? That is what would make me think you are genuine.'

Luckily for Siggi, side-stepping the gender stereotyping that she seemed to expect had taken the wind out of her sails. Suddenly, she looked tired.

'I'm sorry,' she said, unzipping her coat and pulling it off, dumping it on a chair while she unzipped the next layer to reveal a well-worn knitted sweater. 'I've just got off a plane from Hawaii and I wanted to go and set up some equipment before a well-meaning colleague from the IMO tells me there is no need and that I can use the data they are already collecting.'

'And their data is not good enough for you?'

She sighed. 'It's not exactly what I want. It's hard to explain.'

'Well, you are convincing me; even so, we cannot take you. That area is out of bounds because of the warnings.'

'Like, literally, they've barricaded the roads in and out of the peninsula?'

'Well—'

'I know they haven't. Do you know how I know? Because they're waiting for me to tell them whether or not that ought to happen. The data they're collecting is brilliant, and it's got them this far, but now there's more at stake. They need my data. It goes deeper and is more accurate. I've been working on my model for years.'

'So,' Siggi peered at the computer and brought the email up from earlier. 'Iris. If I call someone I know at the IMO, they will know who you are?'

'Couldn't you just google me? I'd rather get some stuff set up before I have to start bargaining with people about whether it's a good idea or not. Although that already seems to be happening.'

'Would you like a coffee while I google you?'

'Thank you. That'd be lovely.'

Iris sat on the chair opposite him on the other side of the desk and sipped the coffee he'd made for her while he looked her up.

It was incredible. She actually was a leading expert on predicting eruptions. She was working on a project that was looking not only at whether an eruption was imminent, but more detailed information about what kind of eruption, what kinds of problems might be caused by gases or ash, and even how long it might last.

'Um, sorry, I don't know your name. But are you still looking or have you started looking at something else and forgotten I'm here?'

Siggi looked across at her. The person he'd just been reading about seemed at odds with the woman sat across from him. Perhaps her irritation and impatience was down to jet-lag if she really had just flown in from Hawaii because the woman he'd googled was accomplished in a way that no one could achieve without a kind of quiet determination.

'My name is Siggi and you can consider yourself verified,' he said, smiling, and surprisingly drawing a smile from her in return.

'Does that get me a ride to Reykjanes?'

'I cannot decide that. I need to ask a colleague and also, I would like to check with a friend at the IMO.' He held his hands up as she opened her mouth to protest. 'It will be off the record, but you have not yet seen the lay of the land. I want to know what we are dealing with if I take you out there.'

'Okay, fair enough. So you'll take me.'

'If it all checks out, I will.'

'Thank you. Now, can you suggest somewhere I could stay?'

He had to stop himself from suggesting his place because if he'd heard that question from any other woman he thought was attractive, he'd have seen it as an invitation for him to ask. But she wasn't the kind of woman he would want a casual hook-up with. He could already tell that she was very different from the women he usually had relationships with. Not that he could really call any of them relationships.

'I have a friend who owns a hotel a few minutes from here. Does this look okay?' He pulled up the website for Anders' hotel and pushed the mouse towards her.

'This looks great. Which way is it?'

'Why don't I take you? I can help with your bags.'

'Are you sure? Don't you have to man the office?'

He shook his head. 'I can close for five minutes. It is no

problem.'

'Thank you.' This time, she smiled widely. It transformed her face and made her blue eyes sparkle in a completely different way. Siggi found himself intrigued and desperate for her not to leave the office without him knowing he would see her again.

3

Iris was beginning to wonder whether it had been a mistake to beat such a hasty retreat from Hawaii. It felt like a new low to be standing in a tour office in Reykjavik trying to explain her credentials to an Icelandic man who obviously thought he was still in his twenties judging by the collar-length surfer dude hairstyle that would look more at home on Dylan. And now he was offering to accompany her to a hotel.

As it was, she was too tired to argue. It'd be nice to have some help with her bags. That was the only downside of travelling as much as she did; her whole life was in those bags and she couldn't seem to travel light.

Siggi went through a door at the back of the small office and came back with his coat, which he pulled on, along with a knitted hat which frankly looked ridiculous.

'Nice hat.' She couldn't help herself.

'You think so? My boss's wife knitted it for me.' He tipped his head and shot her a resigned smile.

Iris thought she must be more jet-lagged than she felt because the fact he was wearing the hat so as to not hurt the feelings of the woman who made it for him, never mind what he looked like, was very endearing.

'What can I say? It suits you.'

His blue eyes, a lighter shade than her own, seemed to hypnotise her for a second as his gaze locked onto hers. Then he looked away, breaking the spell, as he reached and picked up her holdall, landing it easily on his shoulder.

'You can manage the case?' he asked.

'Yes, of course.' Iris pulled her own coat and hat back on and wheeled the case back outside, waiting while Siggi locked the door before he led the way along the street.

'I thought it was supposed to be spring,' she said, having to turn her head to stop the wind from hitting her square in the face.

'Yes, it is. This is good weather for Iceland. There has been no snow for two weeks.'

'You still get snow in March?'

'And April. It starts to warm up in May and then it is beautiful.'

Iris clutched at her hood with one hand as they turned a corner and the wind came from a different direction.

'Here,' said Siggi, standing aside to allow her to enter the building first.

'Oh, that was close.'

'It is a small city. Most things are close.'

The foyer was bright and modern but welcoming, with a gently trickling water feature that would be at home in a high-end spa, right in the middle.

Siggi went up to the woman on the desk and said something to her in Icelandic. She picked up a phone and spoke into it, all the time giving Siggi the dirtiest look Iris had ever seen.

'She is just calling Anders,' he said.

'I don't mind checking in. You don't have to get your friend involved. You've done enough already. Honestly, thank you, but there's no need.'

At that moment, a man who Iris assumed to be Anders

came through a door behind the reception desk.

'*Hæ, Siggi!*' he said.

'*Hæ,*' said Siggi, as they had a brief hug. The manly kind where they both clapped each other on the back.

'Excuse us for a moment,' Siggi said to Iris, and the two men started conversing in Icelandic.

It wasn't too much of a stretch for Iris to realise that Siggi was asking Anders for something he couldn't do. He kept shaking his head, but Siggi seemed undeterred. She hoped he wasn't trying to negotiate a discount or something like that. She'd just met the man, so she wasn't sure why he was doing anything to help her out.

'Siggi,' she interjected. 'I'm fine with checking in myself.' She smiled at him in a way she hoped conveyed that there was no need for further discussion, and headed to the desk herself.

'Hello. I'd like to take a room please. For two weeks, but I may need to extend if that's possible?'

Suddenly, Anders was next to her. 'I am sorry. What is your name? Iris…?'

'Bellingham.'

'Please check Ms Bellingham into room fourteen.'

The receptionist raised her eyebrows but took the almost imperceptible nod that Anders gave her in response as confirmation.

'Thank you, Anders,' Iris said.

'You are welcome. You have a very persuasive friend.'

Iris was about to launch into an explanation about how they weren't friends because they'd only met twenty minutes ago, but Siggi had helped her find a lovely hotel in a good location, and in record time, so she wasn't going to start arguing. Instead, she smiled and thanked him again before he disappeared through the door he'd come through.

'I'm also very happy to pay the advertised rate,' she said to the receptionist, out of earshot of Siggi, who was busy looking at his phone. 'I'm not sure what Siggi arranged with Anders, but it's not necessary.'

'He was asking Anders to find a room for you even though we are full,' the woman said without cracking a smile.

'Oh.' Iris was taken aback. 'But you do have room?'

'Anders is going to move someone else's booking to another hotel.'

Siggi had joined her by the desk, overhearing the end of the conversation.

'No, it is not what you think,' he said, his face the picture of innocence as he turned to Iris. 'There is room.'

'I didn't ask you to do anything like this for me. All I wanted was a hotel room. In any hotel. I don't want other people to be inconvenienced because of me.' Because the reception area was quiet, and because by now, Siggi's expression was that of a disappointed puppy, Iris managed to contain her annoyance to a low whisper. 'Why would you try and pull strings for me?'

'I'm sorry. You look tired and this is the closest place. It is good luck that I know Anders.'

Suddenly, almost as if him mentioning it made her realise, she felt tired. Right to her bones.

'I am tired and the thought of having to find another hotel isn't that appealing. If it helps, I'm happy to look for somewhere else tomorrow.' She said this last part to the receptionist.

The sullen woman managed a tight smile and said, 'There is no need, Ms Bellingham. Anders is happy to make the arrangements for you to stay here.' Then she shot Siggi a quick look of disgust.

Siggi was grinning from ear-to-ear, seemingly unbothered about what this woman thought of him. There was probably some history there, Iris realised.

'Do you need help with any bags?'

'I'll take the bags,' said Siggi, before Iris could answer. He was already heaving her holdall back onto his shoulder and had picked up her case and started up the stairs, so there seemed little point in making a fuss.

'Thank you. I think we have it covered.' She gave the receptionist a weary smile in a final attempt to get on her good side, if she had one.

'Your room is on the third floor. Breakfast is between seven and ten and here is a card with the code for access to the rooftop spa.'

Iris thanked her again and headed up the stairs after Siggi, ready to forgive him everything now that she'd found out there was a spa.

'Thank you,' she said, stopping outside room fourteen, where Siggi stood with her bags. 'I wasn't expecting this when I emailed you this morning. Your tour company really goes the extra mile.'

'It's no problem,' he said, putting his hands in his coat pockets. 'Have a good rest. I will reply to your email when I have spoken to the boss.'

'That'd be great, thanks.' She'd almost forgotten why she'd been in his office in the first place. Hopefully, after a few hours' sleep, she'd be refreshed enough to make a proper plan for her visit.

'Nice to meet you, Iris.' He backed away slowly, a half-smile playing on his lips as he shifted his gaze to the floor and then turned away, walking towards the staircase.

Iris watched him walk away, then opened the door to room fourteen and dragged her bags across the threshold. Without even looking out of the window, she drew the heavy curtains across, then stripped off all of her clothes and climbed into bed.

When she woke, she lay still, taking in the sumptuous bed

that had cocooned her as she slept. The mattress was so squooshy, and the duvet so soft and voluminous that she briefly wondered whether to go back to sleep. After another few minutes, her brain kicked in and reminded her she had instruments to set. She reached for her phone and saw that she'd slept for the whole day. It was just after seven in the evening and her stomach was urging her to find something for dinner.

With a sigh, she sat up and pushed the duvet aside, swinging her legs over the edge of the bed and setting her feet down on some thoroughly plush carpet. How much was she paying a night? Perhaps she'd misunderstood, because it had sounded affordable, but it definitely wasn't enough for this level of luxury. Then she remembered the back and forth between Siggi and Anders, rolling her eyes and smiling as it all fell into place. As much as it had annoyed her this morning, she was grateful to Siggi and Anders for showing her — an absolute stranger — such kindness.

After a steaming hot shower, she dressed, then opened the curtains. Reykjavik was before her; silhouettes of buildings, lights twinkling in the darkness, and people bustling along the street below. This place had a heart, she already knew that, and she was excited to explore it.

'Hi,' she said to a different receptionist than the one this morning. 'I wonder if you could suggest somewhere nearby where I can grab some dinner.'

'Of course,' she said, smiling. 'There is a pizza restaurant along the road this way,' she said, gesturing with hand signals. 'Or there is a fish and chips place if you go this way, and then towards the harbour. And there are lots of other places, so you may see somewhere your prefer on your way.'

'I might try the fish and chips.' It was a taste of home that she hadn't had, or even thought about, in a long time.

'Good choice.'

'Thank you. Sorry, what's your name?'

'You're welcome. I am Bríet. Enjoy your meal.'

Iris hesitated, and then asked, 'And who was your colleague on the desk this morning?'

'That was Embla.' Bríet glanced around. 'You came in with Siggi Ólafsson. Embla used to be with Siggi.'

'Oh. Okay. Thanks Bríet.'

'Embla is always angry with Siggi. It is not you.'

Iris stepped from the warmth of the hotel into the fresh air. She took a deep breath, enjoying the feeling of the cold on her face while the rest of her was bundled up in layers of clothes. It was almost the opposite of Hawaii, and most of the other places she went more frequently, where the inside was air-conditioned and cooler than the outside.

She walked along the road, taking the turn she hoped would lead her towards the harbour, but not minding if she took a wrong turn because there was nothing like being somewhere for the first time and taking it all in. Iris always felt that her first impressions of a place stayed with her, and however many times she went back, the same feelings were evoked again and again. In this area of Reykjavik, the streets were lined with two-storey buildings, each a little different from its neighbours and each painted, some in bright colours. The trees lining the street were laden with fairy lights through their branches and spiralling down their trunks, giving a festive feeling even though it was March.

Iris took her time. Although she was hungry, she didn't want to miss anything. She paused now and again to look in shop windows, left the street altogether on a couple of occasions to explore tiny side streets, and made a mental note of a couple of places that might be nice to eat at on a night when she wasn't craving fish and chips like she was since Bríet's suggestion. Then the road opened out onto a wider, busier road with the sea and harbour on the other side and a huge glass building that dominated the sea-front. Curious, and because she was headed that way anyway, Iris crossed the road and walked across the plaza in front of the building. A sign told her it was a concert hall called the Harpa. The doors slid open automatically as she approached them and she went inside. It was cavernous with the front wall, made up of elongated hexagons of glass, soaring above her and continuing across the ceiling. Opposite, the wall was dark grey, probably lava rock, Iris thought, and the foyer narrowed towards one end where the two walls met. A staircase rose majestically along the length of the building, with sofas on the many landings, making Iris think it would be the perfect place to while away an hour or two with a coffee, watching the world go by.

Her phone was buzzing in her pocket. She pulled it out and saw that Jay was calling her. The temptation to ignore his call was strong, but he never called out-of-hours unless it was important.

'Jay.'

'Hey, Iris. I've been speaking to my opposite number at the Icelandic Met Office and arranged for you to go in and meet them the day after tomorrow. That gives you a day to get settled before you get started.'

So, not that important. 'Okay, that's fine. Can you email the details?'

'Of course. So, how is Reykjavik?'

She could have told him that the city had all but won her over already, but she didn't want to share it with him. 'Yes, great, thanks. I've found a nice hotel and hopefully have someone who can take me to the Reykjanes peninsula tomorrow.'

'That's fast work,' he said, sounding impressed.

'Well, best to get a handle on it as soon as we can.'

'Quite. Let me know how it goes on Friday.'

'Will do. Bye.'

Iris left the Harpa, the spell broken, and headed in the direction she hoped the fish and chip shop was. If only she could put her feelings about Jay aside, she thought for the millionth time.

Her phone buzzed again and she pulled it out, barely looking at who was calling, assuming Jay had forgotten to tell her something.

'Yes?'

'Iris.' Her brother Finn sounded surprised.

'Finn! Sorry, I thought it was Jay calling again.'

'Is this a bad time?'

'No, I'm wandering around Reykjavik trying to find fish and chips.'

He laughed. 'Well, I won't keep you. I just thought since you're almost in the same time zone for once, I'd try and actually speak to you.'

'I've missed you.'

'Me too.'

'How're Mum and Dad?'

'They're good. They're away with Don and Carol until next week.' Their parents always went to Tenerife for a few weeks in February and March for some winter sun.

'And how are you?'

'I'm okay.'

Iris was used to this from Finn. It was an automatic response, one he was more likely to use when she was away, not wanting her to worry about him. But she did worry because he'd had a lot of ups and downs in his life that he'd struggled to weather.

'Really? I worry about you when Mum and Dad are away.'

'Iris. I'm almost forty. I can be left by myself sometimes now,' he joked.

'I know,' she said affectionately. 'But now I'm on the same

side of the world as you, we can talk more often.'

'I'll let you go and find your fish and chips. Call me tomorrow when you have chance.'

'Okay, love you, Finn.'

'Love you.'

Not for the first time, Iris wondered what price she was paying for the nomadic lifestyle she led. It meant she was always at arm's length from her family because it was hard to keep in touch enough to be involved in their lives like she would be if she saw them more often. And more recently, she could blame the fact that she'd never had more than a fling with anyone in the past few years on the travelling too. What was the point of letting herself catch feelings for someone she was going to have to leave behind? Because that was what she had chosen. Her career over everything else and most of the time she was happy with that. But deep down, she knew that her career had saved her. She could devote herself to that without fear of rejection and, in fact, the single-minded way she had thrown herself into work after the split with Patrick was the reason why she was about to become the person who could predict volcanos more accurately than anyone else in the world. That had to be worth sacrificing her personal life.

4

The following morning, Siggi had opened up the Iceland Adventures office and for once, wished it was one of the days when Jonas couldn't stay away from the place. He still hadn't had chance to ask him whether it was okay to accompany Iris after all, now that they'd established her credentials. And he was itching to see for himself how things were developing.

When he'd come back to the office the day before, after taking Iris to the hotel, he picked up googling her where he'd left off. Reading more about her had left him feeling somewhere between impressed and intimidated. Not only was she a volcanologist, she was one of the leading ones in the field of using data for predicting what might happen in the course of an eruption. There was a lot more to it than that, but Siggi had skimmed over the more technical aspects of her career in favour of finding out as much as he could about the rest of her life.

Most of the information available to him online was to do with her work. Papers she'd written, news reports where she'd given a quote, her work history on some random Who's Who in volcanology website, but hardly anything about the rest of her life. He knew she was thirty-three and came from a place called Cheltenham in the middle of the UK. He found out she went to university in Lancaster and that since then she'd worked at British Geology Labs. She had a Facebook page people tagged her on but that she hardly ever updated, and when she did, it was about a volcano. He certainly didn't feel the need to contact his friend at the IMO to clarify anything. There was no doubt that Iris Bellingham knew more than most people about what she might be getting into by requesting a trip to a volatile part of the country.

Siggi felt a kind of affinity with Iris. He was nowhere near having a work ethic like hers, but he assumed that to travel around the world, she must want to do that regardless of the volcanos involved. She was looking at data, so he wondered why she was the one who had to come out to the Reykjanes peninsula, unless she wanted to.

Thanks to his own wanderlust nature, he had a terrible track record with relationships and he wondered whether that might be the same for Iris. He always began by being super-invested, but when things got more serious, he ended up leaving. It was never how he planned things would go, but that was the way they went. The day before, he'd been amazed by the expression on Embla's face while she'd checked Iris into the hotel. He understood entirely why Embla was angry with him. He couldn't give her what she'd wanted, and he'd been honest with her about that, but accepted that from her perspective, the conversations hadn't been over when he'd upped and left for Thailand. The need to leave sometimes overwhelmed him to the point of almost paralysing him to do anything except flee. And it had never been the wrong choice, even if he felt the choice had been made for him.

Having established that all signs pointed to Iris being a workaholic, Siggi wanted to respond to her email before she turned up on the doorstep as he fully expected she would at any moment. He called Jonas.

'Jonas, it's Siggi.'

'Is everything okay?'

'Sure. The email we had yesterday about the Reykjanes trip? The woman is a volcanologist. It seems legitimate.'

'Ah, okay. When does she want to go out there?'

Siggi preempted Jonas offering his services by saying, 'I told her I'd take her today, if it was okay with you.'

'If you're sure. I can come in and cover the office this afternoon. I have some paperwork to do.'

They made arrangements around timings and what vehicle would be best to take, then Siggi emailed Iris with the details.

Half an hour before the time he had told her he would pick her up from her hotel, she arrived. She had a rucksack and a silver ruggedised case that presumably held her equipment.

'I thought it'd be quicker if I came here,' she said, making no move to put anything down or take her coat off.

'I am sorry, I need to wait for Jonas to arrive to take over the office,' Siggi said, suppressing a smile. Her assumption that she was their only concern this afternoon amused him.

'Oh. Right.' She shrugged off her rucksack and took off her coat and hat.

'While we wait for Jonas, shall we have a look at where you would like to go?'

Iris pulled out her laptop and showed him a detailed map of the area with an overlay of information that he didn't understand.

'This is the road west out of Reykjavik, route 41,' Siggi pointed out.

'Okay. Then I'd like to take this road south to Hraunvik.'

'To the town?'

'Yes.'

'But the volcano is west of there. Or do you mean the Gunnuhver volcano on the tip of the peninsula?'

'I need to go to the town. I could explain on the way, if that helps?'

It shouldn't have surprised Siggi that Iris might be single-minded about this and might not feel the need to justify where she wanted to go, but if a volcanologist wasn't that interested in seeing the volcano, he wondered what else could interest someone predicting eruptions.

'Okay, that would be great,' he said, genuinely meaning it.

Iris smiled. 'Thanks. I really appreciate you taking me today. It's important to get this set up before I meet the team over here.' She gestured to her silver case.

'This is not something they would help you with?'

She shook her head. 'It's an unorthodox theory, so I might be in the position of needing the data it's going to give me to prove my point.'

'There is nothing I like more than being a rebel.'

Iris laughed. 'I don't think anyone has thought I'm a rebel before, but it is something like that.'

Her entire face lit up when she laughed and Siggi beamed at her, intrigued by this clever woman who had just walked into his life yesterday.

Their heads were bent over the laptop again, assessing exactly where in Hraunvik Iris wanted to go, when Jonas came into the office.

'Jonas, this is Iris Bellingham,' said Siggi, more formal than he would usually be. For some reason, Iris's trip made him feel like he needed to be more professional than normal. This was a serious business, far from the tours they usually did for visitors. He felt the gravity of the situation.

'Pleased to meet you, Iris,' Jonas said warmly, shaking her hand.

'Thank you for helping me. If I'm honest, I asked a few other companies as well, but as Siggi was so helpful to me yesterday, I feel in very capable hands with him and that's important.'

Jonas raised his eyebrows at Siggi, a hint of humour in his eyes. 'I am happy that Siggi has been such a good representative of our company,' he said.

Iris seemed to miss the nuance in his tone, but Siggi felt himself blush. Jonas would definitely think Siggi was going above and beyond because he found Iris attractive. And while that was true to a point, there was much more to Iris than met the eye. And that was what intrigued Siggi far more than her blue eyes or the curls that kissed the edges of her face.

'Siggi is our most experienced guide for that area of the country. He knows it very well.'

This time, Siggi shot Jonas a warning look. There was no need to explain to Iris what his credentials were for taking her to Hraunvik or why he knew it so well.

'Okay, Jonas, so we will be off.'

'Take care and make sure you take a satellite phone with you.'

'It is already packed,' said Siggi, patting his own small rucksack.

'It seems as if you are the perfect person for the job,' Iris said to him as they walked the short distance to where one of the company's jeeps was parked. She was smiling, but even that didn't make Siggi feel like elaborating. He would much rather get underway and grill her about what data she was after in Hraunvik than talk about himself.

'It's a nice day for a drive,' said Iris, taking her coat off and settling herself into the front seat.

'For now. It looks like we will see some rain or snow later this afternoon. It depends how long we are.' He didn't mind how long they were. He was looking forward to getting to know her better on the journey.

'It might take an hour to set up the equipment once we find a good spot.'

'We will not get trapped anywhere because of the snow at

this time of year,' he said. 'Although Jonas got caught out a few years ago and had to camp in a summer cottage with one of our clients. They're married now.'

'Wow, that's an intense way to start a relationship. So you and Jonas are friends outside of work?'

'Yes, we went to school together. A few of us work for him. He's a good guy. I like to travel and he lets me pick up where I left off when I am back here.'

'Where have you been recently?'

'I spent a couple of months in Thailand and then went to Hawaii on my way back.'

'Hawaii? Really? I came straight here from Hawaii. I was working on The Big Island.'

Siggi's heart leapt inexplicably, as if the fact that they had been in the same place before somehow cosmically linked them. 'I was on the Big Island until a couple of weeks ago.' He turned to smile at her and saw in her face that she was just as thrilled as him at having found this in common. 'I enjoy surfing and although we have good waves here, it is too cold and dangerous to surf in the winter.'

'My colleague, Dylan, learned to surf, so I used to go with him.'

'You surfed too?' Siggi tried not to focus too hard on the image that flashed up in his head of Iris in a close-fitting wetsuit.

'Oh, god no. I'd be hopeless,' she said, laughing. I mostly watched and occasionally swam if the waves weren't too wild.'

'We might have been on the same beach.' This time when he glanced at her, she looked more thoughtfully at him.

'We used to go to Kahaluu Beach. It's close to Mount Kilauea.'

'I did surf at that beach! Small world.' It was crazy, but he started replaying those visits to the beach in his mind as if he might somehow see that Iris had been there.

'It's mad to think we might have been there at the same time,' she said.

'It is worrying me that if you were there, it is because you thought the volcano was going to erupt?'

She laughed. 'Well, there had been some rumblings, but it came to nothing. You'd have been okay. It wouldn't have been a big one if it had happened.'

'And how about this one?' Siggi looked across at her. 'This could be big?'

He could almost see her switch into work-mode. 'It's hard to say at this stage. But it's being closely monitored.'

They drove in silence for a few minutes, Siggi sensing the gravity of the situation, even though Iris hadn't said in so many words. They were getting closer now, having turned south on the road to Hraunvik, a small, traditional fishing village near the coast. Grey clouds had started to build. If he'd been with anyone else, Siggi would have suggested stopping off to look at some geysers and steaming hot springs, but Iris was all business. Keen to get her work underway.

'How will you know where to put your equipment?' he asked her as they got closer to the village.

'I have a detailed map of seismic data from the past week. I'll use GPS to pinpoint the places when we're there.'

They drove into the town, along the main road, which was familiar to Siggi. He pulled over on the side of the road while Iris fired up her laptop to check where she wanted to go.

'Okay, can we go east of here?' She looked through the windscreen. 'Maybe take that road.'

He did as she asked, pulling up outside a pair of houses when she asked him to stop.

'Do you think you could come with me?' she asked. 'I'd like to ask the people who live in that house there,' she said, pointing to the house on the right, 'whether it would be okay to set some equipment up in their garden.'

'Here? You want me to knock on the door and ask them?'

'Yes, please.'

'It has to be that house?'

'I'd prefer that one. It's marginally closer to where I'm predicting a fissure might appear. I can do the knocking, if that helps?'

She was teasing him. But that was because she didn't know that it wasn't the knocking on the door that was the problem. It was who might answer it.

'Everyone speaks English,' he said.

Iris looked at him, confused. 'You think they'll understand if I start wittering on about lava tubes and mantle plumes?'

'I am sure they will.'

'I'm not. Come on, please Siggi. It's really important. This is the main reason I needed you to come with me. Don't you think I could have hired a car if I just needed to plonk some equipment down anywhere?'

He should have let Jonas come.

Almost every conceivable scenario was playing out in his head as he sat there, crippled with anxiety.

In some ways, it would get the moment he'd been dreading for years over with. He might be about to meet his teenage daughter for the first time. And Iris instigating it should take the pressure off him. There was no time to overthink or plan how he might introduce himself; often the stumbling block when he'd considered knocking on the door in the past. It could happen right now.

But what frightened him most, what had kept him away from her until now, was the thought of explaining to Arna why he'd taken that decision so long ago not to be part of her life. Why he'd decided he'd rather not have a daughter.

The shame and regret he'd carried with him since was like

a stone in his heart. He couldn't imagine how he could explain to Arna that he'd thought she was a mistake. How could she see it as anything except her father abandoning her?

'Siggi?'

He looked at Iris and wished that this moment hadn't come now. With her. It was one thing to meet his daughter at last, but quite another to have his two worlds collide at the same time. Just as he was getting to know Iris, to have to explain all of this, it was too much. But he couldn't see a way out of it.

5

Siggi wasn't moving from the passenger seat. There was obviously some particular reason he was reluctant to help her out with the translating. She knew he was chatty and personable, so she was at a loss to understand why he suddenly looked like a rabbit in the headlights.

'You don't know the Icelandic words for the volcanology terms? Is that it? We could do google translate, if that helps?'

His face brightened. '*You* could use google translate.'

'I could, but the point is that I would be a random English person knocking on their door. Whereas you, at least until a minute ago, are a friendly-faced native-speaker who they're more likely to trust.'

He sighed. 'I might know someone who lives in that house.'

'Ah.' Now it was starting to make sense. 'Is it a woman? Someone like Embla?'

His head spun, a look of surprise on his face. 'What did Embla say?'

'Look. I'm sorry if I've stumbled across the one house in Hraunvik that is a no-go area for you, but it is quite important.'

With a dramatic sigh, Siggi undid his seatbelt and climbed

out of the jeep. 'Okay. Come on then,' he said, zipping his coat and pulling his hat so far down his forehead that his eyes were barely visible.

'I have a scarf in my bag if you want to disguise yourself a bit more?' Iris said, earning a side-eye from a sulky-looking Siggi.

She pulled her equipment case from the back seat and headed up the steps to the front door of the house, and knocked. Siggi trailed up the steps behind her and stood with his head down. After a few more seconds, Iris knocked again, but after a minute, had to accept that there was no one home.

'Oh, that's annoying.'

Siggi grinned, a look of relief sweeping across his face as he headed down the steps.

'We'll try next door,' Iris said. 'Any issues waiting behind this door?'

Shooting her another side-eye, Siggi nevertheless followed her up the steps as she knocked on the door. This time, the door was opened by a man in his forties, Iris would guess.

'Hello. My name is Iris and I work for British Geology Labs. I was wondering whether you would be willing to let me set some equipment up in your garden?'

She turned to Siggi and raised her eyebrows, encouraging him to jump in. Thankfully he did, and there was some back-and-forth conversation between them. Siggi gestured towards Iris and her case a couple of times.

'He's asking whether it's to do with the earthquakes they've been having.'

'Yes, it is. Kind of.'

In the end the man shrugged and said, 'Where do you want to put it?' in English, making Iris wonder whether Siggi was right after all, and that she could have managed perfectly well on her own.

'Over there, if that's okay.' She pointed to the corner of the front garden closest to the neighbours, where she really would have liked to set up. 'Do you know whether your neighbours would mind if I set up in their garden?'

'They would mind,' Siggi interjected. 'He has already told me that.'

The man guffawed.

Iris couldn't be bothered to get into whatever subtext was going on. 'Thank you. I'll get started.'

'I will wait inside,' said Siggi, and to Iris's surprise, turned and went inside the house.

By the time she had set up her modified seismometer, it was almost dark. Satisfied that it was working and the data was being collected, she closed her laptop and climbed the steps, knocking on the door again. Concentrating on the job in hand had taken her mind off how cold it was, but now she realised she'd started shivering.

'Hey,' said Siggi, opening the door and closing it behind him. 'Are you ready to leave?'

'Yes,' said Iris. 'Are you?'

'It seemed crazy to wait in the car.'

'Do you know him?'

'Um, yes, sort of.'

Clearly this was related to the issue Siggi had with the house next door.

'Let's go.'

Irritated, but not really sure why, Iris climbed into the jeep.

'You want to take your coat off?' Siggi asked.

'No, thanks.' She shivered again.

'Here.' Siggi turned and grabbed his rucksack from the back seat, pulling out a flask and handing it to her.

'Thank you. What is it?'

'Tea. I know it is what English people drink. Three of my friends have English partners and they drink it all the time.'

Iris laughed, her annoyance dissipating. 'That's really

thoughtful, thank you. I haven't had a good cup of tea for ages.'

'This is probably also not a good cup of tea.'

But it was the best cup of tea Iris had had in a long time, and it warmed her from the inside out.

'Thank you for bringing me here today, Siggi,' she said once she'd warmed up and could sit back and enjoy the drive through the dark wilderness back to Reykjavik, cocooned in the jeep's warmth, with Siggi capably in the driving seat.

'No problem,' he said softly.

It occurred to Iris to ask about Siggi's links to Hraunvik, to find out why he'd been so reluctant to knock on the door of the house in the first place, but she didn't. She never enjoyed having to answer personal questions, and she knew that if Siggi had a reason he wanted to share with her, that would have happened before they were standing on the doorstep. She respected the fact that although she felt as if she'd known him a while, they were still practically strangers.

'Where's your next trip?' Iris asked once she'd finished her tea and was feeling human again.

'I am not sure. I have been thinking about Indonesia but I will wait until the autumn.'

'Will you work for Jonas all summer?'

Siggi nodded. 'It is a busy time and the excursions are more exciting this time of the year. In the winter, we mostly do Northern Lights trips and Golden Circle tours, you know, to see the geyser and where the tectonic plates meet. In the summer we can do diving, kayaking, climbing, hiking, all sorts of things.'

'I'd love to see the tectonic plates. Iceland is the only place on earth where they're visible on the surface.'

Siggi laughed. 'I should be telling you that.'

'Sorry.' She felt ridiculous. Of course he would know that. Not only did he live here, but he showed people around his country for a living. 'I'm sure you know all sorts of fascinating information about the geology here.'

'I expect you know more than me. I have to admit, I am a person who will always do the bare minimum to get by.'

'You could say that's an efficient approach to life,' said Iris, trying to sound understanding, although she was the complete opposite; wanting to know everything there was to know about anything that interested her.

Siggi gave her a self-deprecating smile and raked his fingers through his hair to push it back from his face. 'That is one way to look at it. People don't usually get behind the idea.'

'I must admit, I'm not really like that.'

'I already know that.' Siggi was smiling while he kept his eyes on the road. It did something strange to Iris to see him smile like that. Was it thinking about her that made that smile happen?

Iris drew her eyes away from him. If he looked at her now, she didn't know what she'd do. She must be tired. That was the only explanation.

As the lights of Reykjavik appeared in the distance, Iris asked Siggi whether he could recommend a taxi company. 'I need to go to the IMO tomorrow.'

'I could take you,' he said.

'I can't ask you to do that. It's just a ride. No need to wait or anything like today.'

'The offer is there. And if you need to go back to Hraunvik, I will take you. You know more than I do about what is happening there, but if something does happen, I know how to get you home safely.'

Iris looked at Siggi, marvelling at this protective side to him that seemed at odds with the impression she had of him bending the rules of the world to suit him. What made a person who worked to live, travelling the world alone, as far as she knew at least, care about a stranger he'd just met? It made no sense. But she wanted Siggi to look after her. To take her to Hraunvik and know how to get out again if things went south.

'Thank you. I really appreciate that. I hope I won't be there if that happens, and hopefully no one else will be either if we can get some useful data.'

'So, tell me Iris. What is the difference you will make by being here?' His tone was interested rather than challenging her. Maybe he genuinely wanted to know.

'I hope it's the difference between people having time to move out of the way of whatever happens and not being hurried from their homes. Time to prepare when something devastating is on the horizon can make all the difference.'

'Devastating,' he said quietly

'We don't know yet. I'm talking hypothetically.'

'But you wouldn't be here if nothing was happening.' It wasn't a question.

'There's time. You know people in Hraunvik?'

He nodded. 'Some distant family.' Now, as he stared through the windscreen, he looked serious and thoughtful. 'Iceland is a small country. We are all family somehow.'

'I understand. You know the IMO is incredible. They are already across it. I'm hardly adding to what they already know.'

'We understand what it is to live in Iceland. The land of ice and fire. It is in our bones.'

'But it's different when it threatens you so directly.'

Siggi turned to look at Iris and gave her a small nod.

'I've been to Hawaii once before. In 2018. Two thousand people lost their homes. I know how hard it was for those people to leave, even though they knew they lived next to one of the world's most active volcanoes.'

'It is true,' he said ruefully. 'Every day we take people to see these places where the planet is showing us what is beneath the surface, and I guess we forget what that could do.'

It had begun to rain. Iris could imagine how cold that would be, hitting her face, assisted by a keen wind.

As if he was reading her mind, Siggi said, 'I will take you to the hotel.'

'Oh, there's no need. It's not far from the office.' Her default English setting of not wanting to put anyone out had kicked in, almost against her will. She hoped Siggi would protest because now she had warmed up, all she wanted to do was dive straight from the jeep into the cosiest bed in the world that was waiting in her hotel room.

'You would like to walk in this?' The rain had morphed into sleet.

'I would have walked in the rain, but now it's turned into a snowstorm I'd be very grateful for a lift to the hotel.'

'This is not a snowstorm by Icelandic standards, but I can understand that for an English person it looks extreme,' he teased.

'In the UK, this kind of weather would have people panicking about whether they'd make it home from work. I'm not joking,' she added when Siggi laughed.

'There is not much weather that would make us think that,' he said.

'What's the worst snowstorm you've ever seen?'

'Aside from this one,' he said, rubbing his stubbly chin. 'I would have to say seven years ago. It was the most snow ever recorded in Reykjavik. It was half a metre deep everywhere, and deeper where the snow had drifted. We had to cancel all our tours for a week because no one could leave their houses. Luckily, February is not a busy month for us. I had just come back from spending Christmas in Australia. Bad timing for me.'

'You wouldn't have wanted to miss that, surely? I bet it was amazing.'

'I think the magic of weather like that is only seen by people who do not have it as often as we do.'

'Be careful what you wish for.'

'Exactly.'

Siggi pulled up outside Iris's hotel.

'Thanks so much for today.'

'The offer is still there for tomorrow.'

'You're not working?'

He shook his head, picked up his phone and handed it to Iris. 'Put your number in here and I will message you when I get home. Call me tomorrow if you would like me to take you.'

'Thank you,' she said again, passing the phone back. 'Bye.'

It crossed her mind to give him a peck on the cheek. It also crossed her mind that she'd like to put a hand behind his head and pull him in for a full-on kiss, so she settled for quickly patting his hand where it rested on the gearstick, then she opened the door and climbed out before grabbing her stuff. She didn't look back, but she didn't hear him pull away until she was inside.

When she got into her room, she stood with her back to the door and exhaled. Siggi. It was a feeling she was unfamiliar with. She wasn't in the habit of falling for anyone. It made life complicated, and she thought that over time, she'd become immune to the charms of men. The thing was, Siggi wasn't trying to be charming. He was down-to-earth, looked like he'd just stepped off that beach in Hawaii and coasted through life on his own terms. But that, combined with the protective streak he'd shown today, was hitting Iris right in the heart.

It had taken her a long time to get over what she thought of as her one true love. It had seemed impossible that she would ever feel ready to face the thought of being hurt again, and even dating had seemed too risky. So she'd concentrated on work, which had enough challenges of its own to keep her busy, and she hadn't felt like she was missing out. Until now.

Siggi was the first man for as long as she could remember who made her *feel*. She had to acknowledge that she was attracted to him, foolish as that was, because it wasn't as if it could go anywhere. They were from different places, had very different outlooks on life and lifestyles that meant, even if something developed, it would be rare for them both to be in the same place at the same time.

But there was a connection that Iris couldn't ignore. She'd enjoyed being with him today, even for the frustrating few minutes when he'd been so reluctant to knock on that door.

Perhaps she'd reached a point where enough time had lapsed that she was ready to look for love again? But she didn't think that was it. Whatever this was, it was specific to Siggi. A man who clearly had a rocky past with women, a man who, given his age, seemed incapable of settling down, and was probably a commitment-phobe as well. But these things paled into insignificance when Iris thought about how caring and thoughtful he was. There was something loveable about him, so if he was alone, it suggested that was because he wanted to be. And in that sense, they couldn't be more alike.

6

It was crazy to ask Siggi to take her to the IMO. Wasn't it? Iris had made an appointment for that afternoon with Bjarkey, someone Jay had suggested she get in touch with. Apparently, he was the remote monitoring expert at the IMO. She wasn't exactly looking forward to it, well aware that she could easily come across as someone flouncing into their office and telling them she knew better. How she was interpreting the data was unconventional, but she was slowly gathering enough data to prove her point. So stressing about whether to take Siggi up on his offer was a welcome distraction.

Iris had found a coffee shop along the street from the hotel, so after breakfast she took her laptop there, ordered a flat white and sat at a table for two in a cosy corner while she checked in on the data that her seismometer had hopefully been retrieving in Hraunvik. Thankfully, the signal was good and there was some data there, consistent with what the IMO had been gathering, according to what they'd published. That would make this afternoon easier. She could correlate her data to theirs and then explain the nuances that she would spend the rest of the morning deciphering.

After an hour or so, Iris got up to order another coffee, then checked her phone before she engrossed herself in work again. There was a text from Siggi.

What time shall I collect you?

His confidence in assuming she was planning to take him up on his offer made her smile.

Don't you have anything better to do?

No

How long does it take to get there?

15 mins

He either knew where it was, or he'd looked. Iris hoped it was the latter. She paused, then decided, why not?

Meet you at your office at 13.15?

Siggi replied with a thumbs up emoji. It was a done deal.

That afternoon, she arrived at his office just after one o'clock. He was standing talking to another man who was sitting at the desk.

'Hi,' she said.

'Hey, Iris,' Siggi said, with a warm smile. 'Olafur, this is Iris, the volcanologist I was telling you about.'

'Welcome, Iris,' said Olafur, holding out a huge hand for her to shake. He was about twice the size of Siggi and looked a bit like a viking. Perhaps more typical of what she imagined an Icelander to look like than Siggi was.

'This is Olafur, a friend and a colleague.'

'Nice to meet you,' said Iris.

'Has Siggi asked you to come to the bar tonight?'

All sorts of things whipped through Iris's head. Did Olafur somehow think she and Siggi were an item, and if he did, did that mean Siggi bizarrely thought the same? Did Olafur think she and Siggi somehow already knew each other and hadn't just met two days ago? Thankfully, Siggi stepped in, speaking Icelandic to Olafur.

Then he turned to Iris and said, 'I am sorry. My friends

assume that everyone we meet who is travelling alone needs to be entertained. It happens all the time.'

'Siggi, invite her properly, please. Or Gudrun will have something to say about it.'

Siggi rolled his eyes. 'Would you like to come to the bar tonight? There is a group of us, some English people. It might be fun.'

He wasn't making it sound fun. And Iris wasn't getting the impression from him that he'd like her to go, and really, what other reason would there be?

'Thanks for the invitation. Do you mind if I see how this afternoon goes? I'm still quite jet-lagged.'

'Of course,' said Olafur. 'We will see you if we see you. And take no notice of Siggi. He is quite grumpy.'

Iris laughed partly at Olafur's stark assessment of Siggi and partly at Siggi's look of resignation.

Siggi was mumbling under his breath in Icelandic as they walked to the jeep together.

'I'm not going to come. Don't worry,' she said. If he was that annoyed that Olafur had asked her, he was making it simple for her to say no.

'No, I would like you to come. I was thinking about asking you because it is interesting to see a city with someone who lives there. You see a different side of things. I am annoyed with Olafur for interfering. As if I cannot manage my own life.'

They reached the jeep and settled inside. Iris left her coat on, since it was going to be a brief journey.

'Do you think they're trying to set us up?' she asked.

'Probably.'

She didn't know what to say to that, but Siggi felt the need to fill the silence.

'It is not just Olafur,' he said. 'If you had walked into the office the other day and any of the others had been there, they would have asked you to join in with something like this as soon as they knew you were staying for a while and travelling alone. I prefer to wait. You might not be a person who wants to be involved in anything.'

'And you might not like me,' Iris added, helpfully.

Siggi laughed. 'That is not the case,' he said, smiling across at her.

'You mean you prefer to sit back and get the lie of the land before jumping into anything.'

'Yes, that is it. My friend Brun was working with an author last year. She came for a book tour and he was taking her everywhere she needed to go. He invited her to the open mic night and she went round to Rachel and Jonas's house to make bread.'

'Okay,' Iris said, laughing.

'And I am not sure you would want to do that.'

'I'm not sure either. Can't I just come to the bar for a drink without having to go to anyone's house and make bread?'

'You think it is funny, but they are together now.'

'Are your friends that amazing that I'll want to get together with you just to be in the gang?' She blushed as she said it, feeling bold for even suggesting out loud that she and Siggi might get together.

'I don't know what I am saying,' Siggi said, laughing and banging his hand on the steering wheel. 'But I do know that you would not be the first person to say yes to a night out and end up staying in Iceland forever.'

'God, really? I mean, I am drawn to the volcanoes, but I'm not sure even that's enough to make me want to stay here.'

Siggi pulled up outside the IMO building. It was a huge concrete cube with windows in a vertical line down the side that faced the road. 'If you end up staying forever, I will not be here. Just to be clear.'

'So you're saying I'm safe to come for a drink?'

'Yes, Iris,' he said, smiling at her. 'It is safe. I would recommend you accept the invitation.'

Iris's stomach did a somersault. It was probably nerves about meeting Bjarkey. 'So where shall I meet you?' She was fully intending to take a taxi back to the hotel.

'Here, as soon as you're finished?'

'No. You're not waiting for me.' She climbed out of the jeep. 'I'm not going in until you've driven away. All the way down the road,' she said, nodding towards the busy dual-carriageway they'd just left. 'I'm getting a taxi. Where shall I meet you?'

He smiled as if he was enjoying her getting cross with him. Iris imagined that could be infuriating if you were in a relationship with him.

'I'll call you when I'm outside your hotel. Around eight?'

'Okay. And thank you for the lift.' She slammed the door of the jeep and stood, waiting until he drove away. She was pretty sure he would be there when she came out otherwise. He saluted her with two fingers tapped to his forehead then drove off. It was mildly annoying that she thought that was cute.

Iris gathered herself, put Siggi out of her mind, and walked to the side of the building, looking for the entrance. She pushed the huge revolving glass door around and went to the reception desk to announce herself. A friendly man on the desk called Bjarkey for her.

Bjarkey was a smiley woman, a little older than Iris, with a blonde bob. Iris hadn't been able to tell from the name whether she was a man or a woman and, to her shame, had assumed it was a man.

'Welcome Iris!'

'Thank you for agreeing to meet me.'

'When I heard about the research you are doing, I was very excited.'

'Thank you,' said Iris, flattered. 'I've been looking at some of your data. You've got an unbelievable amount.'

They took a lift to the fourth floor, then Bjarkey led the way into a room where the walls were lined with multiple screens. 'This is our monitoring room. We have around fifty seismic stations around Iceland which all send live data. We also monitor the different frequencies and waves of the data to pinpoint locations more accurately. And we have live webcam feeds from some of the most active places.'

The sheer amount of information in front of Iris astounded her. 'I'm not sure I can add much to this,' she said. 'I bet you already have what I was planning to show you.' They just might not know they had it, but Iris didn't want to point out to Bjarkey that they could be sitting on valuable data that they weren't analysing.

'I am not sure about that,' Bjarkey said, smiling. 'Why don't we grab a coffee and we can take a look?'

Over coffee, Iris opened her laptop and showed Bjarkey the data she'd been collecting from Hraunvik.

Bjarkey frowned. 'I do not understand. You have a seismometer set up somewhere in the town?'

'Yes. I set it up yesterday. Do you have any in that area?'

'We do.' She pulled up the data on her own screen.

'Okay, so we can see the readings are very similar, but I have mine set to record a different frequency besides the normal stuff we would look at,' said Iris. Now she was hitting her stride. She'd forgotten any of the worries she'd had before she'd arrived. And Bjarkey's open-minded response had helped.

'This low frequency is not something we would normally look at because it indicates something further away. Not relevant to the area we are interested in.'

'Right. But if you amplify the frequency like this.' Iris clicked a button to show the change in her data. 'It shows you that the low frequency is actually a pre-cursor to what is happening later on on the higher frequencies.'

Bjarkey clicked the button, toggling the view on the screen between the two examples. 'But how have you done this?'

'It's an adjustment to the seismometer settings and also a change in how the raw data is logged.'

'Can you show me where you have got to? Have you any data leading up to an eruption event?'

They pored over Iris's data for the rest of the day, and it was six o'clock before they finished.

'It's incredible,' said Bjarkey. 'And it is great timing for you to be here now.'

Iris didn't like to point out that her visit was entirely intentional, and instead asked Bjarkey for the number of a taxi firm.

'Don't be silly, I can drop you at your hotel. I am going that way, anyway.'

'Thanks, that would be great.'

'Do you have any plans for the weekend?' Bjarkey asked once they were in her car and speeding back the way Siggi had come earlier. Iris smiled at the thought that Siggi would have been waiting outside for four hours if she hadn't insisted he leave.

'I'm going out with some locals tonight.'

Bjarkey laughed. 'How have you already met locals after two days?'

'I walked into a tour company office and came across the most helpful guy in the country.'

'Ah, a guy?'

'It's not like that.'

'Of course not. I am sure he is helpful to everybody who walks in off the street.'

'I think he is!' Iris laughed. 'Anyway, he travels a lot and thinks it's good to spend time with locals to really get the feel of a place.'

'He is probably right about that. Is this your hotel?'

'Yes. Thank you so much, Bjarkey. It's been great to meet you.'

'Email me. We will take a trip to Hraunvik next week, yes?'

'Okay.' Iris was thrilled. 'I can't wait.'

'Enjoy yourself tonight!'

Back in her room, Iris contemplated what she might wear for a night on the town. All she had at her disposal was a reasonable pair of jeans. They were dark, at least. Having not planned on a night out in Iceland, she had nothing fancier than a long-sleeved t-shirt and short-sleeved t-shirt layering situation to fall back on. If it had been warmer, she had a couple of pretty tops she'd bought in Hawaii but she'd freeze in those here, even in a centrally heated bar. Luckily one of her t-shirts was a vintage Fleetwood Mac one that she'd taken from her mother's drawer back in the sixth-form. She put it on and thought she looked okay. After all, how dressed up did anyone need to be if they were going to a bar?

She ran some hair oil through her fingers and scrunched it into the ends of her curls to take some of the frizz out, then finished with a lick of mascara and some lipstick. At that moment, her phone buzzed with a message from Siggi saying he was outside.

Iris grabbed her coat, betting on the fact that the bar wouldn't be too far away because she left her hat behind, not wanting to flatten her hair, which looked better than she would normally expect for such minimal effort.

She flew down the stairs and out of the hotel, finding Siggi waiting, leaning against the wall with his hat on and his hands in his pockets. His face broke into a smile when he saw her.

'You look great,' he said easily, as if they did this kind of thing all the time.

'Thanks. So do you.' He actually looked exactly the same as every other time she'd seen him, but he was the kind of guy that probably always looked effortlessly good.

'You had a good day?' He took Iris's hand and tucked it into the crook of his arm.

'Yes, and it was a good job you didn't wait for me because I only got back an hour ago.'

He shrugged. 'I would not have minded.'

They walked only for another minute or so before Siggi stopped beside some concrete steps that led up into the building on the corner of the street.

'Here we are,' he said. 'This is where they come every Friday. Islenski Barinn.'

Iris went up the steps, thinking that it was a little odd that Siggi was distancing himself from his group of friends by saying "they" come here every Friday.

'You don't come all the time?' she asked before she pulled the door open.

He shook his head. 'I am not always here. And I don't mind working on a Friday so that they can come here.'

The bar was lively, dimly lit and pretty traditional from what Iris could see. Certainly it wasn't trying to be trendy and didn't seem to follow any particular theme. It was welcoming and comfortable.

'Over here,' Siggi said, holding his arm out, gesturing for Iris to go ahead of him. His friends had commandeered a table next to one of the windows that looked out onto the street. There were six of them. Iris recognised Olafur from the office earlier that day. Siggi did some quick introductions, but basically they were three couples. Jonas, who owned the tour company that Siggi and Olafur worked for, his wife Rachel, who was English, then Olafur and his girlfriend Gudrun and Brun and his girlfriend Fliss, also English.

'Ned and Anna are in London this weekend, but they're

usually part of the gang too,' said Rachel.

'It's great to meet you all,' Iris said, feeling a little overwhelmed. She hadn't had a night out like this in a group since she was at university. It felt good, and everyone was so welcoming.

Siggi suggested they go up to the bar together and took orders from his friends,which he repeated to Iris. 'I'll never remember,' he said. 'What would you like?'

Iris scanned the bar and opted for a locally brewed beer.

'It's a good choice,' Siggi said, then adding his and everyone else's drinks to the order.

'Your friends are so —'

'Friendly?' He'd jumped in so quickly, it made her laugh.

'Yes!'

'I did warn you,' he said, raising his eyebrows and grinning.

'Well, I think it's nice,' she said. Because it was. She felt like she was part of something, and even if it was only for a little while, only for as long as she was in Reykjavik, she was going to take it. 'Thank you for asking me to come.'

For a moment, she thought Siggi might joke that Olafur had asked her, not him. But his expression turned from playful to something more thoughtful. 'You're welcome, Iris. I enjoy spending time with you.'

Her stomach flipped and she was lost in his gaze for a second. Then the barman interrupted them, setting out their drinks order on the bar.

'I'll take some of these over,' she said, tearing her eyes from his.

'Iris.'

She stopped breathing for a moment, as if by inhaling she might miss something he said.

'Thank you for coming.'

She exhaled as she smiled. And for the rest of the evening,

she kept playing his words over and over in her head. *I enjoy spending time with you.* Had any words ever had such a significant effect on her? She didn't think so. She hugged them to herself as she enjoyed the rest of the night and then fell asleep with them humming in her ears like a lullaby.

7

Iris woke up, groaned, and reached for the glass of water beside her bed. It was a long time since she'd drunk as much beer as that and her head was reminding her she wasn't used to it anymore. She took a few gulps and lay back on the pillows, thinking about last night.

It was no surprise to her now that Fliss had been drawn into the group so quickly. They were welcoming and great fun to be with. The men, having grown up together, had a straightforward relationship, knowing each other inside out. But for some reason, Siggi wasn't as comfortable with that as Brun, Olafur and Jonas were. He'd joined in with the gentle ribbing they gave each other, but he hadn't said much, Iris realised. Perhaps it was because he travelled so much, he missed a lot of what went on, when the others were working together, socialising together and very much part of each other's lives.

She reached for her phone and replied to a couple of messages on the family WhatsApp, then her phone pinged with a message from Siggi.

Wondered if some fresh air might help?

She laughed. Had it been that obvious?

I'm going round to Rachel's to bake cakes

I hope you are joking. But it sounds possible…
What can you offer instead?

Iris felt bold. She bit her lip waiting for his reply.

A visit to a volcano, unless you need a break from them at the weekend…

Can we have breakfast first?

Outside your place in half an hour

She sent a thumbs up emoji and immediately felt better at the thought of a carb-laden breakfast. She got up, showered, scrunch-dried her hair and then layered multiple items of clothes on, finishing with her Icelandic style wool jumper that her nan had knitted. The weather forecast, for what it was worth, was saying it would be a bright but cold day.

Half an hour later when she went downstairs, Siggi was waiting in the foyer, leaning on the reception desk, talking to Bríet.

'Good morning, Iris,' she said with a smile. Iris was envious of how bright and non-hungover she looked.

'Morning.'

'Ready?' Siggi asked.

Iris nodded.

'Have a great day!' Bríet said.

'Thanks, you too,' said Iris.

'Feeling rough?' Siggi asked her with a wry smile.

'A bit. You?'

'Not too bad, but I know how easy it is to get carried away, so I pace myself,' he said smugly.

'Well, thanks for sharing.'

Siggi laughed. 'We are going to have the best breakfast and lots of coffee and then you will feel back to normal.'

The breakfast place, Café Babalú, was just a couple of streets away from the hotel. It was painted in a sunny shade of orange and had a cosy and welcoming look.

'This is on me,' Iris said. 'No, you've done so much for me,' she said as he tried to protest. 'Let me. Please.'

He gave in gracefully. They ordered a croissant and a breakfast crepe each at the counter, then taking their coffees, they chose a table for two in the window and sat down.

'Your friends are great,' Iris said, grinning at the thought of the night before.

'Yes, they are. They welcome me back every time I have been away, and we all look out for each other.'

'I guess because you travel, you don't see them as much as they see each other?'

He nodded. 'A few years ago, we were still all the same, all single men. And gradually they have all moved on and I haven't.' He said it simply, with no bitterness. Maybe because he wasn't interested or searching for the same lives that his friends had. 'Do you find that too with being away from home?'

'I suppose so. My best friend from school is married with two little girls, but I never had a group of friends like you do. It's nice to have that constancy to come back to after you've been away.'

'You don't have that?'

'I have my family. My brothers are brilliant. They're twins and they're older than me and always looked out for me when we were younger. We always have a big get-together when I go home.'

'How often is that?'

'Not often enough. Even if I'm working in the UK, my lab is a couple of hours' drive from where my parents and my one brother live, and my other brother is in London, which makes us into a triangle if you plotted it on a map. How about you? Are your parents in Reykjavik?'

Siggi shook his head. 'No, they retired and moved to the north.'

'Do you see them much?'

'Not as much as I should,' he said with a rueful smile. 'Have you ever visited anywhere else that you think could be home instead?'

'That's a brilliant question. I went to the west coast of Canada for a conference, to Vancouver. It was so beautiful, I could definitely see myself living there.'

'Not many volcanoes in Canada, though.'

'There are, but there's nothing going on with them. I think the rest of the scenery might make up for the lack of volcanic activity on offer. How about you? You come back here because you know you can get regular work, I suppose?'

'Yes, exactly. I loved Australia. I have been there a few times, and it is easy to pick up some casual work and I did that so I could stay longer, but it is not possible to live there. There are things that keep me in Iceland.'

Iris wasn't sure whether he was referring to his job again or something else. Maybe family that he didn't want to leave behind? She didn't want to pry. He'd tell her if he wanted to.

When they'd finished eating, he opened his backpack. 'Okay, I think we should get coffee to go as well,' he said, taking out two thermal flasks. 'Do you want a pastry for the road? There is nowhere to get food.'

'In that case, maybe two?'

'Good idea.'

Siggi left the table and went back to the counter while Iris munched on her last piece of croissant, thinking that this might be the best day out she'd had in a while and it hadn't even started yet.

Siggi came back to the table, put his backpack on the chair and began putting his coat on.

'We will need to walk to the office. Jonas is letting us take the jeep.'

'So which volcano are we visiting?' Iris asked as they made their way back along the road the way they'd come.

'It's Fagradalsfjall.'

'Wow, that's really exciting,' Iris said, recognising the name. 'I think it might be the only time I've visited a volcano and it wasn't for work.'

'That is the same for me,' Siggi said, after a thoughtful pause.

'You don't feel like you're taking me on one of your tours?'

'Not at all. Unless you want me to give you a running commentary on the drive. Then I would feel like I was at work.'

'No, that's okay. I don't think I'm recovered enough to bear that.'

As it was, Siggi ended up pointing out all sorts of things to Iris. They even pulled over a couple of times so that he could show her something of interest. A waterfall, which was running but still had vast swathes of ice clinging to the rock next to where the water cascaded over the edge. There were plumes of steam emerging from the lying snow at the sides of the road as they drove through the wintery landscape and enormous boulders, seemingly dumped in the middle of nowhere, where they had been discarded by a glacier flow thousands of years ago.

'I can't believe I've never been to Iceland before,' said Iris.

'How is that possible? For a volcanologist, it must be the best place in the world.'

'I'm focused on the data collection side of things more than the geology, so until a couple of years ago, I spent most of my time in the lab, monitoring and trawling through data. Now that I'm researching this new thing, I've only been out in the field for a couple of years. I have colleagues who spend a lot of time here, though.'

'I cannot imagine being inside all the time.'

'This is going to sound a bit weird, but when you get engrossed in the data, it's like you're seeing it happen in front of you.'

'Wow. I also cannot imagine being so passionate about something.'

'You don't feel passionate about what you do?'

He shrugged. 'It doesn't feel like work, but I don't think that's the same thing.'

'If you could do anything for a job, what would it be?'

'I would be a pilot, ' he said, without missing a beat.

'So you could see the world and get paid for it?'

'I think the feeling of freedom would be amazing. Imagine living in an archipelago and being the pilot everyone relies on to get them from island to island. I don't know where that place is.'

'Maybe Scotland?'

'Maybe somewhere warmer like Indonesia?'

'Mmm, that would be better.'

'Here we are.' Siggi pulled off the road into a clearing that had been turned into a makeshift car park by spreading crushed-up lava, like gravel across the surface.

'There's a car park for the volcano?'

'They cannot stop people from coming to see it, so they make it as safe as possible. It is better to do this than have people driving too close.'

The contrast between here and other places she'd visited was stark. She had already heard from Bjarkey that the IMO had daily meetings with the civil defence agency to discuss things like road closures and other measures but she'd not imagined they'd actually manage the risk for people who wanted to visit rather than just restrict it entirely. In Hawaii, an entire area of the national park near Mount Kilauea had been closed off to the public since the last eruption.

Even from this distance, Iris could see the steam rising up around the eruption site, and a thrill coursed through her. It never ceased to amaze her that she could witness the planet adjusting itself in spectacular style. Literally getting itself comfortable. And to witness in real life what she'd spent years seeing on the screens in front of her was incredible. This was only the third live volcano she'd visited.

They made their way along the path towards the volcano. It had been erupting for a while so there was nothing spectacularly being blown up in the air, and the lava flow, once they approached it, was moving at a constant yet sluggish pace. The risk of being caught out by anything was fairly low. And although she probably knew far more about the risks involved in this kind of of situation, Siggi was a reassuring presence.

They stuck to the well-trodden path that would lead them closer to the volcano. The smell of sulphur hung in the air, but somehow the crisp coldness helped to mitigate the assault on your senses.

'This is incredible,' said Iris, unable to take her eyes off the volcano.

'Let's head this way,' Siggi said, grabbing her hand and veering away from the path, almost heading around the back of the cone.

Iris took a deep breath, finding it difficult to assess the merits of following Siggi away from the beaten track and into an uncertain terrain, because all she could think about was his hand holding hers. All she could think was that she wished it wasn't so cold that they both had gloves on, because she'd like nothing more than to feel the actual warmth of him.

Holding hands proved to be practical, as well as something that was giving Iris butterflies. They had to hike over very uneven ground, negotiating rocks and loose stones as they went. Iris found that she was having to look at the ground all the time so that she didn't twist an ankle. But eventually, Siggi said, 'Look.'

They were overlooking the lava flow. It glowed red and orange, and even from this distance, they could see molten rock spurting into the air.

'This is incredible,' Iris said again.

'I know, it is amazing,' he said, looking at Iris. He had a look of satisfaction that was purely because of her reaction to where they were. This was why his job didn't feel like work to him; because he got so much out of seeing people's reactions to the places he took them. Or was this look for her? Did anyone else get this version of Siggi on a tour?

Iris dropped his hand. She'd caught sight of a rock strata and took her glove off, compelled to run her hand over it. 'You see this? It's a colonnade structure.' The rock had vertical ridges in it, fairly uniformly spaced, making it look almost stripy.

'Are you auditioning for my job?'

She tried to look affronted, but he had taken his own glove off and was running his hand over the rock now as if he was trying to feel the same way about it that she did.

'Feel how that part is so smooth, and this is more granular,' she said. 'You can hardly see by looking at it because it's such a similar colour, but you can feel it.'

'I can,' Siggi said. 'We learned about some of this stuff at school and we went on a couple of trips, but we didn't see any cool stuff like this.'

'Well, cool might be stretching it.'

They grinned at each other.

'Come on, put your glove back on before your hand freezes.' He put his own glove on, then took Iris's hand again. This time, he looked her in the eye as he did so. It was a look that told her it meant something. Her heart gave a small leap, and she had to swallow a gasp of surprise as he turned away. Was it surprise or was it pleasure that a closely guarded hope was coming to life?

They gave the lava flow a wide berth as they skirted around the base towards the area not visible from the direction they'd come.

'Oh my god!' Iris exclaimed when she saw what Siggi wanted to show her. 'It's a pahoehoe lava flow!' Again, she dropped Siggi's hand and went to take a closer look. Now that they were further around the volcano, they also had a better view of the current, very active lava stream that was regularly spewing fire about a metre into the air. The pahoehoe lava behaved differently to the main flow and was breaking away from it. 'I've never been so close to this kind of lava when it's been moving before. I saw it from a distance in Hawaii, but we couldn't get this close because the crater had collapsed.'

Siggi asked her why it was so interesting. 'I just thought you would like to get closer to the flow. I did not know it was anything special.'

'I guess to most people, it's just lava. I don't want to bore you with the science,' Iris said, wary that she didn't want to break the spell and would rather stroll around holding Siggi's hand again than get involved in a geology lesson.

'You won't bore me, Iris.'

What was happening? A man who wanted to hold her hand *and* wanted to know about pahoehoe lava. It seemed so unlikely.

She gave him the briefest explanation that she could, checking every sentence or so for signs of fatigue in his face. But all she saw were his eyes, bright, watching her, interested. And it was overwhelming.

They carried on talking, discussing the volcano, as they walked back the way they'd come, periodically turning to admire the lava firing into the air.

'Thanks for bringing me here, Siggi.'

'It has been my pleasure,' he said, squeezing her hand. 'I

am ready for a coffee and a cinnamon bun.'

'Me too.'

Iris walked back to the jeep in a haze of emotions. Seeing this volcano close up, in all its glory, was one of the most amazing experiences of her career. Of her life. And this man understood what she wanted. More than anyone else ever had. What was she supposed to think about that?

8

Siggi was in uncharted territory. On some level, he was working on auto-pilot; his charms with women well-known amongst his friends. It was second nature to him and he didn't know any other way to behave with women he met for the first time. The only exception to this was his friends' partners. Because he knew where the line was and he would never cross it.

But Iris made him feel different, and although he was well aware of the fact that on the surface he was going down the same familiar road as he always did, there was something else going on too.

The look on her face when she'd seen that lava was incredible. She was passionate about what she did, and Siggi found it quite intoxicating. It made him want to be with her, feed off this remarkable energy that she had for her work. He hadn't met a woman who had a similarly nomadic, you might say unsettled, lifestyle, and it made him think she might understand him. What made him tick. Maybe more than anyone else ever had.

He held the door of the jeep open for her, then closed it after she'd climbed in. Waiting for a second, he took a deep breath and walked around to the driver's side. He'd grabbed her hand without really thinking about what it might mean. What did it mean? He was probably about to find out.

He pulled his gloves and hat off and unzipped his coat, then opened the back door of the jeep and threw them on the back seat. Then he climbed inside and grabbed his backpack from the footwell behind Iris.

'It was such a great idea to bring a picnic,' she said. 'What a spot.'

From here, they couldn't quite see the glow of the lava. The best of the action was hidden behind the cone of the volcano. But perhaps Iris didn't care about the showier parts of a volcano. Perhaps the geology that was all around them was just as good.

'Here.' He handed her one of the thermal mugs and the bag of pastries, letting her choose first.

'Ooh, this one for me. Thank you.'

He watched her take a bite, her eyes still fixed on the view, bright and smiling. Neither of them addressing the fact that they'd shared… something, felt uncomfortable.

'Hey, Iris.' He needed to see her face, to know whether she was fixed on the view to avoid looking at him, or just because she was captivated by it. She turned to look at him expectantly, and his heart leapt a little with relief. Then, a second later her face fell.

'It's okay. I know it's easy to get carried away in the moment,' she said.

'What do you mean?'

'Well, you know, the holding hands. I get that it was just one of those things. I didn't read anything into it. You don't have to worry.'

Siggi didn't know how to respond. She was either giving him the brush-off, or she was getting in there first to say it was a mistake, assuming that's what he was going to say. And he wasn't sure it was a mistake. 'Oh. I guess I thought maybe...'

'I'm not really into starting something when I'm not going to be here for very long.'

Her eyes were firmly fixed ahead of her, and Siggi got the feeling that what she'd said was more of a well-practised response rather than how she actually felt. At least, he hoped it was.

'I thought perhaps there was something there,' he began, never more aware of how far he was straying from his comfort zone. His safe place of never catching feelings for anyone. Never risking being tied down. 'I don't normally hold hands with anyone, Iris.' That was true. It usually went straight to kissing and then quickly developed even further, by which time the holding hands phase was well and truly over.

'You're a great guy, Siggi, but I'm only here for two weeks. However I might feel now, it can't come to anything, can it?'

'I guess not.' There was no point pretending that he would want it to be anything more than a fling. Because she was right. What else could it be?

The conversation paused while they tucked into their pastries.

'You're quite something, you know,' he said.

Iris looked at him questioningly.

'I don't think I have ever met a woman who is so certain about what she wants. I can accept that you would like to be friends, but nothing more,' he said gently.

'Thank you.'

It wasn't lost on Siggi that normally, he'd be desperate for the women he was seeing to be as pragmatic as Iris. To give him the out he usually wanted. Except, this time, he didn't think that was what he wanted. What he wanted was to get to know Iris. Discover the hidden depths that made her afraid to let herself go. Because for all the logic she had spoken in the past few minutes, he knew what he'd seen in her eyes when he'd grabbed her hand. She felt the same way he did. She just didn't want to admit it to him, or maybe even to herself. Perhaps it was as she'd said, that there was no point starting something that had no future, but Siggi thought there was probably more to it.

'So no more holding hands?' he said, trying to lighten the mood.

'I liked it,' Iris admitted. 'Would you hold hands with a friend?'

Siggi didn't want to admit that he'd never been friends with a woman. 'Maybe. I mean, not Rachel or Gudrun. But in theory.'

'Hmm, I wonder if you're the type of guy who is never friends with women.'

Was she reading his mind?

'That is like a knife to my heart,' Siggi said, dramatically clutching his chest. 'I am not a womaniser, Iris.' But in his heart of hearts, he knew that's exactly what he was.

'Friends works for me. I had a friend in Hawaii who I worked with and we went to the beach together a lot.'

'So we can hang out?'

She shrugged. 'I have no objections to that. We both know where we stand.'

'In that case, would you like to go out for dinner tonight?'

'Two nights out in a row?'

'Is that against the rules?'

'No, but I'm not sure my head can take another night like last night.'

He laughed. 'We will not have the bad influence of my friends. We could share a bottle of wine instead of drinking four beers each.'

'That sounds good to me.'

They were quiet on the drive back to Reykjavik, mainly

because Iris fell asleep, her curls falling over her forehead as her head lolled to the side. Siggi kept glancing at her, taking in her long dark eyelashes against her pale cheeks. Her full lips, slightly apart.

Siggi exhaled deeply. What had he just agreed to? Being friends with this woman was going to be difficult. He wasn't sure where to go after the exchange of looks and the hand-holding. Were men and women ever just friends? Not in his experience, and he felt that by the time Iris left Iceland, he was likely to be an expert on why that was.

Siggi dropped Iris at her hotel, having gently awoken her as they reached the city limits, giving her time to gather herself.

'Oh, we're here.' She pushed her hair back and blinked a few times.

'Shall I pick you up in an hour?'

'Actually, I feel wiped out now. I'm not sure I'd be very good company for dinner. Another time, maybe?'

'Oh, sure,' he said, his heart sinking in the way it definitely wouldn't if one of his friends suggested a rain check.

'Thank you so much for an amazing day.'

She leant over and kissed his cheek. He'd have read something entirely wrong into that gesture if they hadn't had the conversation earlier, but now he knew where he stood, so there was nothing to question. But it was hard to ignore how good it felt to have her kiss his cheek. Her hair smelled amazing.

'I enjoyed it too,' he managed to say. 'You are a very interesting friend to have.'

'Thanks, Siggi,' she said, grinning from ear to ear. 'I'm sorry about tonight. I'll see you soon?'

He nodded and smiled, inwardly desperate to pin her down as to exactly when that was going to be. She got out of the jeep, then grabbed her things from the back seat before heading into the hotel.

Siggi sat and watched until she was out of sight and even though he spent most evenings alone, he suddenly felt bereft and had no idea what he was going to do. What he didn't want to do was go home to his empty flat.

He parked the jeep back at the office and then headed for Olafur and Gudrun's house. It wasn't far away, so if they were out, it wasn't much of a detour to get home.

As he walked up the path, which still had mounds of snow piled at either side after the last storm, he could see the lights were on and he felt a deep sense of contentment at knowing what he was going to find inside; friends who wouldn't judge him; friends who would be on his side.

'Hey,' he said as Gudrun opened the door.

'Come in, come in,' she said, turning and going inside without waiting for him.

He closed the door, took his boots and coat off and went into the small lounge where Olafur was lying on the sofa, reading. He sat up as his friend came in.

'Siggi, this is a pleasant surprise,' he said.

'Beer?' Gudrun asked.

'Yes, please,' they both answered at the same time.

'What's going on?' Olafur asked. It was because he was concerned, not because he minded Siggi calling round.

'Iris.'

'Ah.'

'Tell us everything!' Gudrun said, coming in from the kitchen with three open bottles of beer.

'I took her to Fagradalsfjall.'

'Siggi! That is very thoughtful. Did she enjoy it?'

'Yes, it was interesting to see it from her point of view. She was very excited about a particular kind of lava.' He smiled as he remembered.

'Oh my god!' said Gudrun, whose level of excitement was

getting a little wearing. 'You like her.'

'Ah,' said Olafur again. 'This is not the Siggi we know and love.'

'I do like her, but she is not interested. She said there is no point starting anything when she will be leaving in a couple of weeks.'

'And you are sad that she is not such an easy conquest?' Gudrun asked, her face the picture of innocence.

'Well...' That's exactly what he'd thought three days ago when Iris had walked into the Iceland Adventures office. But now, it wasn't. 'It is different this time. I want more than that.'

'What?' Gudrun looked genuinely shocked, and exchanged a worried glance with Olafur. 'But you never want anything serious.'

Siggi shrugged. 'She is different. I want to know her. Everything about her. Before she decided we could only be friends, we held hands, and I thought I saw in her eyes the same feelings I have. And if that is how she feels, why would she not give herself a chance to see what happens?'

'Maybe she is trying to save herself from being hurt,' Gudrun said.

'It is like with Rachel and Jonas. He loved her but tried to end things when he thought she was leaving, to save both of them from being hurt,' Olafur said.

'So what should I do?' Siggi swigged his beer and looked at his friends, hoping that they would tell him something that might help him get Iris to change her mind.

'I don't know,' said Gudrun. 'I think you know better than me what it takes to make a woman fall at your feet.' There was a glint in her eye. 'But if she is immune to your charms, maybe you need to respect that.'

Olafur nodded, stifling a laugh at the same time. 'Siggi, you are now experiencing what used to happen to me, Brun, and Jonas most of the time. You are luckier in love than we ever were, all of us together.'

'None of it was ever love,' Siggi said.

'Is it love with Iris?' Gudrun was a romantic who believed strongly in love at first sight.

'I am not sure what love is, but I know Iris is the only person that has made me interested in finding out.'

'Oh, Siggi,' Gudrun said, her eyes full of happily ever afters.

'Siggi. You are in trouble,' said Olafur with a wry smile.

After another beer, Siggi said goodnight and headed home. As the chilly night air hit his face when he turned onto the street from the cobbled path that led to Olafur and Gudrun's house, he realised he felt better after talking to his friends. He smiled. He could be friends with Iris. It was better to be friends and have half a chance that she might like him enough to stay in touch with him after she left Iceland, than to throw away any chance of ever seeing her again, by insisting that they give it a go, or nothing at all.

But it was going to be difficult to navigate, since his default setting was seduction. This was a chance to show everyone that he wasn't that guy. He knew he'd put up barriers in the past, stopping short of allowing anyone close enough to get to know the real him. It was driven by the shame he carried at having abandoned his daughter and her mother. What kind of guy did that? He didn't want to be the guy that did that, and yet he was. And there was nothing he could do to change that. And the idea of people knowing he was capable of that kind of behaviour crippled him. However he felt about Iris, it was going to take a lot for him to feel able to share that with her, and yet that's what he would have to do if he was serious about her. Perhaps just being friends was the best thing after all.

9

Iris had organised the trip to Hraunvik with Bjarkey. It was Tuesday morning, and she'd not heard from Siggi since their volcano trip on Saturday. And she missed him.

When he said he thought there had been something between them, she couldn't bring herself to open up and say that yes, she felt something too. It felt too dangerous. What if he'd gone on to say, *I thought there was something between us, but I think you have the wrong idea?* That would have been terrible. The safest thing was to deny it until she made sense of the feelings she had for him. She had long ago resigned herself to being single. Flings didn't interest her because she knew from bitter experience that when she liked someone, she fell hard. So it was easier to glide above any emotions like that until she felt ready, one day, to let her career take a back seat. That time wasn't now.

The problem — and it was a nice one to have — was that Siggi had forced her to dip into her emotions, and that hadn't happened for a long time. He was so kind and thoughtful, and that wasn't something she came across very often. She led a very independent, sometimes lonely life and wasn't used to anyone going out of their way for her. She didn't know Siggi well enough to know whether this was usual behaviour, in which case she'd be an idiot to think he was treating her any differently to anyone else. But the alternative, that maybe she was special to him, and that was why he took her to see one of the most amazing volcanoes she was ever likely to see, was just as hard to accept.

Bjarkey picked Iris up, and they travelled to Hraunvik on the same route as she'd taken with Siggi the week before. It was a grey, overcast day and it felt as if the sun hadn't quite risen. It made the landscape look more desolate and imposing, without the sun to glint off the lying snow or to illuminate the drifts that were swept in clouds from the sides of the mountains in the wind.

Since it had looked so cold, Iris had put an extra layer on just to be sure, and packed a spare set of clothes in her backpack in case they got drenched either by snow or rain. She'd also been to the closest bakery and bought two cinnamon buns. She hoped Bjarkey would think about bringing a hot drink for them both since Iris had no means to do that herself, but she packed some water as a backup.

They chatted easily about their work. Bjarkey periodically pointed things out as they crossed the Reykjanes peninsula, showing Iris areas where there had been activity before and a couple of places where their own seismometers were located.

When they arrived in Hraunvik, Iris directed Bjarkey to the street where her seismometer was located. There was nothing to see, but Iris wanted to check in with the homeowner to make sure they were still happy to have it in their garden, and to check that it hadn't been disturbed at all. The data she was getting looked good, so she didn't expect anything to be wrong.

'Do you mind coming with me?' she asked Bjarkey when they pulled up outside.

'Sure! We may as well leave the car here while we survey.'

They got their things together, then Iris went up to the

door of the house she'd been to with Siggi and knocked. The same man answered.

'Hello. I just wanted to check that it's still okay to leave my equipment here?'

He nodded. 'Of course.'

'Thank you. I'll just check on it and then we'll be off.'

He frowned, and Bjarkey took over in Icelandic. The conversation extended beyond a quick translation of the last sentence, so Iris smiled politely and went back down the steps over to her seismometer, which was exactly as she'd left it.

'Everything all right?' She asked Bjarkey when she'd finished talking and come over to see the equipment.

'He was asking where your friend was. Siggi is it?'

Iris blushed. 'Oh yes. He works for a tour company and he agreed to come out here with me when I set this up.'

'Apparently, he knows the family in the house next door. That's how the guy knows him.'

'Oh, he didn't say.' Well, that was confusing. If Siggi knew who lived in that house, why had he been so reluctant to knock on the door?

'I wonder why he did not suggest putting it in their garden?' Bjarkey said with a frown.

'We did try their door, but there was no one in. Here is as good as there.' Why she felt the need to defend Siggi, she had no idea.

'Of course,' Bjarkey said with a smile. 'So this is your special seismometer. What made you decide to site it here?'

'Based on your data, I tried to triangulate a location where we might expect to see the most activity and this was the ideal place.'

'Ah. And has this picked up anything more than we have seen from our own monitoring?'

'Yes. What you saw the other day, that trend is increasing,

and the activity is becoming more regular. There is a seismic event every few hours, according to the data.'

'That is what we were predicting would happen, so it is exciting that you have data that supports it. Maybe tomorrow you could come into the office again and we can have a proper look?'

'Of course, I'd be happy to.' Iris knew this was her big chance to prove that her method worked. To be here, in such close proximity to where something big was going to happen, knowing it was only a matter of time before her predictions would become reality, was exhilarating. If she pinpointed the event accurately enough, gave people time to evacuate, it could make all the difference to the town, and would give her the data she needed to support her research paper.

'We will walk around the town to see if there are any physical signs yet that support what we have seen so far in the monitoring. And perhaps stop somewhere for a coffee?'

'Lovely!' said Iris. She hadn't imagined that this remote little town would have much to offer, but Bjarkey took her to a cafe called Hjá Höllu. It was located back on the main road they'd come in on, near the only roundabout in town, and offered everything from pastries to lunches. The wonderful scent of homemade bread hit them as they went in, making Iris feel hungry. She and Bjarkey both ordered coffee and a pastry each. Iris chose something that looked like a figure-of-eight of light flaky pastry with what she hoped was custard, filling the holes. Bjarkey was far more restrained and opted for something that looked like a tiny pain au chocolat.

Once they'd settled themselves at a table, Bjarkey asked, 'Which tour company did you use to come out here last week?'

'Iceland Adventures. I'd emailed a few places to ask, and they were the only ones that responded and actually, they said no.' Iris smiled because it seemed pretty funny now that she knew Siggi.

'I expect they thought you were a tourist.'

'That's what they said. I had to ask them to google me to prove my credentials.'

Bjarkey laughed. 'I do not know what other way there would be to prove it, but I am not sure I would have thought of suggesting that.'

'And I'm not sure they said no because of the risk, because on Saturday Siggi took me to Fagradalsfjall.'

'On a tour?'

'Not really. More of a day out.'

'So you guys are friends now?' Bjarkey raised an eyebrow and smiled.

'Yes, I think so.'

Bjarkey raised her eyebrows and tipped her head, encouraging Iris to elaborate.

'It's a bit awkward. We held hands at the volcano and then on the way home, I think he was trying to tell me he likes me.' It felt odd, sharing what felt like intimacies with Bjarkey, but Iris liked her and wanted to forge a friendship, so she didn't think too hard about it.

'You think? What did he say?'

Iris thought for a moment. Because what did he say? 'I'm not sure I gave him the chance to explain himself properly. The thing is, I travel a lot. There never seems any point starting anything with someone I'm going to leave in a week or two.'

'Not for some fun?' Iris may have looked shocked, because Bjarkey quickly added, 'I am sorry. I have been married a long time. I love my husband, but I live for conversations like this.'

Iris laughed at Bjarkey's candour. 'I don't know if I'd be able to have the fun without the feelings that might go along with it. I don't want to get hurt, and I don't want anyone else to.'

'Does it need to be so deep?' Bjarkey asked gently.

'It does.' Because what was the point otherwise? Letting down the defences that she had spent so long building could be disastrous if it was for the wrong man. The last thing she wanted was to have made herself as resilient as possible, only to have her heart broken by someone who wasn't as invested in a relationship as she was.

Bjarkey dropped Iris off at the hotel, and after they'd made plans for her to go into the IMO office the following day, she dumped her things in her room and headed back out in search of food. The fish and chips she'd had on the first night had been so delicious, it was tempting to head there again, but there were other places she'd seen as she'd walked around that she was keen to try too. She headed for the church, Hallgrímskirkja, remembering that she'd seen somewhere at the other end of the road from there that she wanted to try. It was on the street where the road was painted with rainbow stripes. The only way Iris could remember where that was, was to use the church as a reference.

101 Reykjavik Street Food was a cross between a street-food eatery and a casual restaurant. Iris ordered the house special, which was fish stew and rye bread. Authentic Icelandic food was something she had yet to try, and this felt like a safe choice. She sat on a high stool at the bar that faced the window so that she could watch the world go by. The food was delicious. Hearty, full of flavour, and it warmed her from the inside out. It was the best meal she'd had, well, since the fish and chips.

When she finished eating, she sipped her beer and gazed out of the window. She was so busy daydreaming that she jumped out of her skin when someone rapped on the window.

'Oh my god!' she said, smacking her hand to her chest. Siggi was on the other side of the glass, laughing so hard he was shaking.

Iris began laughing and tapped on the window, trying to encourage him inside. He finally noticed and came in, taking the stool beside her. He brought the cold in, like an aura around him.

'You have already eaten?' he asked, pulling his hat and gloves off and unzipping his coat, but not taking it off.

'Yes. I had the fish stew.'

'That is good here,' he said. 'And what are you doing when you have finished that beer?'

'Heading back to the hotel. What are you doing?'

'I am on my way to see Brun play at the open mic night. Want to come?'

Iris was quite surprised. It was hard to imagine Brun as a performer. 'He sings?'

'And plays guitar. I think everyone will be there, apart from Ned and Anna. They are still in London.'

It was too tempting an idea to pass up. Iris knew it was going to further blur the lines of friendship between her and Siggi, but when he was sitting there next to her, his blue eyes glistening, creased in the corners because he was smiling at her, it was hard to listen to the logic that she was trying to remind herself of.

'I'd love to come, thanks.' She finished the last of her beer and put her coat on. It felt good to be doing something on the spur of the moment. And it felt great to be with Siggi again.

As they began walking down the road, towards the Harpa, Iris wished they hadn't had that conversation at the volcano, because right now, she'd love to be holding his hand. More than anything, she wished she had waited to see what Siggi was going to say instead of assuming the worst. Why did she think so little of herself that she would let herself believe he had already regretted the hand-holding at that point?

'Are you alright?' he asked.

'Yes, sorry. Just lost in thought for a second.'

'So what have you been doing since I saw you?'

'I went to Hraunvik today with Bjarkey, from the IMO. We visited my seismometer and did a brief survey to establish whether there has been any significant movement.'

'And?' Having family in Hraunvik gave him a vested interest.

Iris made a mental note to temper the information she shared with him with that in mind. It was important not to be alarmist. 'There is nothing at the moment, but the activity is becoming more regular. I'm going to the IMO tomorrow to look at the data with them.'

He nodded. 'So, I am wondering where we will go on our next excursion.'

Iris frowned in confusion. 'Our next excursion? I didn't realise it was a regular thing.'

'Of course. But this is what we will do now that we are friends. Do you have time this week, or maybe Saturday again?'

'So we're friends who do stuff like that together? Coupley stuff.'

'I do not know what makes it... coupley. Don't friends do things like this? It is no different to you going to the beach with your friend in Hawaii.'

'You're right,' she said, smiling. 'It's the same.' But it wasn't the same. She hadn't looked forward to seeing Dylan in the same way that she was already looking forward to what she and Siggi were going to do next, even though she didn't know what it was yet. And her heart hadn't leapt at the sight of Dylan like it had when she'd seen Siggi tonight, and not just because he made her jump. No one had made her feel like that for a long time.

They crossed the road and headed past the Harpa towards an unassuming single-storey building that backed onto the water.

Inside, the bar was busy and cosy, with low-lighting. The bar itself stretched along one wall, stopping short of reaching the far wall to allow space for a stage area in the corner where a woman was singing. There were a few large tables at the back of the room and smaller ones nearer the front.

Siggi waved at his friends who were sitting at a table near the back of the room, and then asked Iris what she'd like to drink, and ordered the same thing for himself.

'This place is really cool,' she said. It was the kind of place you'd hope to stumble across on your travels, but in reality, unless you were a local, it was unlikely.

'Yes, it is,' Siggi said, grinning at her. 'Shall we go and join them?'

Iris nodded and led the way to the table where Gudrun, Rachel, Brun, Jonas, and Olafur were waiting. Rachel and Gudrun greeted her as if she were an old friend, and she remembered what Siggi had said; that just a night out with them would make you want to stay in Iceland. After one night out already, Iris could totally understand that. She wanted to be friends with these people, and not just for a couple of weeks. She was almost as excited to see them as she had been to see Siggi tonight. This wasn't what happened if you spent a couple of weeks somewhere. You didn't come away with lifelong friends. You didn't think you might be falling in love with a man who you'd spent only a few hours with. Was Siggi right? There was some kind of strange Icelandic magic going on, or did this kind of thing happen to people all the time? Iris had spent so long concentrating on work, perhaps she'd closed herself off from more than falling in love with someone. And perhaps now was the perfect chance to make up for lost time.

10

Bumping into Iris on Tuesday night had been a stroke of luck. He'd been in turmoil, wondering whether to contact her, and what to say if he did. The open mic night was perfect because it was casual and he already knew she got on with his friends. There was no pressure, they'd just had a lovely night hanging out with everyone.

His friends were reading more into it. He didn't blame them for assuming that things were getting serious between him and Iris, despite his protestations. He'd never taken a woman to the open mic night before. In fact, he'd never taken a woman to anything he did with his friends. Realising that scared him a bit, because it reinforced what he already knew; that Iris was special.

He was on his way to collect her from the hotel. He had an amazing day planned for them. They would need to make a quick stop on the way, but he'd factored that into his timings. Since it was Thursday, and he was back on the tour rota with Iceland Adventures, he had swapped days off with Olafur. Any of them would have swapped with him. They were so thrilled that he was taking Iris out on a date, as they thought of it.

Siggi had been busy telling himself that it was not a date. It was two friends going on an outing. It was the only way to keep himself in check, to stop his emotions from running away and beginning to hope. While he wanted to respect that she didn't want to start anything with him, on some level, he knew he was trying to change her mind. And if taking her on an excursion that would blow her mind might help his cause, that was what he'd do.

He pulled up outside the hotel, the engine running because the road wasn't wide enough to park there and go inside to fetch her, but he knew Iris well enough now that he'd bet on her being on time. He was right. Less than a minute later, she walked out of the hotel, opened the back door of the jeep to throw her stuff on the back seat and climbed in the front next to him. Siggi watched her do all of this as if it were something she did every day and took it as a good sign that she felt comfortable to make herself at home with him.

'Góður morgunn!'

'Morning!' She put her seatbelt on, and then gave him a bright smile that lit her face up.

'Coffee?' He handed her a thermal mug from the cup-holder in between them.

'You're a mind-reader, thank you. What's the plan?'

'We have to make a stop to pick up some equipment.'

'Oh, it's a surprise?'

'I think it will be a good surprise,' Siggi said, glancing over at her. She looked pleased. 'How did it go at the IMO yesterday?'

'It was great. We modelled some of the data I've collected and Bjarkey thinks it's giving some extra depth to what they're picking up from their own monitoring, which is great. She's getting hold of a couple more portable seismometers that we can set up in other places in Hraunvik to see if that enhances it even more.'

Iris's enthusiasm was infectious and Siggi was happy to

hear all about her data and her monitoring, even if he didn't understand what it all meant. 'That's great,' he said.

'Yes. It's very positive. Now I need to write up what I have so far and send it back to my lab. I'm hoping that they'll let me extend my stay.'

'Really?'

'I hope so. The outcomes are very positive. It would be a shame to leave now, before I can see it through to a proper conclusion.'

'You mean before an eruption?'

'Or whatever is going to happen. The data is pointing to it not being an eruption of a volcano but something else.'

'Because there is no volcano in Hraunvik, and yet you are monitoring it.' Only now had it dawned on Siggi that this was the case. He knew the entire country was constantly monitored for seismic activity that predicted volcanic activity and eruptions, yet he knew that the closest volcano to Hraunvik was the one he had taken Iris to at the weekend, and that was some way from the town. 'What do you think will happen?'

'We think there are some old lava tubes filling with magma.' She glanced at him and he could see that she wasn't telling him everything.

'Near the town?'

'Perhaps. It's too soon to say.'

'I need to know, Iris. I have people in that town.' He needed her to understand why it mattered to him.

'I know. But I don't understand why you wouldn't knock on their door if they're your family?'

'It is complicated.' He hated himself for replying with such a cliché, in an attempt to close down this line of questioning.

'Okay.'

He could hear the confusion in Iris's voice. He didn't blame her. He was being vague. But he wasn't about to explain his life story to Iris. Not now, not today, when they should be enjoying themselves.

They pulled up at the industrial unit on the outskirts of Reykjavik where Iceland Adventures stored all of their equipment.

'This looks interesting,' Iris said. The note of sarcasm in her voice wasn't lost on Siggi, and he knew he needed to turn things around if it was going to be the day he'd hoped for. He needed Iris not to care what his connection to Hraunvik was. For now.

'Come on,' he said. 'And bring your coat. It'll be cold inside.'

Iris followed him, pulling her coat on as they walked over to the door.

'Wow, this is impressive,' she said, as Siggi flicked the lights on and revealed the well-organised equipment store.

'It does not look like this at the end of the summer,' he said. He began pulling dry suits from a rail, holding them up in front of him and squinting at Iris to see which would be a good fit.

'We're not going diving?'

'Not quite.'

'Swimming?'

He shrugged, trying to keep the secret a little longer. 'I think this one looks like it will be a good fit. He held it up closer to her and nodded, then began sorting through a pile of neatly-folded inner suits. They were basically insulated jumpsuits to wear inside the dry suit.

'Can you dive?' she asked him.

'Yes. Can you?'

'I did a PADI course before I went to Indonesia, but I didn't have chance to dive in the end.'

He hadn't expected her to be able to dive, but anyway, it wasn't necessary for what he had planned.

'Choose a pair of these for yourself,' he said, handing her a plastic box full of goggles. 'And then some of these.' He pointed to a box of neoprene gloves and thick woolly socks.

'We're going snorkelling,' she said triumphantly.

'Yes. Is that okay?'

'Of course! I love swimming. I don't know if I love swimming in Iceland, but I'm willing to give it a go.'

Relief swept over Siggi. 'I hope the only part of you that will be cold is your face.'

'I can cope with that. And don't tell me where we're going. I want it to be a surprise.'

'You like surprises?'

'Love them. And how often does anyone actually get a surprise, especially a good surprise? It's a very thoughtful thing to do. Thank you.' She blushed and looked away from him.

'You are welcome, Iris.' His mood lifted. She thought it was a good surprise. His heart swelled and not for the first time, he wondered what he was getting himself into.

They reached Thingvellir National Park around an hour later. It was a windy day, but bright with fluffy white clouds being blown across the blue sky. The water was sparkling, inviting-looking, although at a couple of degrees warmer than freezing, it wouldn't feel like it looked.

'Oh my god!' Iris said as they pulled up into the carpark. 'We're going to snorkel in a fissure!'

Siggi nodded happily 'It is the Silfra fissure. It was created almost three hundred years ago by an earthquake.'

'And it's between the tectonic plates,' Iris said, almost reverently. 'I knew you could walk between them in Iceland, but I didn't know about this.'

'That is my job.'

'No,' Iris said, looking at him with tears in her eyes. 'You didn't bring me here because it's your job, Siggi. You brought me here because you knew what it would mean to me.'

Their eyes locked for a moment. Then Iris leaned in and softly kissed his cheek.

It was so quiet, he could hear them both breathing. He had hoped he might break down her barriers, but he wasn't sure what to do now that he seemed to have made some progress. He wanted to cup her head in his hand and kiss her, properly, but he was also certain that wasn't a good move. It could break the spell he'd begun to weave.

'Ready?' he asked.

She nodded. 'Never been more ready for anything.'

As he'd suspected she would be, Iris was already wearing thermal under layers, so they both sat on the tailgate of the jeep, took off their top layers, pulled on their inner suits and woolly socks, then stepped into the drysuits. The back had an opening across the shoulders that closed with a heavy metal zip. After stepping in, you had to put your head through the tight neck opening, put your arms in the sleeves and then have a friend zip you up. Siggi was halfway into his suit when he heard Iris laughing. The kind of laugh that makes you weak. He popped his head out and adjusted the neck of his suit so that it didn't feel like it was choking him, then turned to see that Iris was bent double, with no sign of her head.

'Help me!' she said.

'Here.' He put his hand through the neck hole and found the top of her head, guiding her to the opening.

'Oh!' she gasped as she popped her head through. 'That was harder than it looked!'

They zipped each other up, put on hoods, and the goggles and snorkels before finishing with flippers and gloves.

'Ready?' Siggi asked.

Iris nodded, her eyes glistening with excitement. He turned to walk towards the metal steps that led into the water and felt her grab his hand. This was no time to ask what that might mean; it was probably just because it was awkward walking with flippers on your feet, so he gave her hand a squeeze and led the way to the water.

'I'll go first,' he said, and went down the steps. He waited on the bottom step, his hands ready to help guide Iris in if she needed him to, but she confidently came down the steps, and he moved to the side to allow her into the water next to him.

'This is amazing,' she said, treading water as she scrabbled to find the end of her snorkel.

'It is amazing,' he said, 'but it is important to make sure that you do not get cold. As soon as you feel a chill, it is time to get out. It may be only a few minutes.'

She nodded earnestly. He knew she was used to working with risk and that she'd take him seriously.

'Let's go.' He settled his snorkel into his mouth, then reached for Iris's hand again, and they floated onto the top of the water, face down.

He looked over to her but couldn't see her expression since she was busy looking down into the fissure below them. Some people freaked out at this point and got straight out, unable to cope with the unknown depths beneath them, but Iris's grip on his hand didn't waiver and he took that as a sign that she was in her absolute element. He pointed ahead of them and gently kicked away from the edge, further into the stretch of water. The water was always crystal clear and you could see around a hundred metres down because of it. The colours of the rocks mesmerised Siggi, and he knew Iris would know how they came to be those colours, what their composition was, and everything about how the fissure had come to be. And that excited him.

In the end, they spent around fifteen minutes in the water, floating along near the surface for around the two hundred and fifty metres' length between the entry and exit platforms.

Siggi climbed up the steps and waited as Iris continued to float for another minute or so before she climbed out too.

'My face is numb,' she said, trying to lift her goggles up. 'But it was worth it.' She was glowing.

Siggi grinned and helped her to take the goggles off. She mirrored the action with his goggles and they stood for just a moment, their hands either side of each other's faces, before Iris leaned into him and kissed him. On his mouth.

'That is not fair,' Siggi said, softly. 'My lips are too cold to feel that kiss.'

'I'll try again later, then.'

He knew it was the intensity of the moment that had led to the kiss. That Iris's emotions were heightened by the adrenaline of what they'd just experienced. But he wanted to believe she meant it.

He bent down to undo her flippers, helping to take them off before he did the same himself. They carried the goggles and flippers in one hand while they held hands with the other on the short walk back to the car park.

'Siggi. That is the most amazing thing I've ever done,' she said, once they'd got their suits off, dressed and were sitting in the jeep with the heater on.

Siggi poured hot chocolate into two cups from a flask that he'd retrieved from the boot.

'Here. I think you are the only person I have ever met that I knew exactly where you would love to go the most.'

'It was so incredible. To think that even while we were swimming in the fissure, the plates were moving further apart.'

'Incredible,' he echoed, watching the look on her face of sheer joy.

'And the colours of the rocks. I mean, I've never seen anything so clear underwater before. There was almost no sense of there being anything between us and the bottom of the fissure.'

'I know,' he grinned.

'I'm sorry. I'm going on,' she said with a bashful smile, looking down at the drink in her hand.

'Don't be sorry, Iris. It is wonderful that you enjoyed it so much. That is why I wanted to bring you, to make you feel like this.'

She brought her gaze up to meet his and reached for his hand. 'Can we have another go at the kiss?'

He could see in her eyes that it had taken a lot for her to ask him that, and he wanted to reassure her that there was nothing he'd rather do. He touched her cheek with one hand, resting his thumb gently on her bottom lip. Their eyes were on each other all the time, the intensity between them building.

'Just checking that you have warmed up,' he said.

She gave an almost imperceptible nod.

He leaned in and kissed her softly, moving his hand to cup the nape of her neck as they kissed more deeply. This was it. Everything he'd been hoping for.

They kissed for what felt like hours, neither of them wanting to pull away, except for the briefest time to exchange a smile, their eyes glinting just as they had after they'd swum the fissure, but now for entirely different reasons.

But where it would lead, and what they had started by giving in to the kiss, Siggi had no idea. And right at this minute, he didn't care.

11

Iris had spent the whole of the walk back to the jeep, and the time it took for them to change out of the drysuits wondering what had come over her. She'd kissed Siggi. And far from the instant regret she'd been expecting to feel, all that was there was a surge of emotion towards him.

Why was she fighting this? Okay, so it wasn't practical when she was leaving in a week or so, but she'd never wanted to kiss anyone as badly as she'd wanted to kiss Siggi when she'd climbed out of the water. It wasn't something she could ignore any more, and she'd concluded that trying to suppress the feelings she had for Siggi was going to make her just as miserable in the long run as she might be if she fell for him and then had to leave him behind. At least this way, she'd have some lovely memories to take with her.

'So you have changed your mind,' Siggi said softly once they'd tried the kiss again. More than tried it again. More like leant into it for a good while.

Not wanting to ruin the moment, but feeling the need to clarify, Iris said, 'I'll still have to leave next week.'

He nodded, amused. 'I am not sure a kiss is a declaration of anything except that you wanted to kiss me.'

'There might be more to it,' she said with a shy smile. 'You know, no one has ever done stuff like this for me before. This, and the volcano the other day. You know what makes me tick. And it's quite… hot.' She had a feeling that telling Siggi she thought he was hot would go straight to his head.

'You think I'm hot?' He had exactly the look Iris had predicted. He was pleased. And preening.

'Is that what I said?'

'It could also translate to be sexy.'

'Okay,' she said with a laugh. 'But I think what I mean is that your thoughtfulness is making you…hot. Sexy. Whatever.' She felt her cheeks flush.

'You are sexy when you are flustered.'

'Oh, shush.' She pulled him in for another kiss, full of joy that he'd said she was sexy. No one had ever told her she was sexy. His stubble was grazing her chin in the most delicious way, and all she could imagine was how it might feel if he kissed her in places other than her lips.

'So we are doing this? More than friends now?' he murmured, in a brief pause between kisses.

She nodded. 'I'm not used to doing this kind of thing.'

He looked bashful and said nothing, leading Iris to assume that wasn't the case for him, but she already knew that because of Embla from the hotel. Bríet had said she was always angry with Siggi, but she was probably hurt.

Iris knew that even if she hadn't as much control over her emotions as she'd like, she had to control something. 'But I know enough to realise that it isn't something that can carry on after I leave. It won't work for either of us.'

'I understand, Iris. And for the next however many days you are here, you are mine and I am yours.'

That sounded so good. Any thoughts of what happen after she left, that she might be broken-hearted by then if she fell too hard for him, vanished. Siggi consumed all her thoughts. Here, now, and turning her on like she'd never imagined possible.

They drove back to Reykjavik, calling in at the unit again to clean and drop off the equipment they'd used. All the time they were in the jeep, on the straight roads, at least, Siggi had his hand on Iris's thigh, with hers on top. They kept stealing glances at each other, but Iris loved watching him when he wasn't looking at her. The way his hair grazed the collar of his fleece, the back of his hands, tanned and capable as he drove the car. And the creases in the corner of his eyes that made it look like he was smiling all the time.

'You don't think this is a bad idea?' She hated herself for asking. For second-guessing herself, but she needed reassurance.

'Of course not,' he said. 'I think we are two people who like each other and why should we not enjoy that while we can? Life is too short to deny ourselves things that we want.'

'That's true. Do you think we can be friends afterwards?' Iris doubted it would be possible. Self-preservation would probably mean it wouldn't be a good idea.

'Do you?'

Perhaps that response meant that Siggi was thinking along the same lines.

'I want to, but it might be hard.'

'You are not friends with any of your old boyfriends?'

'No. And I don't have that many old boyfriends.'

'That cannot be true.'

'Don't humour me,' she said, not interested in being flattered.

'I'm not.' He looked surprised that she thought he was joking. 'You are very smart and beautiful. Is it work that gets in the way of having a boyfriend?'

'The very few men I've been out with are never interested in what I do. Not even a little bit. And the one time I did find someone I liked who was in a similar field, it didn't end well.'

'Because?'

'Because I got drunk and accidentally kissed someone else. By mistake. He couldn't get over it, so we split up.' She didn't add that she had thought he was the love of her life and it had left her heartbroken.

'That is sad.'

She shrugged. 'It was sad for quite a long time, but if he couldn't trust me, it wasn't going to go anywhere after that.'

'And why could he not trust you if it was a mistake?'

'The person I kissed was someone I worked with. He's my boss now, unfortunately. And my ex-boyfriend couldn't handle me seeing Jay every day.'

'Could you have moved jobs?'

'Not really. The place I work for is one of the few labs in the UK where I can get paid and be researching at the same time. It could have been the end of my career before it had even started if I'd left back then.'

'How long ago was it?'

'About ten years ago.'

'And you have not had a boyfriend since? No one serious?'

'Is that weird?'

'It is sad, Iris.' He didn't say it unkindly, but it brought tears to her eyes because he sounded sad about it himself.

'Well, don't be thinking that you're some kind of miracle man who has brought my heart back to life,' she said, trying to lighten the mood, but looking out of the window next to her while she blinked the tears away.

'And don't *you* think that I kiss every woman I take to the Silfra fissure,' he said with a smile. 'That was the first time for me.'

As they drove into the city, nearing the hotel, Iris asked, 'What shall we do now?'

'If you are asking what I would like to do, I would like to take you out to dinner, finally.'

She smiled. 'I'd love that. Can I have an hour to get ready?'

'Sure. I will meet you back here.'

'Thank you.'

He stopped the jeep outside the hotel and left the engine running while they kissed again, then reluctantly, Iris climbed out and waved goodbye as he drove away. She went into the foyer and was greeted with a filthy look from Embla. She might have felt worse, but Embla had been throwing dirty looks the very first time she'd set eyes on Iris, so the fact that she was with Siggi now should make no difference.

After she'd showered, Iris surveyed her clothes and wished she had something more exciting to choose from. She wouldn't want to wear a dress, but a pair of boots that weren't practical hiking boots might be nice, or a top in a more interesting shade than grey or navy blue. In the end, she settled on her newest jeans, skinny fit with a high waist, a black t-shirt where the hem just skimmed the waistband of her jeans and a relatively new dark green hoodie that was made of a light knit fabric which made it smarter than her only other options of a sweatshirt or fleece. There wasn't much she could do about the boot situation, but she felt certain that Siggi probably didn't go for smart clothes either, so it would probably be okay. She put some extra make-up on; eyeliner and some liquid eyeshadow that her sister-in-law, Bec, had given her, her usual mascara and then a slick of plummy-brown lipstick, another gift from Bec.

She scrunch-dried her hair and pulled some hair-oil through the ends, hoping it would stop the frizz, then looked at herself in the mirror. She looked okay. Hopefully, different from the other times Siggi had seen her because now things between them *were* different and she wanted to make an impression.

'Where are we going?' she asked when she skipped down the hotel steps to meet him.

He put an arm around her shoulders as if he'd done it a hundred times before, and pulled her into his side. 'You look beautiful,' he said, twisting to kiss her.

'Thanks. So do you.'

He laughed. 'Thank you. I am thinking a bar that has good food?'

'That sounds perfect.' She was relieved that he wasn't interested in showing off by choosing somewhere fancy where they might end up feeling uncomfortable.

She loved walking along the street wrapped in each other's arms. Her arm was around his waist, feeling like they were the perfect fit for each other, even with their bulky coats on.

They walked further than Iris had ventured before, to the part of the city that lay beyond the Harpa, to the west. The buildings there were more architectural in style and there were fewer of the small, colourful-clad houses. They stopped at a place called Slippbarinn.

'Is this okay?' Siggi asked, his eyebrows raised.

'Definitely. I could eat a burger and fries,' Iris said, having scanned the menu that was on the wall outside.

Siggi opened the door and held it for Iris to go in first. He waved at the guy behind the bar, who waved back, and they chose a table near the back, where the lighting was intimate and there were more empty tables, so it'd be quieter for chatting.

'You know that guy?' Iris asked, nodding to the barman, after Siggi had come back to the table with two pints of beer, having ordered the food.

'That is the hazard of living in the town you grew up in,' he said, setting the beers down and wiping his hands on his jeans.

'I think that's nice, that you're still friends with people you grew up with.'

'Is it like that for you?'

Iris shook her head. 'No, my parents moved away from the village where I grew up. They wanted to live in a town once they retired, so they didn't have to drive everywhere. I'm still in touch with my best friend from school, though. We catch up when I'm in the UK.'

'Have you always travelled a lot for work?'

She tipped her head from side-to-side. 'Only for the past couple of years. The first few years after my Master's degree, I worked in the lab all the time, monitoring seismic activity all around the world. Data came in from places like the IMO and we'd analyse it, especially for countries who don't have the resources themselves.'

Siggi was still looking interested, which surprised Iris. Perhaps it shouldn't have done; she'd be pretty interested in anything he had to say after what had happened today.

'Then I started getting interested in the way things were being monitored. The equipment, how it worked, what we wanted to know, and how good it was at delivering that. I started travelling because I was installing portable devices in places that were starting to see more activity on their standard monitoring equipment. It sometimes makes a difference. And now I'm researching how looking at different frequencies with a modified seismometer might help with predictions.'

'Wow, that's impressive. You are an expert in your field.'

'I'm getting there.'

'It must be an amazing feeling to have a job that really makes a difference to people.'

'It feels disjointed. It's not like we're responsible for deciding to evacuate or anything. We just pass on the information to the people that make the decisions.'

'It is still impressive,' he insisted.

'Thank you.' It felt wonderful to be here with Siggi. The way he was looking at her with a hint of what she could only describe as adoration in his eyes was out of this world. And she was sure he was seeing the same thing mirrored in her own eyes.

'I did not expect this to happen today,' he said, smiling, his eyes crinkling at the corners.

'Neither did I. I was trying quite hard not to fancy you.'

Siggi laughed. 'Maybe I am irresistible?'

'Apparently,' Iris said drily. 'Or it was the euphoria that overcame me after snorkelling between *actual* tectonic plates.'

'I don't think so. I have been there a million times and it has never happened before,' he said, taking Iris's fingers and intertwining his own.

She had to stop herself from gasping out loud at the intensity of feelings his touch released within her. She felt lightheaded, and it wasn't the beer. It was intoxicating.

'What happens after dinner?' She knew exactly what she wanted to happen after dinner, but she didn't want to assume that Siggi would want to take that step this quickly. Normally, she wouldn't herself. But time was short. She wanted Siggi. She wanted as much of him as she could get before she had to leave. And she already knew that even if they spent every second of that time together, it wouldn't be enough.

'What happens next is up to you,' he said.

'I'd quite like to do some more kissing. Somewhere more comfortable.' Saying it out loud made her feel shy. Telling someone what she wanted like this was not something she'd ever done before. But she was so sure that this was what she wanted. It was pointless dancing around it or pretending to be coy.

'I'd like that too.'

12

What had happened after dinner was that they ended up back at Siggi's flat. He'd been keen to go to the hotel instead, insisting that his flat wasn't that comfortable, but Iris had insisted for two reasons; she was curious to see where he lived, and she didn't want to risk running into Embla in the hotel. She might have been unfriendly to Iris on every single occasion they'd met, but Iris didn't want to rub her nose in the fact she was with Siggi.

'Are you sure?' he said, pausing by the street that led to Iris's hotel.

'Yes. I want to see where you live,' she said, kissing him in encouragement.

'Okay,' he said, with a resigned roll of his eyes.

The walk to Siggi's was another five minutes. They strolled through the town, enjoying the newfound feeling of being together, their arms wrapped around each other again, lost in their own world.

'Here we are,' Siggi said, stopping outside a grey building that had none of the charm of the pretty little houses in the centre of the town. He unlocked the door and held it open for her. 'I am on the third floor. There is no lift.'

'That's okay. Race you!'

Iris ran up the stairs, trying not to squeal as she felt Siggi right behind her.

'Hey, come back,' he called, laughing as she overshot, going up an extra flight after losing count of how many flights she'd run up.

They fell inside his flat and Siggi closed the door amid the kissing that had suddenly become more urgent. Barely parting as they both pulled off their coats, they made their way over to the sofa, the flat in darkness save for the light from the road outside.

'Are you sure?' This time, he was asking a different question, but Iris had never been more sure of anything in her life.

She nodded and looked at him with intent in her eyes while she pulled off his top layer.

'Okay then,' he said, with a half-smile that made her shiver in anticipation.

He teased his fingers underneath her various layers until he met her skin. His touch made Iris feel as if no one had ever touched her before, and no one had. Not like this. She nuzzled into his neck, breathing him in while his fingers travelled underneath her clothes from her waistband, up the sides of her ribcage, teasing her with the gentlest of caresses. She wanted to pull all of her clothes off and be naked with him, as close to him as she could get, but she was also loving the anticipation of what was to come. And this had been a long time coming.

When she thought she could stand it no more, he ran his hands up her sides, encouraging her to raise her arms, and he lifted her layers off all in one go, leaving her in her jeans and bra.

'Oh, Iris,' he said breathlessly, standing back to appreciate her.

She stepped towards him, determined to reciprocate the

level of teasing she'd endured. She pulled his remaining top off, revealing a tattoo that encircled the top of one arm and another that reached from the top of his shoulder and disappeared onto his back. 'I love this,' she said, running her finger around the tattoo on his arm.

'It's a Maori design.'

'It's sexy.' She never thought she'd say anything like that out loud to someone, but it was almost as if she couldn't help it. She needed him to know that's what she thought.

'You're sexy as hell, Iris.' He grabbed her thighs and lifted her up, forcing her to wrap her legs around his waist. Then he carried her into his bedroom and laid her gently on the bed.

Iris woke to the smell of fresh coffee. The bedroom was dark, but the light coming from the living room and kitchen wasn't the cosy glow she'd expected. She'd not taken much notice last night. They'd been desperate to fall into bed together, so there hadn't been time for a tour.

She reached onto the floor and grabbed the first thing that came to hand, which was thankfully her thermal leggings. There was a sweatshirt neatly folded on the chair, so she grabbed that, loving that it smelled of Siggi. Before she left the bedroom, she ran her fingers through her curls in an attempt at taming them, but it was fruitless, so she swept the front of her hair away from her face, tucked it behind her ears, and followed the smell of the coffee.

'Morning,' she said, walking over to where Siggi was warming a pan of milk on the stove. He was wearing loose jogging bottoms and a tight black t-shirt that showed off the tattoo on his arm. She snuggled into his side and wrapped her arms around his waist. He put one arm around her and kissed her on the top of her head.

'Good morning, beautiful.'

She squeezed her eyes shut and grinned with the sheer joy

of everything. It felt so right and she was thankful for her heart overriding her ridiculously logical head, giving her this chance of happiness, even if it was only for a few days. She would never regret it.

'That coffee smells amazing,' she said.

'There are fresh pastries on the table.'

'You've already been out?' she asked, sitting at the table and beginning to devour a cinnamon bun.

He nodded and smiled at her.

As she munched, she looked around at his flat. It was so sparse, it looked as if no one lived there.

'You don't have much stuff,' she said.

'I don't need much stuff. I did warn you, it is not very nice.'

She tipped her head to acknowledge that she remembered.

'It isn't that it's not nice, it doesn't feel like you, that's all.'

'What would it need to feel like me?' He came and sat down, placing the cups of coffee on the table between them. He looked amused.

'I thought you'd have photos everywhere of the places you've been, lots of souvenirs, that kind of thing. I imagined there would be a surfboard propped up in the corner of the lounge and that you'd have Mexican cushions and Indian throws. Things like that.'

'You think I surf in Iceland?'

'I don't know!' she said, laughing at how surprised he sounded.

'I do,' he said, grinning. 'But it is not as good as surfing in Hawaii. There is nothing like the warmth of the sun on your face.'

'Isn't it too cold here?'

'It is, but you know that saying, there is no such thing as bad weather, just bad clothing choices? That goes for surfing too. You need a thermal wetsuit and you cannot stay in too long. And it is best to avoid any beaches that are throwing ice balls onto the beach.'

'Does that really happen?

'Yes. In the deepest parts of winter, and I do not feel like surfing then. In fact, I am usually surfing somewhere else in the winter.'

'What are you doing today?'

'What are you doing?'

Iris bit her lip and smiled. 'I have nothing pressing to do.'

'I have nothing to do except press myself on you until around six tonight.'

'That is so cheesy,' she said, grinning anyway.

'You can stay for a while, then?'

'Yes.' Iris slid out of her seat and onto Siggi's lap. She wrapped her arms around his neck. 'And what are you doing later?'

'I am taking a Northern Lights tour.'

'Really?'

'Want me to see if you can come?'

'Oh my god, I'd love to come. Do you think that would be alright?'

'I will see if there is a space, and we will rely on the forecast to know whether the aurora are likely tonight, because if not, it will be cancelled.'

'And then what will we do?'

'Perhaps I could show you?'

Iris buried her head in Siggi's shoulder. 'This is so perfect,' she whispered.

He pulled back, put his hands either side of her face, caressing her cheeks with his thumbs. 'It is. For now.'

Iris didn't think too hard about that. It was a little warning that this was temporary, but she already knew that. She wasn't expecting a happily ever after and she knew Siggi wasn't either. They both knew where they stood and living in the here and now was what this was about. So she wrapped herself around Siggi and allowed him to carry her back to the bedroom.

'Hey.' Siggi was sitting on the bed next to her, gently waking her.

'What time is it?'

'It is time for you to go and get ready for the trip, if you still want to come?'

Iris sat up, wide awake. 'Yes! There's room?'

'Yes,' he said, kissing her. 'And there is a good forecast.'

'All the stars have aligned.' She threw the cover off and began gathering her clothes. 'Shall I meet you at the office?'

'If that is okay?'

'Of course it is. Do I need to bring anything special?'

'Just wear all the layers you can. It will be cold while we are hunting.'

'I'm looking forward to seeing you do your thing.'

He caught her wrist. 'I am looking forward to sharing the aurora with you.' He kissed her deeply, and she responded knowing that they would have to restrain themselves for the next however many hours.

Considering how long they spent saying goodbye to each other, which was ridiculous given that they would be together again in no time, Iris still had enough time to get herself ready. She packed some extra layers into her backpack rather than wear them on the way, since it probably wouldn't be cold in whatever vehicle they were going in. She had half an hour to spare before she needed to meet Siggi, so she opened her laptop to catch up on some emails.

There were a couple from Bjarkey with the results of some data they'd run, and an email from Jay asking her to call him. She frowned. Why wouldn't he have called her if he wanted to speak to her?

She pulled her phone out of her coat pocket, finding the battery was dead. Only then did she realise that she hadn't even pulled it out of her pocket since she'd left the hotel yesterday evening to meet Siggi. Almost a whole day since she'd checked it. That was unheard of, but it made her smile because the reason that had happened was so delicious to think about.

She put the phone on to charge, hoping that it would have time to charge enough that she'd be able to take some photos if they were lucky enough to see the Northern Lights. Actually, she'd given hardly any thought to the fact that she might see the phenomenon for the first time in her life. She'd been more excited about going on the tour with Siggi. She had a feeling that she was going to find it as sexy as anything watching him doing his job.

While her phone was plugged in and once it had enough charge to boot up, she found she had eight missed calls from Jay. She hadn't checked in with him since she'd been to the IMO for the first time. He'd had to arrange the first meeting for her, but Iris couldn't think of any reason he'd need to speak to her so urgently now. Torn between ignoring him, which was the easy option, and calling now to get it out of the way, Iris decided on the latter. At least then, whatever it was would be out of the way and she'd be able to enjoy her evening.

'Jay?'

'Iris. Christ, where have you been?'

She was pleased he was so irritated. The number of times it had been the other way around, well, she'd lost count. 'I had a day off.'

'Right.' He sounded like he was going to dispute that she was allowed a day off, but thought better of it. 'I've been expecting a report from you.'

'I haven't finished the first phase of testing yet.'

'I assumed you would have sent something over once you'd met with the contact at the IMO.'

'We're still looking at my data in conjunction with theirs. The activity is starting to increase, so the next few days could give me something more solid to report on. I don't think we should rush.'

He exhaled in impatience. 'Iris, we're not sending you here, there and everywhere for you to swan around taking days off.'

'I didn't have a single day off in Hawaii. I was on site every day and writing the results up on the weekends. I flew straight to Reykjavik with no break, worked the first three days and have had two days off since. I don't think you could call that swanning around.'

Jay was silent for a moment, presumably trying to think of a comeback. 'I'll expect the report by the end of the week. You're due back next week, right?'

'Right.' She might be due back next week, but it was looking less likely that the activity in Hraunvik was going to increase enough by then to give her what she'd come for. 'I'll have the report across as soon as I have something meaningful pulled together.' That was all she was willing to promise. And leaving Reykjavik wasn't on her radar. Especially now.

'Okay. I'll expect it as soon as.'

'Okay.'

'Thanks, Iris. Bye.'

She ended the call and resisted the urge to throw her phone against the wall. Why did he have to micromanage her? His boss's boss had agreed that Iris could work in the field, testing her theory until she had enough data to prove that it worked in real-life situations. Hawaii hadn't been the hotbed of activity they'd hoped for, but Iceland was still looking very hopeful. And whatever Jay thought, there was no way she was heading back to the UK before the seismic activity at Hraunvik came to a head.

Before she left, she checked her seismometer readings. It was still sending the data, and there was slightly more regular activity still, but nothing more to get excited about. Yet.

Iris gathered her things, unplugged her phone at the very last moment, and headed out to the Iceland Adventures office. There were six people waiting outside already, all bundled up against the cold. One man had a camera and tripod and a large bag of what Iris assumed was more camera equipment.

'Hi,' she said, feeling shy, but wanting to make an effort.

Everyone murmured hello back and smiled.

Another couple came and joined the group. 'Is this the right place for the Northern Lights trip?'

'Yes,' Iris said. And right then, a minibus pulled up next to them and Siggi jumped out.

'Welcome, everybody! Let's go aurora hunting!'

13

Siggi looked thrilled to see Iris waiting outside with the rest of the tour party when he pulled up in the minibus. Even though it had only been an hour since they'd been together, she felt a buzz of anticipation at seeing him again. He had ten people on the tour, as well as her.

He greeted everyone, then checked them off his list. The last couple arrived just as everyone else had got onto the bus. Iris hung back until everyone else was settled.

'Maybe sit in the back on the way?' he suggested. 'I need to do a lot of talking to start with and you might be a distraction.'

Iris had no problem with that. She respected the fact that he was working, not here to be with her this time, and it might be more fun to be part of the crowd. 'Okay,' she said, smiling and climbing into the minibus where there was one pair of seats spare.

Siggi slid the door closed and went around the other side to get into the driver's seat.

'Okay, aurora hunters!' he said through the microphone that he'd tucked around his ear. 'Let's go!'

Iris leant into the aisle and looked to the front of the bus. She could see a screen on the dashboard which showed what she thought was a weather radar.

'We are heading to the south-east of Reykjavik tonight. The skies are clear but there is some cloud to the west, so we will try to get ahead of that. For anyone who has not been on a Northern Lights hunt before, we are looking for three things. The first thing, we need it to be dark.'

There was a rumble of laughter at Siggi stating the obvious.

'Yes, it's sounds funny, but there are many weeks in the summer when it is hard to find a dark enough sky. Number two, we need to see stars. That is the best sign for us that the skies are clear, and number three is that we need a strong aurora forecast.'

He explained what made a good forecast and said that tonight the KP index, which is used to measure the strength of the lights, and how far south of the North Pole they might be seen, was a solid four. 'The usual forecast is a two to three, and we would have a chance even at that level, so a four is very good news.'

Everyone cheered, and Iris laughed, loving the camaraderie that was building up on the bus.

'You're on vacation alone?' an American man, probably in his sixties, asked her.

'Ronald,' his wife said. 'I'm sorry, honey. It was unusual in our day, that's all.'

'Oh, it's fine,' Iris said, smiling at poor Ronald. 'I'm here for work. I was lucky enough to get a spot on the trip tonight, but I'm not really on holiday.'

'What do you do?'

'I monitor volcanic activity.'

'Well, you're in the right place, I guess,' Ronald said.

'Is something going to happen?' Ronald's wife looked panic-stricken.

Iris didn't want to alarm the woman, but surely, being on

holiday in Iceland, it was hard to ignore the fact that there was volcanic activity on some level, almost everywhere.

'How do you think they get the Blue Lagoon hot, Barb?' Ronald said.

'There is a lot of activity all the time,' Iris said, trying to reassure Barb. 'That's why it's a great place for me to come. And you don't need to worry because they have some of the best data anywhere in the world for predicting really big events like volcanos erupting.'

'You'd tell me if that's why you're here,' Barb said, staring Iris right in the eye.

'Of course.'

Luckily, at that point, Siggi began talking again, which distracted Barb at just the right moment. This time, he was giving advice on how to take a great photo of the lights. 'Sometimes the lights are not visible with the naked eye,' he said. 'On your phones, set your camera to the longest exposure you can. If you have a camera, you probably know better than me what to do, but I am happy to help if you need it.'

Iris pulled her phone out and began fiddling with the camera settings until she thought she'd found what Siggi was talking about. She was getting pretty excited at the prospect of seeing the aurora. Everyone was looking out of the minibus windows, looking for stars or even a glimpse of the lights themselves.

After a few more minutes, Siggi turned off the main road and pulled up in a small clearing. There were a couple of other vehicles there, so perhaps they were not the only aurora hunters out that night. Maybe that was a good sign.

'Okay guys. We will spend about twenty minutes here. That will give us time for our eyes to adjust to the darkness and have a good look for the aurora. If they are putting on a good show, we will stay.'

They all piled out of the minibus and ventured in their pairs a little way from the bus. Iris did the same, training her eyes on the sky, looking for stars. There were stars. The longer she looked, the more she could see.

'Oh, look!' Someone was exclaiming at a photo they'd taken on their camera. Iris could see the colours on the screen from where she was, and pulled out her own phone.

Siggi came up behind her, and hooked his arm around her waist, then pointed up at the sky. 'You see that? It looks like a wave of mist, maybe a cloud? Take a picture of it.'

Iris did as he suggested, her breath momentarily taken away by the surprise of his body enveloping hers.

'Oh my god! Look!' The wisp of cloud was actually a wave of bright green. 'But why can't we see it?'

'It is not strong enough yet. The camera is building the light in the time your exposure is open.'

'It's still amazing, even through the camera.'

'I'll be back,' he whispered into her ear, squeezing her around her waist before he went to check on his guests.

Iris was mesmerised, taking photo after photo of the sky. Some images were better than others but there was something there in all of them. Then after another few minutes, she thought she could see colour in the darkness. She took a photo to see if there was anything there or if she was imagining it. Yes! The photo was the best yet, and the green waves were starting to be more visible. The others were pointing and telling each other where to look. It wasn't long before they were all treated to the most spectacular show. What had begun as green lights, gradually morphed into purple shades, reaching almost as bright as a neon red.

'This is a very interesting colour,' Siggi said to the group as they gathered together again, all the cameras forgotten in favour of watching the lights live in front of them. 'The red colours are because there is very high altitude oxygen mixing with the solar particles. The green is the normal oxygen in the atmosphere which is why the green lights are more common. The red is wonderful.'

Iris watched Siggi watching the lights, thinking how amazing it was that he could find the wonder in it as much as the rest of the group even though he must have seen them countless times before.

'Is the red unusual?' One of the men asked.

'Very,' said Siggi. 'Green and purple are the most common. I have never seen the red as strong as this before.'

It was as if the lights had put on a special show just for them. The guy with the tripod, Pieter, on holiday with his wife, from Germany, took photos of all the couples under the lights, promising to email them to the tour office for Siggi to distribute to everyone. Everyone, without exception had huge grins on their faces.

'And you?' he asked Iris.

'Oh, yes, please, that'd be great.' She'd seen some of the photos he'd taken and the colours were more vibrant and the waves more defined in his pictures than anyone else's. 'And one with Siggi?'

Siggi grinned and put his arm around her shoulders.

'You make a cute couple,' said Barb, presumably unaware that they were just that.

'Would you like to stay for a while?' Siggi asked them all. Everyone agreed that they'd like to, to make the most of the experience for as long as no one was freezing cold. He opened the back of the minibus and revealed two huge flasks. 'Hot chocolate for everyone?'

By the red light on his head torch, to preserve everyone's night vision, Siggi poured cups of hot chocolate for everyone and offered butter cookies. He and Iris stood close to the bus, poised to collect in the empty cups or provide anyone who wanted one with a refill.

'This was a good night for aurora hunting,' she said. 'How often do you go out and not see them?'

'Not that often. Usually, if the forecast is bad, the trip does not run, and everyone gets bumped to the next night.'

'So they could end up going home without seeing them?'

'It does happen.'

'I feel so lucky. My first time of looking for them and I see this.' The lights were still dancing across the sky, the energy of them almost palpable as they moved, growing alternately brighter before fading a little and then coming back.

'It is incredible luck,' Siggi agreed. He tucked his arm around her waist. 'You could come again tomorrow night, if you would like to.'

Iris wanted nothing more than to replicate the day she'd had with Siggi today. To laze around in bed, getting to know each other in every sense. But the report was weighing on her mind and she knew she had to make a start on it.

'I'd love to, but I should work tomorrow.'

'All day?' His expression was so forlorn that Iris imagined for a moment that the best thing to do was to quit her job, tell Jay to stuff his report and spend tomorrow and every day forever more with Siggi.

'Maybe not all day,' she relented. 'I'm going in to meet Bjarkey again on Monday and hopefully we can run my data alongside theirs so I can get some analysis for my report. But I suppose I could get some work done, enough to prepare for Monday, and then we could hang out?'

'That sounds good to me,' he said. 'And we have tonight.'

'We do,' Iris said, grinning. And when she'd left the hotel, Embla hadn't been on the desk, so Iris knew they were safe to be there tonight without fear of a look that could kill on the way in.

He kissed her, no longer caring that anyone might see. It didn't matter. Now that everyone had seen the Northern

Lights, they were too happy to care about the tour guide canoodling with one of the guests. And anyway, their eyes were still trained on the sky.

'I think it is time to go,' he said. 'I am starting to feel a little bit cold.'

He rounded everyone up, and they all climbed aboard the minibus again. Iris sat up at the front with Siggi this time.

'See? I told you they were a couple,' she heard Barb say to her husband.

Siggi turned and looked at Iris, his eyes shining. Iris could see he liked what Barb had said, and Iris loved that. They were a couple.

The lights were visible almost all the way back to Reykjavik. Everyone in the back was sitting in a peaceful silence, the darkness and the late hour lulling a couple of them to sleep. Iris kept stealing looks at Siggi and occasionally, he glanced across at her and gave her the most wonderful look that told her he couldn't wait for them to be alone again.

It was after eleven o'clock by the time they got back to Reykjavik. This time, Siggi dropped everyone directly at their various hotels. Barb and Ronald were the last, since their hotel was closest to the place where Siggi had to park the minibus.

'Thank you, Siggi. We had the best time,' Barb said, giving him a hug once she'd climbed out of the bus. 'That was on my bucket list and it's well and truly ticked off now.'

'You're welcome,' Siggi said, shaking Ronald's hand once Barb had turned her hugs over to Iris instead, who had also climbed out to say goodbye.

'And you'll send the photos from Pieter?' Barb asked.

'Of course,' Siggi said. 'We have your email address from the booking.'

'And you look after this one,' she said, patting Iris on the arm. 'She's a keeper.'

'Thank you, that is good advice,' Siggi said sincerely.

'It was lovely to meet you both,' Iris said.

'You too, honey,' said Barb.

Once Ronald and Barb had gone inside their hotel, Siggi drove them to the car park on the edge of the oldest part of town, where they left the minibus.

'We'll leave everything for tonight,' said Siggi when Iris asked whether they should take the cups and flasks with them. 'I'll pick it up tomorrow in the jeep.'

They walked through the quiet streets together, hand in hand.

'Would you like to stay in my room tonight?'

Siggi beamed at her. 'I would love to.'

Iris was glad she'd decided not to work all day Saturday after all. She could hardly bear to contemplate spending an entire day without him. It was ridiculous, she knew that, but also such an overwhelming feeling. She'd never had that feeling of missing someone when you're still with them. If she felt like this at the prospect of a day apart, what would it be like when she finally went home?

'Have you explored the rooftop yet?' Siggi asked once they were in Iris's room and had taken off most of their layers.

'No.' Until he'd said, she'd forgotten the rooftop spa that had been mentioned when she checked in.

'There's a sauna and hot tub.'

'That sounds tempting after an evening out in the cold. Should I ask if we can go up there?'

Siggi shook his head. 'I know the code for the door and Anders won't mind.'

Iris's heart beat a little faster at the thought of doing something that might be against the rules. She wasn't sure why, but she thought Siggi had probably been a bit of a bad boy in his younger days. Maybe because he didn't seem to have grown up and taken on the usual responsibilities that his friends had, and instead seemed to live the life of an eternal twenty-year-old. It gave him that air of rebellion that Iris found deeply attractive, because she was nothing like that herself.

'Okay, let's do it,' she said, feeling excited. She began digging around for her swimsuit in the holdall that she hadn't unpacked. 'Oh, you don't have any swimming trunks.'

Siggi took a step towards her and put a hand on hers. The one that was now holding her swimming costume.

'You won't need this,' he said.

Relief swept over her because it was the worst example of a swimming costume to wear if you wanted to look sexy in front of your boyfriend. But that was quickly overtaken by embarrassment once she realised he meant they should go naked.

'I don't think that's a good idea. What if there are other people up there?'

'There won't be,' he said with an easy shrug.

'You don't know that.'

'I do. Anders doesn't let guests up there at this time of year after ten in the evening.'

'Oh.'

'So we will leave this behind.' He took the costume from her and tucked it back into the bag, then took her hand and led her out of the room and upstairs. On the landing, there were two doors. He keyed a code into the pin pad by the one in front of them. It opened and they stepped out onto the roof.

Siggi opened a small cupboard and flicked a switch inside. The strings of fairy lights that criss-crossed the rooftop burst into light.

'It's so pretty,' she said.

'Not as pretty as you.'

Somehow, Iris felt it easy to suppress the urge to laugh. It was there for a second, but then she accepted the compliment, however cheesy, because the way Siggi was looking at her made her think he might actually mean it.

They kissed for a minute until Iris shivered.

'Come on, let's go next door and get undressed. The idea is to warm up, not freeze to death,' said Siggi.

'Thank you.' Iris threw her arms around his neck. 'This is the perfect way to end the perfect day.'

He took her hand and led her inside to a warm and pristine changing room with baskets of fluffy white towels and robes hanging on hooks waiting for them.

'Iris, I don't know what is happening, but every minute of today has been a surprise to me. I didn't know I could feel like this about anyone, and all I want is to be with you. You make me feel like a different person.'

'Is that a good thing?'

He sat on the wooden bench that ran around the room and pulled her to him, his arms looped around her waist. 'I feel like myself for the first time in a long time.'

14

It was wonderful to wake up together and for neither of them to have anywhere to be. Iris stretched and then snuggled into Siggi's side, her head lying on his shoulder.

'So you're not working until tonight?' she asked.

'I wish I could switch out with someone, but I can't ask them to do that now it's starting to get busy again.

'We could hang out together today and then I can work later when you're working.'

'You don't want to come again tonight?'

'I'd love to, but I have to try and fit some work in, so if we can both do that at the same time as each other, that kind of makes sense.'

Siggi murmured in agreement. They lay in silence for another couple of minutes, then he propped himself up on his elbow, eyes shining, and said, 'I have an idea.'

'What?' Iris said, laughing at how excited he looked.

'I'm going to take you camping!'

Iris wasn't averse to camping at all. She was outdoorsy and loved that kind of thing. But in the temperamental weather of Iceland? Not so much. But how was she going to say that without bursting his bubble?

'You don't think it's too cold? It did snow on the way back

from the volcano the other day.'

'Trust me. I think you will love it. Also, it is very close to Reykjavik so I can go to work tonight and you can bring your work to do, but it will be like a little holiday for us over the weekend.'

It sounded tempting. They had such a short amount of time together, a break away could make it feel like they'd had longer. And if she could work at the same time, what reason was there to say no?

'Okay, let's do it.'

'Yes, Iris!' Siggi put his arms around her in a bear hug and rolled them both around the bed.

Iris laughed harder than she had for a long time, fuelled by the rush of agreeing to a plan on the spur of the moment.

'I need to make a call,' Siggi said. 'Perhaps I should not have made it sound like a sure thing because I have to check with a friend whether it is possible.'

'You make the call while I shower,' Iris said, shifting further towards the edge of the bed.

'I am not ready to get up yet,' said Siggi, placing an arm around her waist, pinning her to him. 'You stay right there while I make the call and then we can make plans for the day while we relax in bed.'

By the time Siggi had made the call and organised whatever needed organising, and they'd finished relaxing in bed, it was almost lunchtime. It astounded Iris how quickly the time could go when you weren't doing anything in particular.

'I'll go home and pack,' Siggi said, pulling his clothes on while Iris watched appreciatively from the bed. 'Shall I pick you up in an hour?'

'Perfect,' she said. 'I'll pick up some coffee and pastries for the road.'

He bent down to kiss her. 'See you soon.'

Iris showered, dressed and packed, making sure she had her laptop charger, since Siggi had assured her that the camping wasn't basic and that there was electricity and running water. It was exciting, heading off on an adventure without having really planned it and without knowing exactly what it was. This was the side of Siggi that took him off on his travels, Iris supposed. He probably liked spontaneity, whereas she was much more of a planner.

An hour later, she waited outside the hotel with her bags at her feet and the coffees and bags of food in her hands. Not knowing where they were going, as well as pastries, she'd bought fresh bread rolls from the bakery, and had popped into a deli and bought some cheese and cured meat of some sort, in an attempt at a makeshift picnic.

Siggi pulled up and left the engine running while he helped her get everything in the jeep, then they were off. It was a windy day, and grey clouds scudded across the sky with some speed, so the sun was in and out with regularity.

They headed out of the city on a road that Iris hadn't been on before. Unsurprising, since she'd only been to the Reykjanes peninsula or the IMO offices. She sat back, sipping her coffee and enjoying a change of scenery, when Siggi pulled off the road.

'Here we are,' he announced.

'Already?' It couldn't have been more than twenty minutes since they'd left.

'I said it was close by.'

'I know, I wasn't quite expecting it to be just down the road.'

'Let's come back for the bags when we have seen where we are staying,' he said, climbing out of the jeep and opening the back door to fetch his coat.

Iris did the same, then they held hands and walked along a path towards a wooden building that marked the entrance to the camping park.

Siggi held the door open for Iris to go inside.

'Hey, Siggi!' The man behind the desk came out and hugged Siggi. They exchanged a few words in Icelandic before Siggi introduced Iris.

'This is Kristján,' Siggi said. 'Kris, this is Iris.'

'Great to meet you,' Kristján said, pulling Iris in for a hug and kissing her on both cheeks.

'You too,' she said, surprised at the greeting.

'The best tent is available for tonight,' he said. 'I have already lit the fire in there, so it will be toasty.'

Iris sighed with relief and smiled at Siggi. 'So not exactly camping, then?'

Siggi winked at her, which made her weak at the knees. 'Thanks, Kris,' he said.

'Let me show you.'

Kristján led the way outside, heading through a gap in the hedge and into a field. It had eight large white dome tents, each with a chimney pipe coming out of the roof and a wooden hut attached to them. As they walked towards the opposite side of the field, Iris noticed that the front part of the tents were glazed with triangular windows that continued the shape of the domes.

'Wow, this is amazing,' she said. 'You can watch the stars from your bed.'

'That's the idea,' said Kristján.

Siggi glanced at her out of the corner of his eye and smiled.

'This is yours.' They stopped at the farthest dome from the entrance. It had a fantastic view of the mountains yet was tucked in the corner of the field and so had more privacy. 'I have lit the fire under the hot tub too, so it'll be steaming in an hour or so. And I reserved you a table for dinner since we were getting full, but if you don't want it that's okay.'

'That sounds great. Can I let you know? I might have to

take a Northern Lights trip tonight, but otherwise I think we'd love to have dinner.' Siggi raised his eyebrows to check with Iris who nodded.

'You may be lucky, my friend. The forecast is not good for tonight. Anyway, I will leave you to settle in. Enjoy.'

Iris was excited. This place was unimaginably perfect for a romantic getaway, and that type of thing had been non-existent in her life until now. She felt so lucky to be with Siggi. It was his more adventurous nature that was giving her these amazing experiences while she was in Iceland.

'Come on, let's go inside,' he said.

The way in was through a door in the wooden hut at the back of the tent, if you could even call it that. They stepped inside, finding a tiny hallway where they could hang their coats and leave their shoes. To one side, within the hut itself, was a tiny bathroom with a toilet, shower, and sink. It was tiled in dark grey, giving it a luxurious feel. Then the wooden hut led through into the tent itself. There was a kitchenette against the back wall of the hut, and the space opened out under the dome. Sumptuous looking bed linen, fur throws, and cushions adorned the enormous bed that sat in the middle of the room. There were more fur rugs on the wooden floor and, as promised, a fire was burning in an open-fronted stove to one side.

Iris walked over to the window, which had a panoramic view across the hedge at the edge of the field and over the plateau beyond. The mountain was to the left but still gave them uninterrupted views of the northern skies.

'I'm torn between wanting the forecast to be terrible so you can stay here, but then I might see the Northern Lights from here, anyway, if you have to take the trip.'

Siggi came up behind her and wrapped his arms around her waist. 'I will always think of you when I see the aurora now.'

She turned to face him. 'Me too, although it'll happen much less often. Maybe never again.'

They kissed.

'We will see the aurora together before you leave. I am certain of it.'

'How long before you know about tonight?' Iris whispered.

'Long enough for us to try out the hot tub.'

'It won't be warm enough yet.'

'We can find something to do until then.'

Siggi pulled his top layers off all in one go. Iris grinned, loving his lean, tanned body with its tattoos. She took a step towards him and ran her hands across his chest, pinching his nipples between her fingers and thumbs as she looked him straight in the eye and said, 'What do you suggest?'

He pulled his trousers down and she saw exactly what he was suggesting. Suddenly, there was nothing Iris wanted more than that. She wasn't interested in seduction. There would be time for that later. For the first time in her life, she wanted to surrender herself to the feelings that were coursing through her. She pulled off her own clothes as quickly as she could, and with one hand, pushed against Siggi's chest so he fell backwards onto the bed. She straddled him and could see the lust in his eyes and the excitement when she pinned down his arms with her hands and leant over him, her eyes full of promise.

Siggi unravelled himself from Iris and the various throws that were keeping them cosy, and threw another log on the fire.

'Don't go,' she said.

'I'm going to the car to get our stuff and to call the office. Stay here. I'll check the hot tub on my way back.'

Iris lay there with her eyes closed, a lazy smile on her face, thinking that she hoped the Northern Lights trip was cancelled. She wasn't in the mood to work, and had talked herself into thinking that there wasn't much point in doing anything else on the report until she'd been to the IMO on Monday. She had plenty of holiday days accumulated, and anyway, it was the weekend. Her body felt heavy and more relaxed than she could ever remember it being before, and she could hardly contemplate getting out of bed.

'I am off the hook!' Siggi said triumphantly when he came back from the jeep. 'The forecast is not good, so they have bumped everyone to tomorrow.'

'That's great news,' said Iris, from her snuggly spot in the bed.

'I confirmed about dinner. We can eat at seven.' He came and perched on the bed next to her. 'You want to get up?' he asked, running a finger down her cheek and tucked a stray curl behind her ear.

'Not really.'

'The hot tub is perfect.'

Iris sighed. They should make the most of it, she supposed. 'Okay. Let me get my costume out.'

'Haven't you learnt anything, Iris? We do not need costumes. We just need to shower first.'

'But —'

'But no one can see our hot tub from their tent.'

Iris relented, and settled on using a supplied fluffy dressing gown and nothing else, feeling reckless since it was still daylight, just about.

'You feel naughty?' Siggi asked as they pulled their boots on for the short walk to the hot tub.

'Yes,' she said, laughing. 'It is the opposite of something I would do normally.'

'You know, if you go to a swimming pool in Iceland, you have to shower naked before you go in. No swimming costume. Usually open showers with everyone else.'

'Oh my god, really?'

'Yes, really.'

'In that case, this is fine.'

The hot tub was indeed looking inviting. Great clouds of steam were billowing into the air and the smell of wood smoke from the fire underneath only added to the outdoorsy vibe.

Siggi whipped off his robe and stood with nothing on while he toed off his boots. He laughed and held his arms out wide. 'See? It feels great!'

'You're a nutter!' Iris said, laughing along with him. She took her own robe off and felt the cold air nip at her skin while she took her boots off as well.

Then they both stepped into the steaming water, sinking beneath the surface to banish the cold. Iris thought nothing had ever felt as wonderful as the heat that enveloped her.

'Oh my god,' she groaned. 'It's absolute heaven.'

'Better than the bed?' Siggi murmured, having his own moment of deep appreciation for the hot tub.

'Better in a different way.' Iris leant her head back against the side of the tub and closed her eyes, luxuriating in the warmth.

'Do you know what? I have never been in a hot tub with a woman before. Naked.'

Iris felt him move to sit next to her. She smiled, but kept her eyes shut. 'That's not true. We went in the hot tub on the roof of the hotel the other night.'

'Oh Iris, that does not count. Here, it is you and me in nature. I don't think you would get naked in a hot spring in the middle of nowhere, so this is the next best thing.'

'You think I'm a prude?' She was definitely a prude, but Siggi was bringing out her adventurous side and she wanted him to know how far she'd come.

'You are a lovely prude.'

Iris stood up in the middle of the hot tub. The water was at waist height, thankfully, because she certainly would have been prudish about baring everything. She flung her arms out to the sides and lifted her face to the sky, grinning, and enjoying the feeling of the cold air on her skin, knowing she would plunge back into the heat at any moment.

'Okay, you have convinced me,' Siggi said, laughing. He put his hands on her waist and brought her over to straddle his lap. She felt ready to suggest they went back inside to the bed. 'Oof, you are cold!' he said, as she wrapped her arms around his shoulders and pressed herself against his chest. But he pulled her to him anyway, and Iris didn't think she'd ever feel as happy as she did right now, ever again.

Once the fire underneath the hot tub began to die down, it got colder and Siggi announced it was time to get out. 'It will soon be time to leave for dinner,' he said.

'Where is this dinner place? Can we walk?'

'Yes,' he said, handing her a robe and a towel as she stepped out of the tub. 'It is an amazing place that people travel especially to get to, so it is always booked up, even if no one is staying here. It helps them to keep the business going in the winter months when it is too cold for camping.'

'This isn't camping,' Iris said.

'No,' agreed Siggi. 'This is not camping, *ástin mín*.' He kissed her.

'What does that mean?'

'My love,' he said, and she thought her heart might explode.

My love. That was what he'd called her.

My love.

She was his love.

15

When they'd got back from the camping trip yesterday, they'd spent the night at the hotel together. After not much sleep, it was a wrench to leave Iris, especially after such an incredible weekend. All Siggi wanted was to lie with her in his arms for as long as she'd let him. But she had an appointment with her colleague at the IMO, so he left while she was getting ready and headed back to his place.

From the hotel, he walked along Hverfisgata and headed into Te & Kaffi for a double espresso to take out. Then he strolled along the seafront, enjoying the keen wind that was coming off the sea, sending spray from the tips of the cresting waves through the air. He needed to clear his head. It was as if he was in the grip of something, and he wasn't sure what.

He had taken himself by surprise with what he'd said to Iris over the weekend. It might have seemed insignificant, calling her *ástin mín*, but it was the tip of the iceberg of his feelings towards her. The need to let her know how he was feeling was overwhelming. And it had felt good to say. For years he hadn't had any meaningful relationships, never pursuing women, but then giving in too easily to women who were pursuing him. Iris was the first woman in the longest time that he actually would want to have pursuing him. They had an actual connection. Something that he hadn't known he needed until he had met her. The difficulty was that he was falling for her. Hard. And he didn't know what to do about that, given that she would be leaving. He wasn't sure when that was, and he wasn't sure she knew either, but it was too soon.

For years, as soon as he was back in Reykjavik, working, he started thinking about where he was going to travel to next. He had to have a plan. Something to keep him going while he worked endless Northern Lights excursions and Golden Circle tours. Not that he didn't enjoy his job, but it wasn't what fulfilled him. The next destination did that.

He showered, dressed and lay on his bed, his hands behind his head, staring at the ceiling. The past few days had been slightly surreal. He'd actually enjoyed the Northern Lights tour immensely, and not just because the aurora had put on such an amazing show, but because he'd shared the experience with Iris. It was incredible how being there with her could put a completely different complexion on something he'd done a hundred times before. And it had stunned him. The camping trip had been a way of prolonging that feeling. But this time, with just the two of them, it had actually been magical.

They'd eaten at the restaurant along the road from the campsite, sharing a bottle of wine that paired perfectly with the lamb they both chose as their main course. Then on the walk home, it had begun to snow. Great big, soft flakes of snow that delighted Iris. They'd lain in bed, with the fire stoked up to keep them cosy, and watched through the window as the snow fell, turning the landscape into a winter wonderland, until they'd fallen asleep in each other's arms.

After a yawn that made him realise how tired he was, and that lying on the bed and daydreaming about the weekend probably wasn't the best idea when he needed to get to work, he sighed and got up.

He picked the minibus up and drove to the Icelandic Adventures industrial unit. He wasn't due out for a few hours, but he needed to load the bus with supplies. The door was open, which meant there was somebody else there.

'Hey!' he called out as he went inside.

'Siggi?'

Jonas and Rachel were there. They had the wood-burning stove lit and Jonas was sitting at the table with something in front of him he had taken apart, while Rachel was curled up in the corner of the sofa with her laptop open.

'I guess the lights put on a good show for you last week,' Jonas said. 'We've already had a couple of reviews on the website.'

'It was incredible. I have never seen them so vibrant.'

'The reviewers are singing your praises,' said Rachel. 'They make it sound as if the lights coming out to play was entirely down to you.'

Siggi laughed. 'If it was that easy, we could be out every night. Are you trying to mend that?'

'I was hoping to, but I'm not sure I can remember how it goes back together now,' said Jonas.

'I did tell him it was a long shot, but you know how he always looks on the bright side,' Rachel said.

'What was it before you got your hands on it?' he asked Jonas.

'One of the winches we use to get the heavier equipment up to the top shelves.'

'Ah.' Siggi went over to sit beside Jonas and tried to work out what he had in front of him.

'We haven't seen much of you this week,' Rachel said.

This was what slowly drove him mad when he came home. Everyone lived in each other's pockets, and that was one thing he didn't miss when he was away.

Victoria Walker

'He's on the Northern Lights tours this week,' Jonas said. Siggi was grateful for the implication that he'd have no time for anything else.

So, have you seen Iris since you brought her to the bar?'

'Yes. A couple of times.'

'Really? Because she was lovely. It'd be nice to see her again.'

Siggi suspected Rachel was being careful not to imply that there was anything between him and Iris. Perhaps it was time to open up a little.

'We have been seeing each other. We went to Kristján's place over the weekend.'

'Oh,' Jonas said, grinning and inclining his head. 'That is very romantic.'

Siggi batted him on the arm with one of their excursion leaflets, which was also on the table.

'Gudrun told me what you'd said to her and Olafur, so I wondered how things were going,' said Rachel.

This was the problem. There was no point trying to control the narrative about him and Iris, because his friends were a step ahead of him already. It was one downside to his friends being joined at the hip with their partners; you could never seem to catch any of them alone for a man-to-man talk. Although he at least understood it from their point of view a little more now.

'Gudrun will probably have told you I am in love with Iris.'

Rachel gave him a look that told him that's exactly what she'd said.

'She is wonderful.'

Rachel grinned. 'Siggi? Really? That's fantastic.'

'I am not sure. It feels fantastic now, but we have agreed not to continue with anything when she leaves Iceland.' It felt inconceivable that they might say goodbye to each other in as

134

little as a few days, with no plans in place for seeing each other again. But they had decided. It was the right thing for both of them.

A knowing look passed between Jonas and Rachel, and Siggi knew what was coming.

'That's what we thought,' Rachel said, looking at her husband with hearts in her eyes. 'And we couldn't do it.'

'You will find an answer,' Jonas said knowingly.

'I don't think that will be possible. She travels from one place to the other, wherever the volcanic activity is, and I am travelling too a lot of the time. We might never be in the same place as each other again. That is why we are making the most of what we have now.'

'But you really like her?'

He nodded. All he could think about was the next time he was going to see her. He needed to see her. It was like a primal urge. 'She is working today at the IMO and has some report to write so we might not see each other for a couple of days.'

'And it's two days too long,' said Rachel.

'Yes,' he laughed.

'Do you think if she was the one, there would be some way of being together? Like, Jonas and I, we made things work because we loved each other. That's what makes you willing to compromise.'

'You compromised, my love,' Jonas said, pointing his screwdriver at Rachel, who shrugged and blew him a kiss.

'My point is that Iris might not want to be travelling the world chasing volcanoes. She might want what she's found here,' she said.

'Here. This spring was dislodged.' Siggi couldn't continue with this conversation. What if Rachel was right? What if Iris would be willing to stay? It seemed unlikely, based on less than a couple of weeks in Iceland. Whatever Jonas and Rachel said, it took longer for people to fall in love than that. Didn't it?

'Hey, Siggi.' Jonas spoke in Icelandic and laid his hand on Siggi's arm. 'Don't overthink it. It's been a long time since you felt like this about someone. Don't start thinking too far ahead about things that might not even be true. Iris might not want that. She might be like you and prefer globetrotting to what me and Rachel have.'

'*Takk.*' He nodded at Jonas, grateful that his friend understood. It was hard to think about a different kind of life and far too soon to be thinking about something like that with Iris. They'd known each other a little over a week. That might have been all the time it took for Jonas and Rachel to fall in love, but it wasn't often like that for anyone else.

'Sorry, Siggi.' Rachel didn't speak Icelandic, but after three years in the country, she'd probably picked up enough to get the gist of what Jonas had said.

'It's okay.' He grinned at her. 'I am stuck in my ways. It is hard to imagine sharing my life with someone like you all do.'

'I sometimes forget that what we have isn't what everyone wants, anyway. Despite what Gudrun might think.'

They all laughed. Gudrun was the biggest romantic and was desperate for tales of love amongst her friends.

'It is nice to share a few days with someone like Iris. Both of us are happy with it being only that.' Anything else was too complicated.

'You are out again tonight?' Jonas asked him.

'Yes. The aurora forecast looks good, but I think we may hit some cloud cover if I head back to where we were yesterday. I've been avoiding Reykjanes but that will be the best area tonight.'

'Don't you have an insider in the Met Office now? Iris would tell you if it was too dangerous, wouldn't she?'

'That's true. She has mentioned there is more activity but I haven't heard that it's more than that. Maybe we should not worry yet.' He looked at Jonas for confirmation.

'I agree. We need to be careful, but until we hear something official, we should continue to go to that area if we need to. It will be difficult to keep the Northern Lights tours going if we can't chase them to the best locations, as well as the weather being a problem for us.'

'Have you started looking at your next trip, Siggi?' Rachel asked. They all knew his routine and were always interested in where he was heading to next.

'Not yet.'

'Oh.' Rachel sounded surprised and Siggi knew that she'd be reading too much into why he had made no plans. He wasn't sure what was holding him back either, and he could only assume it was Iris. Because he was having such a great time with her, the urgency he usually felt to escape had left him. Temporarily, he assumed.

'Do you know Iris was in Hawaii at the same time I was?' he said, partly to divert Rachel from asking anything else about whether he was changing his usual plans because of Iris, and partly because he'd forgotten.

'No way!' Rachel said.

'Yes, and she was going to the same beach where I was surfing.'

'You could have been there at the same time and not known.'

'We might have been.'

'Oh my god, Siggi. It's fate.'

'Rachel,' Jonas said, smiling at his wife but with a warning tone in his voice.

'Well, that's an enormous coincidence, if nothing else,' she said.

'Yes,' Siggi agreed. 'And you are right. It felt like fate when we realised.'

'You believe in fate?' Jonas asked him.

'I don't know,' Siggi said, shrugging. 'But I do know that meeting Iris is something out of the ordinary and being in Hawaii at the same time… it seems unusual that our paths might cross twice in places that are so far away from each other.'

'Man,' Jonas said under his breath.

'Shush,' Rachel said. 'It's not so long ago that you were getting just as smooshy over me.'

'I am not being… smooshy,' said Siggi, frowning.

Jonas laughed. 'You are! I have not seen you like this about anyone since we were at school.'

They looked at each other, the greater meaning behind the flippant comment, not lost on either of them.

'You had a serious girlfriend at school?' Rachel asked.

Again, the men shot each other a look. It wasn't something they ever discussed.

'It was a long time ago. It's not the same when you're young. You think you know what love is at that age, but you don't.'

'Right, I'm going to the loo. Do you two want a coffee while I'm up?' Rachel asked.

They both accepted, then when Rachel was out of earshot, Jonas began speaking in Icelandic.

'You haven't told Iris about Arna?'

'No.'

'Should you? I mean, she is working in Hraunvik.'

Siggi sighed. 'She wanted me to knock on their door and ask if she could set her equipment up in their garden.'

'And did you?'

'Yes, because what could I do? Tell her that I can't knock on that door because the fourteen-year-old daughter that I never see lives there?'

'And?'

'There was no one home.'

'That was a lucky escape.'

'I know. But I know how it sounds too. I already knew then that I liked Iris. It wasn't a good way to start out.'

And he was ashamed. Ashamed that fourteen years ago he hadn't wanted to be a father and by the time that changed, his daughter's mother was intent on keeping him away because she'd created the perfect family with someone else to be Arna's father. And who could blame her? Siggi hadn't wanted the job. He'd realised the moment that he'd found out about the pregnancy that he wasn't capable of being the guy who stepped up and took responsibility. He'd hated himself for it, but he hadn't known what else to do other than leave.

'You will have to tell her if things do get more serious. You can't keep a secret about something like that.'

'I know. And I appreciate you not sharing this with Rachel.'

Jonas bumped his fist into Siggi's biceps. 'It's not my business to tell your secrets. But it would not make the difference you think it would to tell everyone. I am not talking about Iris, I'm talking about Rachel, Anna, Gudrun, all of them.'

Siggi would love to believe that was true. But the fact was, he'd walked away from his child. And he would never forgive himself for it. He couldn't defend what he'd done, so he didn't expect anyone to think any better of what he did than he did himself. No. It was better to leave it in the past. It was the biggest regret of his life, but there was nothing to be done. It was too late.

16

Iris spent Monday morning immersed in data from the IMO's monitoring sites. She and Bjarkey had mapped her own data onto it and had come up with what they hoped was a solid prediction of what might be about to happen on the Reykjanes peninsula. Bjarkey had run it past her bosses, making them aware that while it pinpointed the timing of a possible event much more accurately than the current data they were using, it wasn't yet reliable until it had been proven by the thing actually happening.

What was becoming apparent was that there were lava tubes forming underneath Hraunvik, fed by the Sundhnúkur volcano. The data that Iris and Bjarkey now had, was predicting the activity increasing until an eruption of the lava that was currently travelling underneath the ground, in less than a week.

'They already have construction workers building lava walls to try and protect the town if the worst happens,' said Bjarkey. 'This data gives them a timeline that we didn't have before.'

'If it's right,' said Iris.

'I think it is,' Bjarkey said, her eyes shining. 'I think we should go out to Hraunvik today. We could take the two extra seismometers and site them and we can see if anything has changed since our last visit. If we are right about the timing, we should be seeing shifts in the surface by now.'

'Today? That's great.' Iris loved working with Bjarkey. It was a fantastic mixture of crunching the data, which Iris loved, and the fun of actually going out to see where the data was coming from. And if they were right, seeing the changes in reality would give extra weight to Iris's report.

'Okay. Do you have everything with you, or shall we call at your hotel on the way?'

'I have my stuff with me.'

'Let's go, then!'

It wasn't as cold today, but the skies were granite grey and there was a constant drizzle in the air. As they drove towards Hraunvik, the landscape looked less enticing in the gloom, and even in the short time since her first visit with Siggi, Iris could see the snow had receded and there was more of the black lava rock landscape that had peeked out from beneath the snow. It wasn't spring as it would look in England, but it was a start.

They drove straight to Hraunvik, the road looking familiar this time, and parked on the outskirts of the town.

'Oh, look.' Bjarkey pointed at the road. They hadn't walked far. There was a crack in the road's surface. It wasn't big, but it definitely hadn't been there before.

'That's what we were expecting.' The data that they'd put together had indicated that there would be physical evidence of a volcanic event and this was it. Iris was thrilled that her method had helped to predict this, and now it had been proven. Yet seeing the beginning of what could be terrible for the people of the town was sobering.

'Yes, it's fantastic for us,' Bjarkey said. 'But it means that we need to notify the civil authorities. I am not sure they were expecting this kind of timeline. They will need to bring the evacuation plans forward.'

That brought it home to Iris. If the crack in the road wasn't enough, that there were evacuation plans said everything. 'It's terrible. These people are going to lose their homes.'

'They may not. But it is a possibility.'

Bjarkey took some photos of the road and they measured the crack to use as a baseline in the days and weeks to come.

As they carried on into the centre of the town, they saw further evidence of movement. Similar cracks in the ground, mostly visible on the roads since the surface was normally smooth. But then they went to check Iris's seismometer and came across more cracks. This time the crack ran from the street, through the garden where her equipment was and from what they could see, underneath the house.

'Oh my god,' Iris said. 'We should warn them.'

'They will know,' said Bjarkey, gently. 'And they know what it means.'

Iris couldn't imagine living somewhere so precarious. She'd never been anywhere before where people lived so close to a volcanic event she was monitoring. The joy that she normally felt when something was about to happen had been lost to a feeling of dread for these people.

Again, they took photos and measurements of what they could see. They both knew that the house would be compromised within the next day or so. And that this house wouldn't be the only one. If Iris's equipment hadn't been in the garden, they wouldn't have noticed that particular fissure, so it was likely there were others, just as dramatic, that they'd missed.

Using the same technique that Iris had used when she'd first arrived to choose the site of her original seismometer, they chose two new sites. One north of the town and one further to the south. They could see that the fissures would most likely occur on a loose north-south line, so this extra monitoring would help to give them better data about how that might play out.

Iris was quiet on the drive home, contemplating what they'd seen and finding it difficult to feel happy that her theory had finally begun to be proved. Because at what cost?

Her phone rang. It was Jay.

'I was expecting your report today,' he said, with no preamble.

'I've been out in the field. There's firm evidence that the theory is correct. We estimate it'll be less than a week until the activity emerges. I'd really like to stay until it does.'

'Not possible.'

Iris took a breath, knowing that she needed to stay calm to make a persuasive argument for staying. 'But it'd be better for the report if we can show that the culmination in activity matches what we predicted.'

'You don't need to be there for that. The IMO can send the information on.'

'But —'

'Iris. I expect the report tonight and you back in the UK on Wednesday.'

Iris caught Bjarkey's expression out of the corner of her eye. She could probably hear Jay, but if not, she'd caught the gist of the conversation, anyway.

'What would it take for me to stay?'

'It's not an option.'

He rang off, leaving Iris staring at her phone in disbelief.

'Who was that?'

'My boss.'

'He wants you to leave? Now?'

Iris nodded.

'Wow,' Bjarkey said. 'What's gone on? For him to insist you leave when you could leave in a week with a thousand percent more information and data, there has to be something.'

'It's a long story.'

'Come on, we have time,' Bjarkey said, smiling. 'Share the drama.'

'I was at university with him. I was going out with someone else, a guy called Patrick. One night, I got really drunk. That's not an excuse for what happened, but it is the reason it happened.'

'What happened?' Bjarkey still had her eyes on the road, but they were wide in anticipation.

'I kissed Jay, and Patrick saw.'

'Jay is the one who is your boss now?'

'Yes.'

'And did you secretly like Jay? Is that why it happened?'

'No! God, if you ever met Jay, you would understand why that repulses me. Actually, that conversation we just had is a fair representation of what a dick he is most of the time.'

Bjarkey laughed, then Iris carried on.

'We were at a party and it was dark. Jay came up behind me and slipped his hands around my waist. I turned, thinking it was Patrick, because he used to do that all the time. I was drunk and tired and my eyes were closed and I ended up kissing him, thinking it was Patrick.'

Bjarkey shrugged. 'That is not so bad. It was an accident.'

'It *was* an accident, but Patrick didn't believe me. I don't know whether he was using it as an excuse. Maybe he'd wanted to end things anyway. But that's what he did.'

It still hurt to think back at how mortified she'd been when she'd realised what she'd done. How dismissive Patrick had been of her, making her realise he hadn't been in love with her the way she was with him.

'And then you ended up working for the man who ruined your relationship.'

'It feels wrong to blame it on him, and if he was a nicer

person, maybe I wouldn't have.' She gave Bjarkey a rueful smile. 'But from that day on, he's lorded it over me. You know what I mean?'

'I think so. He has never let you forget it and is smug. Is that the right word?'

'That's it exactly.' It was a relief to explain it to someone who understood. 'And now that he's my boss, he tries to control me, even though I have more experience than him in monitoring and especially in this field of experimenting with frequencies.'

'That is what he doesn't like. That you are more knowledgeable than him. He cannot control that, so he has to try and control you in another way.'

'But making me go home now is bad for the project. That's what I don't understand. It's as if his rivalry, or whatever, with me, is forcing him to make poor decisions.'

'A man like that will always put protecting his ego ahead of anything.'

It made total sense what Bjarkey was saying. Jay was jeopardising what she'd been working towards for his own reasons, not for the good of the project. And his priority should be the work as much as it was Iris's.

'Perhaps I should take a stand,' she said. 'I'm not going to hand the report in and leave Iceland. I'm going to stay. I need to see it through.'

'The man is an idiot. If he cannot appreciate that this research could change the way we monitor this kind of activity forever, he has no business running a lab.'

Iris couldn't help grinning. Bjarkey's belligerence against Jay was contagious and had given Iris the courage she'd been lacking for so long. It had taken her years to be in the position of being allowed to do her own fieldwork for her project. Years of biting her tongue and kowtowing to Jay, hoping his attitude might change if only he could see what they might achieve. But he would never change. Bjarkey was right. He saw everything through the prism of what he saw as her rejection of him that night at the party.

'I might lose my job.' The thought of that was actually exciting. In reality, there weren't geological labs in every town begging for a volcanologist with a specialism in monitoring. It would be hard to find another job, but with the completed project under her belt, she'd have a better chance than she might have before.

'You might lose what's been holding you back,' Bjarkey said, patting Iris's hand. 'What you have discovered is incredible. I don't think anyone has told you that. Don't let this man allow you to believe anything less. He will take the credit for this if you are not careful, Iris.'

As they arrived back at the IMO, Bjarkey said, 'I can take you back to your hotel. Do you mind waiting while I finish up here? It will be ten minutes.'

'No, that's fine. I'm happy to wait. Thanks.'

Iris sat with her laptop open, intending to make a start on her report. Though she now had no intention of writing it as quickly as Jay had wanted, it made sense to track the events every day to make sure she didn't miss anything.

'Iris, do you have a moment?' Bjarkey called to her from the doorway of an office on the other side of the room.

She closed the lid on her laptop and went over to the office. Bjarkey held the door open and then closed it behind them.

'Iris, this is Emil. He is the manager of the team here at the IMO.'

'Good to meet you, Iris. Bjarkey has been telling me about your project and what it could mean for the data we are looking at in Hraunvik.'

Iris nodded, ready to explain what she'd been doing with her seismometer, while Emil continued.

'We have a large team here at the IMO and we are always

looking for talented scientists. Bjarkey has told me that you may be in the market for a change and I would like to say that if that is ever the case, we would like the opportunity to be considered.'

'Thank you,' said Iris, looking at Bjarkey, who was standing there smiling. This wasn't what she'd been expecting when she'd walked into Emil's office. It was overwhelming. He spoke as if she'd be doing *them* a favour by considering working at the IMO. Never in her wildest dreams would she ever have thought an internationally renowned place like this would want her as part of their team. Half an hour ago she'd been thinking how tough it would be to contemplate having to look for another job and now one had all but landed in her lap. 'I'm still not sure what my plans are, but I'd love to talk to you more about what a job here might look like for me.'

'Bjarkey can fill you in,' Emil said with a smile. 'She knows what we are looking for and can answer any questions you have about what the role would involve.'

'Thank you,' Iris said again, realising that the meeting was over. She stood up and held out her hand to Emil. 'Great to meet you.'

'And you,' he said. 'I look forward to seeing more of you in the future.'

Iris was floating when she walked out of Emil's office. Bjarkey followed her. 'You see? You are valuable to our world, Iris. You don't need to work for that man if you don't want to. We would not be the only organisation wanting to work with you. The world is your oyster.'

Bjarkey dropped Iris at her hotel and said goodbye, urging her to think seriously about the offer. 'Think about what you want. Where do you see yourself? Even if it is not in Iceland, you know now that there are other options.'

Iris watched her drive away, thinking that for the first time in her career, she could be the master of her own destiny. She'd allowed herself to believe that she had nowhere to go, but that was because Jay had kept her chained to the lab. She'd never had the opportunity to work with other organisations until recently. It was only the modifications that she'd made to the seismometer that had got her noticed by other people who mattered, and they'd seen the potential in her and had gone over his head when he'd suggested she hand over to someone else for the field work. That's when she should have realised. When she should have shouted louder, stood up for herself and been confident in the value of what she'd discovered.

And whatever she did, whether it was stay in Iceland and go for a job at the IMO, or go back home able to confront Jay with a renewed sense of her own value, finally, she felt like the future was hers for the taking.

17

Iris was sorry that she wouldn't be seeing Siggi tonight. He would already be on his chase for the Northern Lights, and in any case, it gave her the opportunity to catch up with her family.

Before she did that, while she was still buoyed from her experience at the IMO and what Bjarkey had said in the car, she emailed Jay and in the most professional tone possible, and copying in the person who had overruled his decision about her being able to do the field study, explained that she would stay in Iceland until after the eruption and that the report would follow shortly afterwards. Pressing send felt hugely cathartic.

She opted to call her brother, Finn. On a weekday, he was the most likely of her family to be available to chat. He worked from home, writing software for companies who paid him a fortune because he was one of the best in his field at doing something that Iris didn't understand.

'Finn! How's things?'

'Ah, finally. We thought you'd fallen into a volcano in Iceland.'

'Sorry, it's been busy.' She'd neglected the family WhatsApp since she'd left Hawaii. Her parents being on holiday made it easier. If they'd been at home, her mum would have been calling daily to find out what was causing the radio silence.

'Is Iceland better than Hawaii? God, even asking you that makes my life sound depressingly boring.'

She laughed. 'They're both great but Iceland has surprised me. I had an idea what Hawaii might be like and that's how it was whereas here…it's not what I expected.'

'What have you been up to? Have you had time to do anything other than work?'

Iris told him about her snorkelling experience and told him about the open mic night.

'You went to that on your own?

'No, I went with a group. I met them through the guide who's been helping me out with getting to the site of what we think will be a major eruption.'

Finn was usually the person Iris told everything to but she wasn't sure how to tell him about Siggi, so held back from mentioning the camping trip because there was no way to spin that as anything other than a romantic getaway. She was worried he would judge her for embarking on what was essentially a fling.

'Nice deflection on the tour guide,' Finn said. Iris could hear the smile in his voice. 'And how's the work going?'

She told him about the job offer, leaving out the part about Jay insisting that she abandon her field work for no valid reason. She didn't want to get into what had happened. Finn would worry about it, share it with Felix, and the last thing she needed was for her brothers to rock up at the lab to warn Jay off. She wouldn't put it past them, especially Felix.

'Wow, that's amazing. It's about time you were recognised for what you're doing. It's a game-changer.'

'Well, I don't know what I'll do about it yet, but it's amazing to be offered something like that.'

'Would you want to stay in Iceland?'

'Honestly, I don't know. It's an amazing set up at the IMO and having volcanic activity on the doorstep is hugely tempting. But it's a big step.' She paused. Again, it was on the tip of her tongue to mention Siggi but she wouldn't want Finn to think that her considering the job offer was driven by anything other than a good career move.

'It is, but you've been travelling a lot for a couple of years. That has to have its downsides?'

'But if you say that to anyone, they'd think you were mad. Who doesn't love the thought of travelling the world for the job they love?'

'Iris, you've always loved routine and consistency. I know the past two years have been out of your comfort zone and I think it's amazing that you've embraced that challenge. We all do. But there's nothing wrong in feeling that you'd want to settle down somewhere again. It's not a sustainable lifestyle for everybody.'

Finn was right. There were lots of downsides. She had lost the feeling of belonging anywhere. Of having a home. And the possibility of finding someone to share the rest of her life with was completely off the cards. She might have been closed off from the idea of falling in love again since Patrick, but Siggi had reawakened that possibility now. And she knew that was something she wanted.

'I've met someone.'

'It's the tour guide, isn't it?'

'Yes, but it's not that cliché type situation.' It wasn't, was it? 'He's not serial dating anyone new who comes into town.'

'Right.' Finn sounded open to more information rather than judgey, and Iris decided she could do with someone else's take.

'He grew up here but he travels a lot, to all sorts of places. In fact, he was in Hawaii at the same time as me before he came back to Iceland to work and save up for his next trip.'

'Wow, that's some coincidence. And you like him?'

'I really like him, Finn. He's fun to be with, he's thoughtful and he's taken me to some amazing places because he knows I'll love them for the geology.'

'So the decision about staying is a bit more complicated.'

'I'm not staying because of him. If I stayed it would be because of the job, and anyway, he'll be off travelling somewhere again in a few months. I'd only consider the job if it's a better career path for me, and I don't know yet if that's the case. At the moment, it's just nice to have been asked.'

'That's great, Iris,' Finn said sincerely. 'About the job and the guy. It's about time you had some fun with someone who appreciates you. Just watch out for yourself.'

Iris glowed. It meant a lot for her brother to give his blessing.

'I will. Thanks, Finn. Have you spoken to Felix lately?'

'Yep, he's in the thick of the exam preparation season so I haven't actually seen him but I gave him a call just to check he's not losing his mind.'

'I won't call him, then. Maybe let him know we've spoken and I'll catch up with you both properly when I get back.'

'And when's that going to be? Or will we lose you forever to your Icelandic tour guide?'

'No, of course not,' Iris laughed. 'I think another week or so, that's all.' She didn't want to think about what little time they had left, or what life would be like without Siggi.

'You know you can stay here when you get back?' She'd given up her rented flat when she began travelling so much for work and instead had stayed with her parents for fleeting visits home, or at Finn's when the parental scrutiny became too much.

'I know. I'll probably start off at Mum and Dad's, but thank you.'

'Enjoy yourself, Iris and take care.'

By the time she'd finished the call with Finn, there was a response from Jay in her inbox. He'd replied to her, removing the other person Iris had copied in to her original message. The gist of his response was a threat that she'd lose her job if she wasn't back by Wednesday. Twenty-four hours ago, Iris would have been worried enough about the prospect of that to be on the next flight out of Keflavik airport, but now it made her smile. The conversation with Bjarkey had changed how she saw him. He was a bully, and by not standing up to him, by believing in the power she thought he had over her, she'd allowed him to bully her for years. But no more.

Iris attached the email trail to a fresh email to the HR department at British Geology Labs asking them to confirm whether Jay had the authority to dismiss her with no warning. She copied Jay in for good measure, knowing that this was the last thing he'd expect her to do, and also knowing already that he didn't have the authority because there was a process that would have to be adhered to.

Feeling energised by what she'd done, Iris lost herself in the data she and Bjarkey had collated that morning, formatting it into meaningful bitesize chunks for her report, roughly drafting the text as she went. It was past midnight the next time she looked up from her laptop. She stretched and closed the lid, pleased with the progress she'd made.

She picked up her phone and saw that she had a text from Siggi.

The lights were amazing again tonight, but I had no fun without you x

Want to meet for breakfast tomorrow? xx

Want to meet for a goodnight kiss now? x

It was tempting. She'd resigned herself to not seeing him until tomorrow, although they'd made no plans. It had been a full-on day and now that she'd stopped working, she was already fighting sleep.

I'm too tired even for kisses. Tomorrow? xx

I'll pick you up at 9 x

She stared at the kiss in his last message. It swelled her heart and reassured her they were both thinking along the same lines. She was falling for him and she knew the same was happening for him.

If only it was just that. That she'd met an amazing guy and was falling for him. It would be so simple. But now, it was going to make it harder to decide about whether the IMO was the right place for her. Iceland was Siggi, as well as everything else she loved about it. Even if she could be objective enough to discount her feelings from the decision, surely they would keep seeing each other if she stayed. Wasn't that inevitable? Because surely the only reason they'd put an expiry date on their relationship in the first place was because of the reality of their situation in the beginning.

The following morning, Iris headed downstairs to meet Siggi. Embla was on the reception desk. Still feeling invincible because of everything that had happened yesterday, Iris greeted her with a smile and received a narrowing of eyes in return.

'*Góður morgunn,*' Siggi greeted her, as she came outside to find him. He took her gloved hands in his and leant in to kiss her.

'I've missed you,' she said, wrapping her arms around him.

'And I have missed you. I had to hang out with Jonas and Rachel yesterday,' he said, as if it was a hardship.

They joined hands and strolled together along the street towards the centre of town.

'Did you see the Northern Lights last night?'

'Yes. It was a good night, but they were not the colours that we saw.'

'Maybe that was especially for us?' Iris said.

'I think you are right,' Siggi said, smiling. 'I hope you are hungry.'

'I'm starving.' Iris hadn't realised until it was too late that she hadn't eaten dinner the night before, having been engrossed in her report. All she'd eaten since she and Bjarkey had stopped for coffee and cake in Hraunvik, were the complimentary biscuits in her room.

The breakfast place was called Sandholt, and was on Laugavegur, nestled amongst the shops. There was a small line forming outside, but Siggi went straight to the front.

'I have a reservation,' he said to Iris when she protested about jumping the queue.

He spoke in Icelandic to the woman who came over to them, and they were shown to a table for two in the busy restaurant.

'I like the shakshouka,' Siggi said, pointing it out on the menu, which usefully had an English translation. It sounded good; stewed tomatoes with egg served with sourdough bread.

'I don't think I can resist the waffles,' Iris said, looking longingly at someone else's table where a steaming plate of fluffy-looking waffles had just been served.

'Coffee?' Siggi asked.

Iris nodded, and when the waitress came over, he ordered their breakfast in Icelandic. It was sexy hearing him speak his native language, but for the first time, Iris thought about it in the context of staying in Iceland, and didn't think it sounded like a language that would be easy to learn. When Bjarkey had said the name of some of the volcanos, the words bore no resemblance to how it looked like they should be pronounced when Iris saw them written. Suddenly, that seemed like a problem when it hadn't mattered before.

'How was your day yesterday?' he asked her, lacing his fingers in between hers across the table.

'Really good. We went to Hraunvik again.'

'Is anything happening there?'

'We saw some evidence of movement on the surface. There were a couple of fissures which Bjarkey reported.' She watched for his reaction. 'And we set up a couple more seismometers now that we have a better idea of what might be happening.' There was something in his eyes that Iris couldn't quite fathom; he definitely didn't look as relaxed as he had before she'd mentioned Hraunvik. 'And something else happened yesterday.'

Iris had been going over and over the best way to tell Siggi about the potential job offer from the IMO. She didn't want it to sound as if she'd engineered the opportunity because of how things were progressing between them. But it was hard to think of it in isolation.

'My boss insisted that I leave Iceland. He wants me back in the office by tomorrow, whether the report is finished or not.'

Siggi shook his head. 'That seems crazy. Isn't it better to wait for the eruption and then you have the whole story.'

'Exactly. Anyway, I've told him that I'm staying, at least until something happens. Because you're right, leaving now jeopardises the past two years of work that I've done.'

'Man, this guy is an idiot,' he said, shaking his head again and grinning. 'You are not worried about going against him?'

'I was. I'm pretty sure he wants to fire me but then I talked things through with Bjarkey and I guess I have options I hadn't considered before.'

'Wow, that's great, Iris.' He beamed at her. It was great to see that he understood what that meant to her.

She nodded enthusiastically and carried on. 'Anyway, Bjarkey introduced me to Emil, he runs the IMO team. When he heard what's been happening with Jay, he basically offered me a position.'

Siggi pulled his hand away, leaned back in his chair and pushed his fingers through his hair. 'Wow, I mean...I don't know what to say.'

His reaction told Iris everything she needed to know. He'd jumped to the conclusion that she was basing her life choices around their relationship. She'd known there was a risk that he'd think that, but it still hurt to see him react so predictably.

'You don't need to say anything. I haven't decided on anything yet. It's made me realise that I have options I hadn't been aware of before, that's all. Whether that's here in Iceland or in other places around the world.'

Their food arrived and Iris was grateful for the pause in conversation while they ate.

'You should not make any decisions with me in mind, Iris,' he said without meeting her eye.

'I wasn't going to, Siggi,' she said gently, trying to catch his eye.

'You know what we decided. You staying doesn't change anything.'

It felt like a punch to her stomach. She was almost physically winded by how much that comment hurt. She'd honestly thought that they'd at least discuss how the future might look in the light of her staying in Iceland and yet it seemed a discussion wasn't what Siggi wanted.

'I don't know what would give you the impression that I would stay in Reykjavik just to continue whatever this is with you.'

He looked at her, now with hurt in his eyes. And that cut into her just as deeply. She didn't want to hurt him, but also, she needed him to know that he had thrown the first punch.

'I am sorry, Iris. Even if you stay, I will not. I will still be leaving at the end of the summer.'

Now he was twisting the knife. Did he know how much

this was hurting? This was rejection. Nothing could be worse than this. Leaving him tomorrow, thinking she might never see him again, would not be worse than this. The coldness in his tone. The way he was avoiding looking at her, when only a couple of days ago she had been his love.

How had it come to this?

Because nothing had changed at all. It was still a hypothetical situation that he was getting upset about. She had to make him understand that.

'I know,' she said, as calmly as she could, trying to hold back tears that were threatening to spill. 'I'm not asking you to stay here for me. I'm not asking you for anything, Siggi. I heard you when you said this wasn't going to become anything.' And if she hadn't known that before this conversation, she knew now. 'I'm sorry. Thank you for breakfast. I need to go.'

She stood up, grabbed her coat off the back of the chair and ran outside.

'Iris! *Skítt!*'

She heard him try to follow her, but he got caught up in having to pay the bill, giving her valuable time to put some space between them.

At the first opportunity, she headed up one of the small side streets that led off Laugavegur so that when Siggi left the restaurant, he wouldn't see her. Because now, the tears were falling down her cheeks and she didn't want him to see the effect he'd had on her. She was freezing. She stood there for a moment, not sure where to go, then pulled her coat on. He'd be sure to assume she'd go back to the hotel. It was better to stay away until she'd gathered herself and thought about what she would say. What could she say? She'd told him he wouldn't factor in any of her decisions and though he'd looked hurt, he'd made it clear that was what he wanted. Whether she stayed or not, what she and Siggi had was over.

18

Having abandoned her much-needed breakfast, Iris went into the first coffee shop she came across, Te & Kaffi, which was further along Laugavegur. She was sure that Siggi would be back at the hotel by now, so the coast was probably clear. She bought a flat white and a cinnamon bun and sat at the table furthermost from the door, where it was dark enough that no one would notice her red eyes.

She should have expected this. She *had* expected this. She was just an idiot for thinking that the feelings she and Siggi had for one another could overcome his typical commitment-phobe reaction. And she was an idiot for thinking that she could have a fling with someone and not fall head over heels for them. There was always going to be an end, and it was always going to hurt. It had come sooner and harder than she'd expected, that's all.

The important thing now was not to let this define what happened next. She was on the verge of a career-defining moment. That was the most important thing. She'd been single for so long, she could easily switch back into that old mindset. She had got over Patrick, and this was no different. In fact, it should be easier because she'd only known Siggi for a matter of days, for goodness sake. How could she even begin to feel heartbroken when that was the case? But she did feel a little bit heartbroken and the only way she knew to deal with that was distraction. By the time she'd finished her coffee, Siggi probably would have been to and left the hotel and she could go back there in peace and spend the rest of the day writing her report. This is what she should be doing. Concentrating on work.

Before she left the coffee shop, Iris went to the bathroom to check how she looked. Not too bad, considering. Her eyes looked okay, but she looked sad. She tried to give herself a peppy smile, which she couldn't manage without looking like a sad puppy, but she made herself laugh. What did she have to cry about, anyway? Even without Siggi, she was still better off than she'd been a couple of weeks ago. She'd never been more excited about work, and she might finally see the back of Jay as a result.

She walked back along Laugavegur towards her hotel. It was nice to feel like she was getting her bearings. As she walked past one of the shops, she noticed a pretty mug in the window. It was large, colourful and something that Iris felt was absolutely essential to making herself feel better.

The shop was full of beautiful things. Iris picked up the mug and clutched it to her chest while she browsed everything else that was on offer. It was a shame she didn't have her own place anymore, although it was probably a blessing for her bank balance. She picked up a candle that was set into a holder made of lava. That would be a great souvenir. Then she decided she'd buy one for her parents and her brothers as well. It wasn't often she went anywhere that had beautiful shops like this, so she made the most of it. Perhaps the retail therapy would help boost her mood.

'Can I take those over to the counter for you?'

'Oh, thank you.'

'Ah, Iris! It is good to see you again.'

Iris took a moment to place the woman. It was Gudrun from the open mic night she'd been to with Siggi. She was part of his group of friends.

'Gudrun.'

'It is so nice to see Siggi with you. He has not been so happy for a long time.'

Iris didn't feel it was her place to have to explain to Gudrun what had happened. She was Siggi's friend and would obviously have to take his side.

'Are you alright?' Gudrun was looking at her in concern, and it tipped Iris over the edge.

The tears fell down her cheeks again before she could stop them. 'I'm sorry. God, how embarrassing!' She wiped her eyes and tried to laugh it off, but inside, she was as devastated as she'd been when she'd left the restaurant. Apparently, half an hour to herself and a new mug wasn't going to help after all.

'Come with me,' said Gudrun, expertly taking Iris's shopping from her, and leaving it at the cash desk. She muttered something in Icelandic to the man behind the counter and took Iris's arm, leading her to some narrow stairs that went into the basement of the shop.

'I'm sorry, I just need a minute,' said Iris, taking the chair that Gudrun offered. They were in a tiny office which had a desk with a computer on it, a couple of easy chairs and a bigger swivel chair that was tucked under the desk.

'What has he done?'

'Nothing,' Iris said, shaking her head, at the same time wondering why Gudrun would assume that her being upset was to do with Siggi.

'Come on, you can tell me. I know when a woman has been upset by a man. He might be Olafur's friend, but we have to stick together. I love Siggi but he has no clue about relationships. That is how I know that it is him.' Gudrun was beginning to sound cross. Iris wasn't sure she was going to be fobbed off.

'We had a misunderstanding, that's all.' Unfortunately, her mind flicked back to the moment when Siggi had felt the need to reiterate that she shouldn't make any decisions with him in mind, and a gulping sob escaped.

Gudrun held out a box of tissues. 'Iris. I am going to tell you about Siggi and maybe it will help you to understand him. I am not telling you any of this to excuse his behaviour. This is for you. So that you know the problem lies with him.'

Iris blew her nose. It was on the tip of her tongue to say to Gudrun that really, it wasn't her business what made Siggi tick, but actually she wanted to know.

'Now, I am not supposed to know any of this, but Olafur and I share everything, so...' She shrugged as if that were explanation enough. 'Siggi was in love with a girl. They were both young, at university in Reykjavik. Olafur says he was besotted with her and she with him. They had plans to travel the world together, then she got pregnant.'

'Siggi has a child?'

'Yes, a daughter. I think she is around fourteen.'

'But he's never mentioned her.' There was a lot that she and Siggi didn't know about each other, but something like this would have come up by now, surely?

Gudrun shook her head. 'Siggi did not want to be a father. Olafur says he was angry that the plans he had made for his life were ruined. He decided to walk away.'

'He left her because she was pregnant?' Iris wasn't sure how to reconcile that with the Siggi she knew, who was thoughtful and kind and unlikely to abandon anyone in their hour of need.

'Yes. He left for a couple of years, travelling. Then he came back, hugely regretful of what he'd done. He tried to make amends but his ex-girlfriend had a new partner and had made a family with him. Siggi did what he thought was the best thing for his daughter and walked away again.'

'So he doesn't see her at all?'

'No, he does not talk about her, even to Olafur and Jonas. It left him broken-hearted, Iris. And when he met you, it was like a new Siggi. Olafur says, it was the old Siggi. You are the first person he has fallen for since all of that happened, so many years ago.' Gudrun had a wistful look in her eyes, as if she were telling Iris a fairy story.

'So you think he pushed me away because he's not used to dealing with his feelings?'

'What I am saying is that he is surprised by how strong his feelings are for you. The two of you deciding to have fun while you're here but not longer than that, it was a safety net for him.'

Iris frowned and looked at Gudrun in confusion.

'He came round to our house and confessed his love for you.'

'Oh my god, did he?'

'Well, perhaps he did not say love,' Gudrun said with a smile. 'But he likes you so much, he was scared. What can I say? I can see the two of you together.'

Gudrun knew more about Siggi than she did. And if he'd confided in her about how he felt, it was probably worth running past Gudrun what had happened. She told her everything. From Jay, to Bjarkey's take on it all, culminating in the job offer.

'It might be my dream job and if I take it, Siggi's going to think it's because of him, although after this morning, that is not the case anymore,' Iris sniffed. 'And I don't want to turn it down just so that I can go along with what he wants and end things between us next week. It seems like lose-lose.'

Gudrun sighed. 'You have to do what is best for you. At least now he is being an arse, you can more easily leave him out of your decision?'

Iris laughed. 'He *was* an arse but at least now I have some clue about why.'

'So you might forgive him?' Gudrun's face was so hopeful, Iris wanted to say what she was waiting to hear. But she couldn't. It was too raw.

'He made it very clear that what we have is a finite thing, not something that could carry on if I happen to decide to stay.'

Gudrun took Iris's hand. 'But you understand that he is scared to let himself love you.'

'I do.' The feeling of rejection and the sudden switch in Siggi from being his usual warm self to the cold, detached person who had crushed her, washed over her again. 'He pushed me away, and however I feel about him, now it makes me question whether I can be with someone who can make me feel as if I've imagined the feelings that have grown between us for the past week or so.'

'I am sorry. I do not want you to think that I am on Siggi's side. He should not have treated you like this. But I know that he loves you, Iris and he is probably devastated that he has done this to you.'

Iris tried to smile. 'Well, I hope so.' She wiped her eyes with a fresh tissue. 'How do I look?'

'You look like a woman who will be cheered up by a store discount.'

Iris laughed. 'That's true. Would it be cheeky to add a few more things to my pile?'

'Not at all. I dragged you away before you had seen everything. I am the store manager so you can use my staff discount which is even better.'

'Thank you, Gudrun. Perhaps it's better not to tell Siggi that we spoke.'

Gudrun ran her finger and thumb across her lips. 'I will

not tell. And you must not tell Siggi that I told you about his daughter.'

'Deal.' Although at this point, she couldn't imagine what it would be like to speak to Siggi again. It felt unimaginable that they'd ever be able to go back to the easy relationship they'd had before.

Iris spent another half an hour browsing the Snug shop, stunned to find out that there were branches in the UK and in a few other European cities. It had completely passed her by until now.

'Okay, I'm done,' she said, placing a beautiful blanket on the counter with the rest of her goodies. It was woven in the softest shades of grey and heathery purples, with a dash of bright pink and green that lifted it.

Gudrun sent the guy who had been manning the till off to tidy some cushions and rang up Iris's sale herself. She packed everything carefully into a huge brown paper carrier bag. 'I think this bag will be okay today,' she said. 'We have plastic ones for when the weather is terrible.'

'Thank you for this. For everything.'

'I hope we see you again soon. And you can always find me here if you need to talk about anything.'

Iris walked back to the hotel reflecting on how remarkable it was that she had found two women here who she'd confided in about things she wouldn't dream of talking about to her friends at home. Whether it was because they had busier lives than her, with husbands and families that made Iris feel as if her issues were insignificant and superficial in comparison, or whether it was because Bjarkey and Gudrun had an openness about them that invited those sorts of conversations. Either way, it was going down on the pro side of the mental pro-con list she was making about the possible job at the IMO.

When she got back to the hotel, Embla was still on the front desk, but wasn't shooting daggers at her for once. She gave Iris a small smile. It was unsettling but probably a sign that Siggi had been here looking for her. No doubt Embla had softened knowing that something had gone wrong between them.

'Iris? I have a note for you.'

Iris backtracked to the reception desk and took the folded sheet of paper that Embla held out to her. She flicked it open for long enough to see that it was from Siggi, then shoved it into her Snug shopping bag.

'Thank you.' She was surprised that Embla would do anything for Siggi given how much she seemed to loathe him.

'No problem.' She gave Iris what seemed to be a genuine smile. 'I am sorry.'

'Thank you,' Iris said again, not sure what Embla was sorry about. Presumably either the rift between her and Siggi, or being a less than welcoming receptionist.

Iris went up to her room, closed the door behind her and, after she'd put her shopping carefully down on the side, took off her coat and boots and lay on the bed. She felt exhausted, and it was only eleven in the morning. Then she remembered the note that she'd stuffed in the bag.

Iris,

I need you to know that what I said is not because I feel nothing for you. I feel everything for you. But I am not a man, someone like Jonas or Olafur, who can share their life with someone. I do not know what my future looks like beyond next week and I cannot imagine how it would look with or without you. Please let me try to explain, Iris. I cannot live with knowing I have hurt you.

S

x

It made Iris feel better that he sounded sorry, but it didn't sound as though he thought any differently about the situation. Perhaps just that he wanted to explain himself properly. Either way, it was too soon and too raw to risk hearing Siggi explain again that he didn't want her. The one word she would have liked to see in the note was "mistake". Whether he made a mistake in saying he wanted no part of a future with her or whether it was simply that he'd made a mistake in the way he'd handled the situation, either way she wished that was how he saw things. All Iris could read into the note was that he couldn't share his life with her, and while he couldn't imagine her not in his life, that probably wasn't enough of a reason to go all-in together.

She folded the note in half again and again until it was tiny. Then she tucked it in her case and tried to forget about it. The fissure in Hraunvik wasn't going to wait for anything and she had more data to analyse from the new seismometers they'd sited yesterday. It was over with Siggi. She had to accept that. Perhaps before she left Iceland, she'd talk to him, try to get some closure, but she had to forget about any future with Siggi in it.

19

If only he hadn't had to pay the bill, he might have caught her up. In the time it had taken for the waitress to fetch the card machine and for him to tap on it, Iris had disappeared.

Siggi pulled his coat on as he strode along Laugavegur towards Iris's hotel. He was angry with himself. Why had he reacted like that? So quick to establish a distance between him and Iris, as if that was really what he wanted. The problem was, he'd spent the past fourteen years making sure that no one got close enough to him that he could ever be held responsible for bringing their world crashing down around them, like he had done to Hekla all those years ago. Since then, he had kept any relationships he'd had superficial. If anyone had got close, that was *their* problem. He'd always been straight with women about what they could expect from him, and they still expected too much.

But Iris had expected nothing. She'd sat there and told him it wasn't about *this* job, it was that she knew now she had options. It might be here, it might not. And he had trampled all over that and made it about him. All he had heard was Iris locking him into her future, just like when Hekla had told him she was pregnant, and in that instant, he'd felt exactly the same as he had back then.

He got to the hotel, having scanned the streets around him as he walked for any glimpse of Iris. And it was just his luck. Embla was on the desk.

'Have you seen Iris in the last few minutes?' he asked her.

'No. I am guessing you have had an argument?' There was an air of satisfaction in the way she said it, making Siggi want to stalk out. But he didn't. He had to find Iris and explain.

'Can I leave a message for her?'

Embla slammed a pad and pen down in front of him. But it wasn't that easy. He took a seat on one of the inviting leather sofas, resting his ankle over his knee and the pad of paper on his thigh. He ran his hands through his hair and closed his eyes, hoping inspiration would strike. It was important not to make excuses. He knew that much. And saying sorry wasn't enough.

'What are you trying to say?' Embla came out from behind the desk and sat on the sofa next to him.

'I need to say sorry, but also I need to talk to her. Explain.'

Embla sighed. 'So she is different from other women you have been with. Different to me?'

'I'm sorry,' he said.

'You know you never said sorry to me before.'

'Really?'

'Yes, really. You made it seem like it was my fault. That I should have known you didn't want anything more than sex.'

Siggi frowned. 'But that is not what I wanted. Not just sex, Embla. We had a good time together —'

'And then you left.'

'But I was always going to leave. You knew that.'

'I suppose I thought we might have had a conversation about me coming with you.'

Siggi shook his head. He had made such a mess of everything. 'I'm sorry.'

'Is that what happened with Iris?'

'No. Not exactly.'

'Look, if you like her, you have to talk to her. Tell her how you feel and what you want. You need to write from your heart.' She tapped the pad, then stood up.

'Thank you, Embla.'

'You're welcome. I can give it to her.'

It took a while, but eventually, Siggi finished the note, hoping that it would be enough. He folded it in half and handed it to Embla. 'Thank you. You deserved better than me.'

She smiled and gave a small shrug. 'You weren't falling in love with me. I knew that. And I also know you are falling in love with Iris. So you are forgiven by me and I will hope for you that she does the same.'

Siggi left and walked along to the office. Brun was manning it today since Siggi was on the Northern Lights tour again later on, but he was interested in whether they had any bookings for tonight. Was there a chance the trip might not run? He needed to know, just in case Iris called.

'Hey, Siggi,' said Brun, looking up from the computer when he heard the door open.

'Brun. I haven't seen you for a while.'

'Not since the open mic night. With Iris.'

And here it was again. 'Yes.' Siggi sank down into a chair in the corner behind the desk.

'How is Iris? Is she still here?' Brun finished what he was doing and swivelled his chair round to face Siggi.

'Yes. I think she's staying until whatever is happening in Hraunvik starts up.'

'Ah, I have heard it will be in the next few days.'

'I think she will leave after that.'

'You think? I thought you two had hit it off.'

Siggi nodded and gave his friend a rueful smile.

'Oh.'

'Yeah.'

'The usual? She is getting too clingy?'

'Right now, she's the one person I wish was more clingy.'

Brun grinned. 'I did not think you would ever say that.'

'I know,' he said, rubbing his eyes with his fingertips. 'And even though that's how I feel about her, when she told me she might be staying in Iceland for work, I told her to back off.'

'Oh, Siggi.'

'It was an automatic response. I have always avoided any relationship that felt like it had a future, and now that a person has come along who makes me think things could be different…'

'You are scared.'

'Maybe.' That was it exactly. He was scared. The moment that Iris mentioned the job, it felt as if her world was aligning with his and he wasn't ready for that.

'What do you think about her staying?'

'Mostly, I feel pleased for her. She deserves the opportunity to shine at a place that knows how great the work is that she's doing. If she'd told me it was anywhere else, we would be out celebrating now.'

'So you don't see a future with her? She has not made that much of a difference?'

'I can't picture the future. Ever since…Hekla.' He paused to gauge Brun's reaction because they never talked about Hekla, even though all of his friends had been around when it had happened. 'Since then, I have focused on not looking any further than the next trip I want to take, or the next stretch of time here, saving up again. I guess everything else that happens in my life is too temporary to factor into any of that.'

'So if Iris hadn't said anything, if she just was here, working without you knowing it might be for longer than a couple of weeks, what would happen then? Because you guys have been having a great time, right?'

'She means a lot to me, Brun. But if she stays, doesn't that automatically mean that we are together because what else would we do?'

'Man, you're thinking too hard about this. If you like her and she likes you, isn't it better that she's here and you can carry on being together, seeing how things grow? What is to be gained by ending things just because she might be here longer? Has she said she would not want you to travel?'

Siggi shrugged. 'We haven't talked about anything like that at all.' Listening to Brun had made him realise he had made a lot of assumptions that perhaps were based on what people other than Iris might want or expect.

'I think you need to talk. You are different now. There is no need to run away from something like this, assuming it is a bad thing. Maybe Iris has reservations as well.'

Now he felt like a total idiot. Of course she might. She had been single for a long time too and perhaps that was because of what had happened with that guy, Patrick. And now he'd reacted as if just by mentioning that there might be a chance for her to stay, as if she'd proposed marriage or something. 'I didn't give her a chance to say what she might be thinking,' he admitted. 'And now it's too late.' He felt sure that if she'd been ready to forgive him, to listen to his side of the story, she'd have messaged him by now.

'It won't be,' Brun said reassuringly. 'Just make sure you're honest with her about how you feel. Apologise. And decide what you want. Don't run away from your feelings. That will lead to more regrets. Maybe you want a future with Iris, maybe not. But whatever you want, it is important to make it work. And you can only do that by listening to yourself.' Brun gave his chest a quick tap.

'Thanks. It's all good advice,' he said with a rueful smile.

'No problem.'

Brun and Fliss had thought they were doomed to live separate lives, and in fact, they'd made a life together, albeit with a foot in both England and Iceland. They'd known what they wanted, and they'd made it work.

Knowing that he wanted Iris was the simple part. As soon as he'd seen the devastation in her eyes that morning when he'd pushed her away, he'd known it was too late to save himself. He loved her. What he was having trouble with was seeing what the future looked like.

'Before you and Fliss worked things out, how did you see the future with her?'

'Much the same as you, I could not imagine it. I could not see anything except the things that would keep us apart.'

'But you knew you could overcome those?'

Brun shrugged. 'I didn't know. I had to be guided by Fliss because of her children. It was not up to me to decide what happened. And she is the one who has made it work. She has compromised more than I have.'

'If Iris ends up living here, that ought to be the answer. If I'm in love with her, why wouldn't I be happy that she is here for longer than the next week or so?'

'Because you have lived on your own terms for so long that you can't imagine having to take account of anyone else. What if you want to go somewhere for a couple of months and she can't go? Do you think it's that?'

'Maybe. Travelling is how I felt like myself again after what happened with Hekla. I could leave all of that behind and pretend it didn't exist. Then, when I wished I had made better decisions about being a father, it became a way to escape the constant reminder of what a failure I had been to my daughter. Because the memories are everywhere. Me and Hekla… we're everywhere.'

'I know. I remember,' Brun said with a smirk.

'Iris makes me forget all of that stuff. It's like I'm not that person when I'm with her. I haven't booked my next trip, or even thought about where I want to go.'

'That says a lot.'

'And I was so busy focusing on what I thought I wanted, I didn't even realise that.'

'Don't be too hard on yourself. Being in love changes you, but you're not going to change overnight. It is a learning curve for you both, to learn what each other wants and how you work your lives together.'

'Assuming she feels the same.'

'Yes. That helps.' Brun grinned and clapped Siggi on the shoulder. 'You will work it out.'

'I have to hope she is willing to speak to me.'

'She will.'

Siggi didn't share his friend's certainty. But he was willing to wait. Whatever it took. He was beginning to understand what Brun was saying. He had to take a moment to think about what he really wanted. This wasn't something he could coast through. If he was serious about Iris, he had to think about what that looked like for him.

He picked up the list of clients for his trip that evening, along with the keys to the minibus, and headed home. The aurora forecast was good, but the weather forecast was not. It seemed likely it would be postponed. He ought to accept that he wouldn't see Iris tonight and instead take advantage of the chance to clear his head. Going back to his empty flat was going to lead to him over-thinking, waiting, and watching his phone. He didn't want to cave in and contact her. The ball was in her court and he had to leave it to her to contact him on her own terms. By the time Iris messaged him, if she ever did, he needed to have worked out what he wanted. And the only way he knew to empty his mind enough to allow him to see clearly was to surf.

'If the tour is cancelled tonight, I think I'm going to camp out at Sandvik,' he said to Brun, following the number one rule of telling someone where he was going. 'Surfing might help.'

'Good idea,' Brun said, smiling and shaking his head. 'I am glad you are not inviting me. Camping and surfing in March is crazy.'

'That's what makes it fun,' Siggi said, looking at Brun as if he didn't know what he was missing.

Siggi hadn't surfed since Hawaii, and he hadn't surfed in Iceland for around a year. He dug his thick winter wetsuit out of the cupboard. Just the smell of it was enough to give him a taste of the buzz he'd get when he stepped into the freezing surf. He packed up other things he'd need like towels, neoprene boots and gloves and plenty of warm layers to dress in afterwards. Everything else he needed, like his surfboard, Jonas let him keep at the company's storage unit. He planned to wild-camp near the coast. The temperatures were still dropping to almost freezing overnight, but with the right equipment, which he had, he'd be fine. And he'd be ready to surf at sunrise.

He packed everything into a large rucksack and put it into the boot of his jeep before he went to pick up the rest of his things from the unit. This impromptu camping trip was exactly what he needed to clear his head and get some perspective.

20

Iris began work on her report, the note from Siggi safely out of sight and out of mind. For now. Hopefully by focusing on work, when she did take a breath to think about everything, the right answer would present itself. She knew she ought to give him the chance to explain, as he'd asked. But she needed to have built some defences back before she could do that. If he came to her now, she'd break again. The memory of it all was too fresh and even though he might be sorry about what happened, it didn't necessarily mean that he didn't still believe the things he'd said.

She logged into the portal Bjarkey had set up for her so that she could get access to the new data they were logging from the extra seismometers and checked her own seismometer data as well. The data from all the units was showing heightened activity; more frequency of events, closer together. It didn't tally with what the traditional data was suggesting, but that was the whole point; her own data should be more accurate. But although she was confident in her data, it was as yet unproven, which was exactly why she was there. She needed to go back to Hraunvik to see for herself.

'Hi Bjarkey.'

'Iris, I was about to call you. I have been looking at your data feed. It looks as if something may be starting.'

'I thought the same.'

'We should go to Hraunvik. I have spoken to Emil, and he wants us to take two others from the team. Also, a team from the civil defence department will meet us there. We will collect you in half an hour.'

Iris felt butterflies in her stomach. This was it. All her work was about to come to fruition. If they could see evidence that her data was flagging up that something was happening ahead of it being picked up by the traditional methods, that was what she'd been waiting for.

All thoughts of Siggi vanished as she focused entirely on gathering her things together. If she'd listened to Jay, she'd be at the airport now and two years of work and research would have been wasted. Whatever happened, she knew she was leaving British Geology Labs. This was proof that Jay was wrong, and no one there seemed to see that what he was doing was undermining everything they were working for.

Half an hour later, she was ready and waiting outside the hotel. The vehicle that pulled up was a massive all-terrain vehicle with huge tyres and a high wheelbase.

'Iris! Climb in the back!' Bjarkey called out of the window.

She threw her stuff in the footwell and climbed in next to a younger man, who smiled and introduced himself with a firm handshake as Kári.

'And this is Aron,' Bjarkey said, indicating the driver. He said hello and waved, catching Iris's eye in the rearview mirror.

'This is exciting,' said Kári. 'I have never been to a site to see what it looks like before the eruption happens.'

'We saw cracks beginning to appear a few days ago,' said Iris. 'I'm expecting to see more of that, maybe some signs of magma beginning to show.'

'They are meeting this afternoon to decide on whether to begin evacuating the town,' Bjarkey said. 'As soon as we meet with the civil defence people, they will be reporting back. We should head to the site of the fissures we saw yesterday first.'

'Good plan,' said Iris.

It was early afternoon, but the brooding skies made it feel as if it were more like dusk. It felt like an omen, and despite Iris's excitement from a professional point of view, she couldn't help but worry about the future of the people who lived in the town. This part of the Reykjanes peninsula hadn't seen any volcanic activity for hundreds of years. Yes, it was the land of ice and fire and there were active volcanoes relatively nearby, but these lava tubes, which she was predicting were going to fill with magma and burst through the surface, were an unknown occurrence. No one had expected that.

Bjarkey spoke in Icelandic to Aron, and Iris could tell she was giving him directions to the house where Iris's seismometer was sited. As soon as they arrived on the outskirts of the town, it was apparent that Iris's data was correct. The surface of the road had bulged in places, with cracks beginning to appear in others. That was alarming enough, but when they pulled up outside the house, that was where everything took on a whole different feeling. The house had essentially split from its neighbour. On either side of the fissure that had appeared a few days ago, the ground was now at entirely different levels. One house appeared to have sunk down into the earth and leaned away from the house it had once been attached to.

'Oh my god,' Iris said. 'Surely they're not still living there?'

'I hope not,' said Aron. 'As soon as the civil defence team see this they will be sure to order an evacuation of the whole town. If the main road becomes impassable, it will be impossible for anyone to leave unless they are in a vehicle like this one.'

'Come on, let's get out and take some measurements,' said Bjarkey.

Aron fetched some camera equipment from a case in the boot and took pictures of the fissure while Kári held a ruler across it, and then vertically to record the movement of one side of the fissure versus the other.

While they were busy, Iris knocked on the door of the house where her seismometer was. There was no response. Taking a deep breath, she knocked on the door of the neighbouring house. The one where Siggi's daughter lived, as far as she knew. Thankfully, no one answered. She could only assume they must have left, which is exactly what she would do if her house was sitting right on top of a fissure like this. Iris felt a wave of relief knowing that Siggi's daughter was away from this immediate danger, but hoped they'd left the town as well as the house.

Iris sat on the steps of the house, opened her laptop, and balanced it on her knees. She checked the data that was coming from the seismometer just metres away from her. Almost immediately, there was a spike in the line of data. Normally, if you saw a spike like that, on the frequencies a normal seismometer monitored, you felt the tremor as it was being recorded. But this was amazing to see. The frequency she was looking at was so low that it couldn't be felt at the surface. But less than a minute later, they all felt the earth shift slightly. There was a groaning sound as it did so, and when Iris looked at the IMO data feed, she could see the spike that corresponded with what they'd felt.

'It's incredible to be literally feeling the data on the screen in real life,' she said to Bjarkey.

Bjarkey nodded. 'I remember the first time I went out in the field. We were monitoring the Eyjafjallajökull volcano, you know the one that closed the airspace in most of Europe because of the ash?'

'I do remember. I was an undergraduate.'

'We did not have very good monitoring of that specific volcano because it had not erupted for at least a hundred and fifty years. I had just started working at the IMO and we began noticing seismic activity in the area and a small group of us went to see for ourselves, to monitor it more closely. The earthquakes were coming so regularly, it was crazy. It was the first time I had ever experienced that.'

'What's going to happen here? I mean, how often do towns need evacuating?'

Bjarkey shook her head. 'It is very rare. I do not remember it before. People know where the danger lies from a volcano. But this is different. No one knew that there were ancient lava tubes underneath this town. And we couldn't have predicted that they would fill with magma. No one would have settled a town here if they had known any of that.'

At that moment, a similar all-terrain vehicle arrived. Two men and a woman climbed out, wearing high-vis jackets. Aron spoke to them in Icelandic and showed them the fissure. Not that it needed pointing out; the state of the houses spelled out what they were dealing with. It only took moments for them to be on their way again.

'They are putting the evacuation notice out,' said Aron. 'They are giving everyone forty-eight hours to leave.'

'Oh my god,' Iris whispered. 'It's horrible.'

Bjarkey sat on the step beside her. 'It is. But everyone will be safe.'

'The town will be lost.'

'Yes, possibly. But everyone will be safe. That is the only thing that matters.'

And of course that was true. But Iris could only imagine how awful it would be to lose her home, if she had one, to a disaster like this. To be uprooted and have to start again somewhere else. It was unthinkable, but it happened to people across the world all the time. Because of other kinds of natural disasters or having to flee from war or oppression. But here, it felt almost personal for Iris. The scientist in her had fallen for Iceland, and her love of volcanology was at odds with the effect it was going to have on these people, but at the same time, she was in awe of the magnificence of what was happening here. It was nature at its most brutal, and it would show itself to be most spectacular in the next couple of days.

Once they'd finished measuring at the house, they packed up and drove along to the next location. The street where Iris and Bjarkey had seen the first fissure on the road surface. They were expecting this to be significantly larger now, especially since they'd seen evidence of other cracks on the way in. But it was shocking to find a long portion of the road had sunk into the ground by at least six inches. Now that they were standing on the open road, it was clear that the cracks were following a line, north-east to south-west, slightly skewed from the north-south that they'd predicted, but the extra seismometers were still providing useful data.

'If this fissure opens up, it'll reach the sea,' said Aron.

They all knew what that meant. The sea would rapidly cool the lava and could produce toxic gases. It wasn't only the physical threat of magma that was a problem for people in the vicinity.

'Come on,' said Bjarkey. 'Let's survey all the areas we looked at the other day for comparative purposes and then we'll get back to base.'

They spent another couple of hours in the town, never wandering too far from where they left the vehicle, just in case.

'Okay,' Aron said, as another tremor hit. 'Let's go.'

'Will we come back again after the eruption starts?' asked

Kári.

'No, it will be too unpredictable. We will use drones to monitor from a safe distance,' Aron explained.

It began raining on their drive back to Reykjavik. Despite the dusk, once they were north of Hraunvik, they could see steam coming from the ground where the icy rain was hitting hot patches of earth.

'It's incredible,' said Iris. 'It's almost mapping out where the activity is bubbling close to the surface.'

She'd seen steam coming from the ground before, from small bubbling pools of water that you could sometimes see from the road when you were driving around. It was commonplace. But this was different. It was almost a curtain of steam rising from the ground over some distance. It was incredible to see.

The twinkling lights of Reykjavik were a welcoming sight.

'Come into the office tomorrow, Iris,' Bjarkey suggested. 'We're only going to brief the rest of the team now, and then call it a day.'

'Okay, thanks.' She was itching to add today's data into her report. Then it would almost be finished, bar the conclusion which she couldn't complete until after the eruption began. And now that she was back in the town, Siggi was on her mind again. She needed to talk to him.

She climbed out of the truck and said goodbye to Bjarkey and the others, grabbed her coat and bag and slammed the door shut, waving as they drove off.

'Iris!'

She turned to see Gudrun and Olafur walking towards her.

'Hi,' she said warmly, pleased to see them both.

'Where have you been?' Gudrun asked.

'To Hraunvik. There's some increased activity, so it looks as if they're going to evacuate the town.'

'Oh my goodness,' said Gudrun. 'It's so awful. The poor

people.'

'It is terrible,' said Olafur. 'People will have to leave their homes, but better that than not knowing what is coming.'

'That's true,' said Iris. 'And where are you off to?'

'The open mic night. Ned is playing tonight. You should come with us!' Gudrun said enthusiastically.

'Oh, I don't think so, but thanks for the invitation.'

'Siggi might be there. The Northern Lights trip is cancelled tonight, isn't it?' Gudrun asked Olafur.

Iris wasn't sure if the fact the Siggi was going to be there was a good thing or not. Seeing Siggi at the open mic night wasn't exactly conducive to being able to have a proper talk. It might be awkward having to spend the evening together.

Olafur shook his head. 'Siggi has gone camping tonight so that he can surf at dawn.'

Gudrun looked at Iris again with renewed enthusiasm. 'Come on! We can wait for you. Ned is always amazing.'

Iris had yet to see Ned Nokes in the flesh, and she had enjoyed the open mic night last time she'd been. Knowing that Siggi wouldn't be there made the decision easier. 'Okay, that'd be great. But don't wait for me. I can catch you up.'

'We will save you a seat!' Gudrun said, as they carried on walking. 'Be quick!'

Iris could hear Olafur say something to Gudrun that sounded like he was perhaps telling her not to be so bossy. She smiled. It was so nice to be part of a community, even in the smallest of ways.

She showered and blasted her hair with the drier so she wouldn't freeze, then ran a tiny blob of hair oil onto her fingers and through her curls to de-frizz them. Choosing jeans and a long-sleeved t-shirt with a short-sleeved one with Guns 'n' Roses emblazoned on the front layered over the top, she felt excited about going out.

She picked up her phone, half-expecting to see a message

from Siggi. There was nothing. But then, she needed to make the next move, so it shouldn't have been a surprise, and it made her heart sink a little that the misunderstanding between them still wasn't resolved.

Thanks for your note. I do want to talk. I hear you have gone camping. Are you mad?! Let me know when you're back x

She felt better having made contact. After everything that had happened today, the sting of how she'd felt that morning had dulled. Hopefully, the tone of her message would tell Siggi that she was ready to listen.

21

Gudrun was looking out for Iris, and waved frantically as soon as she spotted her. Iris waved back and pointed to the bar, showing that she was buying a drink before she went over to sit down. She ordered a pint of locally brewed beer and made her way between the tables towards the other side of the room where the group was gathered around the same table they'd been at a couple of weeks ago. Iris recognised all the faces apart from one.

'Iris, I think you know everyone except Anna and Ned?' said Gudrun. 'Anna, this is Iris. She is working with the Icelandic Met Office. And she is a friend of Siggi.'

'Nice to meet you,' said Anna with a warm smile. 'And where is Siggi tonight?'

'Apparently, he's gone camping,' Iris said, unable to keep the incredulity out of her voice.

'God, really? What a nutter,' said Anna.

Olafur laughed and shook his head. 'He has not gone camping, he has gone surfing. He is camping only to be there to surf at dawn.'

'Oh, well, that makes total sense.' Anna rolled her eyes at Iris, and they all laughed. 'That's Ned over on the stage, faffing around with the guitar.'

Iris looked over, expecting to recognise the global superstar, but with his tousled hair and glasses, he didn't look like the Ned Nokes she remembered from when he'd been part of boy band sensation The Rush.

'I know,' said Anna. 'He's let himself go.'

'Oh, no,' began Iris, but Rachel swiftly interrupted her.

'Anna's teasing. The fact that he doesn't look like Ned Nokes all the time is the only thing that keeps her sane.'

'That's true,' Anna said wistfully. 'It's a nightmare in London if he's tarted up for a night out. We get trailed around by mooning teenagers.'

Iris laughed. 'Not much danger of that here.'

'And that's why we love Iceland,' Anna said.

'What's the latest in the world of volcanology?' Rachel asked.

'They are evacuating Hraunvik,' Gudrun said.

'Really? That's awful.'

'They are building defences right now to try and direct the lava flow away from the town when it starts. Mostly to keep the main road open and keep the flow away from the power station,' Jonas said.

'Will that work?' Anna asked.

'It can work,' said Jonas, 'but it has never been done in Iceland before on this scale.'

They all sat for a moment, sipping their drinks and contemplating the fate of Hraunvik.

'Here's to saving the town,' said Olafur.

'*Skál,*' they all said somberly, raising their glasses towards each other.

'Hey, what are we toasting?' Ned came over to the table, pushing his glasses up his nose with one finger.

Anna explained to him what was happening.

'Christ, what a nightmare.' He lifted his glass to belatedly join in the toast. 'It feels wrong to be playing tonight.'

'I think the word is spreading,' Jonas said, nodding at the television at the opposite end of the room, which was muted, but tuned to a news channel which was showing pictures of Hraunvik. 'If people are here, it is because they want distraction. At the moment, there is nothing we can do.'

'So perhaps the show goes on. I'll ask Thor what he thinks,' said Ned. 'Anyone want another drink while I'm at the bar?'

They all said yes. Iris was hesitant since she had half a pint left, but Anna said, 'Same again, Iris?' So she nodded and thanked her, slightly stunned to be having a drink bought for her by Ned Nokes. Even her brothers would think that was cool.

'Okay, we're on,' said Ned, coming back with a tray of drinks. 'Thor says this kind of thing is something Icelanders take in their stride.'

Jonas and Olafur exchanged glances and a couple of words in Icelandic which made Iris think they may not entirely agree with Thor, but once the music started a few minutes later, everyone in the bar was enjoying themselves as if it were any normal Tuesday night.

'Where has Siggi gone surfing?' Iris asked Olafur when they were chatting between songs.

'I think to Sandvik. That is his usual spot.'

'Is that north of here?'

'No, it is south-west…'

Iris could see by Olafur's face that he knew she was about to put two and two together.

'Near Hraunvik.'

He nodded. 'Siggi knows the dangers. The road to Sandvik does not have to be through Hraunvik and the civil defence will have closed all the roads leading to that area. He will be safe.'

'Right.' But it didn't sit well with Iris that he'd gone to that area, possibly not knowing what was happening in

Hraunvik, and not making an informed decision. She imagined he'd gone to clear his head. That's what it sounded like. And perhaps if she'd messaged him earlier, he might be here now.

'Iris. He will be back before they have finished evacuating Hraunvik. He is not in danger.'

She forced a smile. 'Okay.' Perhaps she should text him. But how likely was he to heed anything she said? Like Olafur said, Siggi was well aware of the dangers. Or thought he was.

It turned out to be a great night and Iris was glad she'd bumped into Olafur and Gudrun. She recognised some performers from the week before, but the clear highlight was Ned. He sang one song she knew and one she didn't, which he said he'd only finished that afternoon.

'He does all of his songwriting here now,' Anna explained. 'I don't know why, but it works for him and we get to spend more time together in Iceland. In London, he's always getting dragged off to do PR stuff.'

'Do you always go back to London with him?' Iris asked, interested in the dynamic of their relationship.

'Mostly, but he spends more time here than I do. I need to be in London for work a lot of the time. I run a music PR company which is very UK based. And I learned early on that he needs his own space.' Anna smiled. 'Are you and Siggi serious enough to have talked about this kind of thing yet? Are you wondering how it could work long term?'

Iris sighed, the beer having lowered her defences. 'We haven't. But I'm not sure Siggi's the settling down type. I had a job offer from the Met Office here and he didn't take it well.'

'Right. I don't know him very well, he's away a lot, but he's a nice guy. Perhaps just set in his ways?'

'Maybe,' Iris said, gauging that Anna didn't know as much of Siggi's story as Gudrun. 'Anyway, it's difficult now to think about the job knowing that he probably wouldn't want to carry on the relationship even if I stayed.'

Anna frowned. 'I don't get why it would make any difference. If you guys like each other, a chance of carrying on seeing each other is great, isn't it?'

'Maybe he feels pushed into it. We'd both agreed it was a short-term thing. A long-distance relationship isn't what either of us wants.'

'And now things have changed, he's run off to surf.'

Iris couldn't help laughing. 'It's fine. He needs time to think.'

'Ned had a massive wobble when we were first seeing each other. I was here visiting Rachel when we met, and he went back to London just when things were starting to get serious. He panicked, I think. I mean, there was a lot of other stuff going on for him as well. He'd just left the band, but I still think it had more to do with the way we were heading. He was scared.'

That resonated with Iris. Siggi was scared. And the job offer had catapulted their relationship from something with a finite end to something else. Another possibility that neither of them could define as easily.

'Hopefully when he gets back from the camping trip, we can have a proper talk about it.'

'But don't turn that job down because of him if it's what you want. It's a small town, but there's room enough for both of you and he's hardly here most of the time. Saying that, neither are we. We're off to London in the morning.'

Anna made it sound so easy. And maybe it was. Being here tonight was a testament to the fact that Iris could find her own way without him by her side. Ignoring the fact that she was out with his friends, she was sure that she could find her own friends if she stayed. Having Bjarkey as a colleague was a good start.

Afterwards, Iris strolled home with Gudrun, Olafur, Anna

and Ned. They all lived just beyond her hotel and it was nice to be part of a group when so often she headed home alone at the end of a rare night out.

'Thanks for taking me out tonight,' she said to Gudrun.

'I hope it will be the start of many nights out together.'

Iris wasn't sure whether Gudrun meant because of the job, or because she'd be with Siggi. Most likely, Gudrun hadn't been thinking so specifically.

She smiled and said good night to them all, then went inside.

'Night,' she said to Bríet as she went past the desk.

'Goodnight, Iris. Sleep well.'

Siggi paddled out as the sun was creeping over the horizon. He'd have loved to see it emerging from the sea as he had done in other places around the world, but he was facing southwest, so he had to settle for seeing it emerge over the mountainous terrain to the east. Still, it was spectacular to see, glowing deep red and orange before it cleared the horizon and brightened. This was what he'd needed. This balance. The solitude. The space.

His phone lost signal somewhere between Keflavik and Sandvik, so he'd heard nothing from Iris and he felt fine about that. Over the past twelve hours, he'd come to realise that he was at a crossroads. But whichever way he chose, he knew that how he felt about Iris was a constant. He loved her. He was sure of that. The only thing he wasn't sure of was whether that could endure in the face of the overwhelming fear he felt about the thought of commitment. Because that was what had driven him to push Iris away, and she hadn't been asking him for anything. She'd made it clear that her decision to stay in Reykjavik wasn't dependent on him, and he hadn't listened to her. He'd jumped to his own conclusion about what she was saying.

Sat astride his board, he let the building waves bob him around before he committed to choosing his first wave of the day. He imagined Iris waiting on the beach for him. It was a nice thought. They could share a flask of hot chocolate like they had on the Northern Lights excursion. That wasn't frightening at all. Being with her had never made him feel trapped. That was his brain working overtime, over thinking.

Glancing behind him, he could see that there were a series of good waves building. He put his hands on the board and flicked his legs up and back so that he was lying on his stomach. He began paddling until he felt the wave lift the board underneath him, then pressed his hands to the board and in one smooth motion, was on his feet. The cold air and spray hit his face as he concentrated on balancing; riding the wave for as long as he could before he jumped off the board into the shallows, whooping at the sheer joy of it all. And then he turned straight back around and started all over again.

It was late morning by the time he was too weary to think about paddling back out to catch another wave. It had been awesome, but despite his thermal wetsuit, he was feeling cold. He picked up his board and jogged up to the back of the beach where he'd parked his jeep. He opened the tailgate and pulled out a towel, stripping his wetsuit down to his waist to dry himself as quickly as he could and get some warm layers on. After doing the same with his bottom half, he then closed the boot and started the engine, putting the heater on full pelt. He loved the feeling of being warm and toasty after the cold of the surf. It was part of the whole experience. Once, when he'd been to the south of England, they'd had a sauna on the beach, which was the best idea ever. Perhaps he ought to call in at the Blue Lagoon on his way back and have a quick go in theirs. He chuckled to himself because that would feel far too much like going to work. The number of excursions he'd taken to the Blue Lagoon on the way to and from the airport was ridiculous.

Once he'd warmed up, he drove the short distance back to where he'd camped the night before. It had been too dark to pack up before he surfed. After a quick lunch of some soup that he heated through on his small stove, he packed everything up and headed towards Hraunvik. That wasn't the way he'd come, but it was a different way to drive back to Reykjavik and he wanted to see for himself if anything had changed since the last time he'd been with Iris. She'd mentioned some cracks beginning to appear in the main road.

He took the coast road towards the town, some eight miles to the east. After just a couple of miles, a roadblock stopped him.

'*Hej*,' he said, rolling his window down to talk to the official.

'The road is closed. You will need to turn around and go via Reykjavik.'

'To get to Hraunvik?'

'Yes. The town is being evacuated.'

Siggi's heart began banging in his chest. 'My daughter is in Hraunvik.'

'I cannot let you through. You are not a resident there.' The guy raised his eyebrows in question, giving him the chance to say if his assumption was wrong.

It crossed Siggi's mind to lie. But also, what was he going to do? Knock on their door and whisk Arna away? 'I'm not. I just wanted to see if she is safe.'

'I can radio in, see if they have left the residence. Do you have the address?'

'Thank you,' Siggi said with a sigh of relief. He turned the engine off while he waited to hear. No one else had come along after him, which was also a sign that people knew what was going on.

'That residence has been cleared.'

'Thank you.'

He had no choice but to turn around, but as soon as his phone had a signal, he pulled over and texted Hekla. They barely corresponded, but she acknowledged Siggi enough to keep him in the loop about important things. Generally, that meant a photo on Arna's birthday and not much else. Siggi had never initiated contact with Hekla before, but he felt that this was important enough to break the rules. He needed to know that not only were they out of the house, they were out of the town.

A text back came almost immediately to say that they were staying with friends in the town. They were aware of the evacuation order and were getting ready to leave.

Siggi couldn't imagine why they wouldn't have left already. Presumably they'd salvaged everything of importance from the house when they'd left there. There was no reason for them to delay. His first instinct was to take another route into Hraunvik and escort them out himself. It was all very well leaving Arna to be brought up by another man, but if he wasn't looking after her, what choice did he have? It was down to him to make sure his daughter was safe.

He continued along the road towards Keflavik but took a right-hand turn onto a road that was barely more than a dirt track, going back east towards Hraunvik, this time with no chance of a road closure getting in his way.

There had been a text from Iris. In his haste to text Hekla, he had barely registered, but he remembered now. He pulled over again, leaving the engine running, and checked his phone. She was ready to talk. A wave of relief swept over him and he tapped out a reply.

I will be back later and would love to see you. I'll call x

When he pressed send, he realised he had no signal , and the send failed. There was nothing else he could do about that now, but he was buoyed by the thought of seeing Iris and explaining.

22

Iris was awake early. She'd tossed and turned all night, wondering whether she should have tried to call Siggi. In the end, she had to accept that however she might feel about him, at this moment, they weren't together. But she couldn't do nothing.

Hope you're okay. Call me when you get back to Reykjavik. We need to talk x

There.

She showered, had breakfast in the hotel for a change, and then asked Bríet to call a taxi to take her to the IMO.

'Have you seen the news about Hraunvik?' Bríet asked.

'Yes, it's awful, isn't it?'

Bríet nodded. 'One of my best friends lives there. They left yesterday and are staying with family in town here. They are hoping that the town can be saved and that they can go back when the eruption finishes.'

'I'm sure everyone is hoping that happens,' said Iris tactfully. It was all very well trying to build defences but even with as much data as they had, these things were unpredictable. And no amount of defending was going to work if a fissure erupted through the middle of the town. That was a distinct possibility given what they'd seen so far.

They just had to hope that the lava might take a different course before that became a reality.

Iris said goodbye and got into the taxi, having a very similar conversation with the taxi driver once he realised she was working with the IMO. His sister-in-law's family lived in Hraunvik. Iris tried to sound reassuring while, at the same time being wary about saying anything that could be construed as a promise that everything was going to be alright.

Thankfully, Bjarkey was also in the office early. Iris had had visions of having to wait on the doorstep for the first person to arrive, but when something like this was afoot, they worked around the clock.

'Look at this drone footage,' Bjarkey said, taking Iris over to a big screen in the monitoring room. 'This is live.'

At first, all Iris saw was the steady stream of vehicles travelling along the main road. But then her eye was drawn to something else as the drone pulled out, showing them a wider area. There was a faint, yet unmistakable, line of red. Stark against the black lava of the landscape.

'It's started,' she said.

Bjarkey nodded. 'And at the moment, it is further north than we thought it would be. If this fissure expands and continues to erupt, it may miss the town.'

'But it's too soon to know for sure,' Iris said, looking at Bjarkey for confirmation. Hoping that perhaps she'd say no, it's a sure thing. But of course, she couldn't know. None of them could.

'It's too soon to know. But we can hope.'

After another couple of minutes, the drone dropped altitude, and they got a better look at the fissure. The lava was spurting above the ground every so often, but as yet, it wasn't looking especially fierce. The drone followed the fissure along, establishing how far the visible crack continued. It was a fair distance but difficult to get much perspective.

'We'll have a better idea of what it looks like once these guys are back at base. They'll have tried to get some measurements.'

'Wow,' said Kári, who had wandered over to watch. 'That's incredible. But that's not the fissure we were looking at yesterday.'

'No, this one is to the north-west. It's only been showing up on the monitoring since last night,' said Bjarkey.

'I'm going to see how the data looks back in town,' Iris said. 'I wish I could get another seismometer set up. It'd be amazing to get some data from a point closer to the eruption. If it misses the town, we're not going to get that. Which is a good thing on so many levels,' she added.

'I could see if the guys will go in and relocate one of the other ones?'

'No. I can't ask them to put themselves at risk,' she said, even though it had crossed her mind to drive to Hraunvik and do just that. 'It's not that important. What we already have is the important part. The early-warning system. What happens now is easier to monitor.'

Bjarkey sighed. 'You're right. But don't tell me you haven't thought about going in and relocating it yourself.'

Iris bit her lip and smiled. 'That would be reckless.'

'But scientifically valid?'

'It might help identify whether this new fissure is the one we need to worry about rather than the ones in the town.'

'I'll go with you,' Kári said, his eyes alight with excitement.

'Alright then. But let's see if we can persuade Aron to drive for us again,' said Bjarkey. 'I don't think we should go by ourselves.'

Aron wasn't as keen as the rest of them to venture back to a quickly evolving volcanic eruption, but once Bjarkey had explained the value of the data they could get by moving one seismometer, he relented. Before they went, they planned exactly what route they were going to take and where they would site the equipment. They'd collect the seismometer they'd placed at the north of the town, then travel west to the new fissure.

They gathered what they needed from the office, then went down into the basement, where there was an underground garage and equipment storage. Aron kitted them all out with high-vis trousers, jackets, and emergency kits that had a torch, first aid kit, flares and other useful things, but it brought home to Iris how dangerous it could be to venture out there now. Even though they were in the best position, with the data at their fingertips, these things were always unpredictable. Everything was packed into the same vehicle they'd been out in the day before, and they headed out.

The weather was overcast but dry. They were all quiet on the journey towards Hraunvik. The regularity with which cars were travelling towards Reykjavik was a sign that people were still leaving the area, because usually Iris had seen only a handful of vehicles on this road the other times that she'd been.

They picked up the seismometer without incident from the north of the town. They'd shown their credentials to the civil defence, who were manning the roadblock that they needed to cross, and he was happy to let them through on the condition they spent no more than an hour in the cordoned off area. That was more than enough time for them to site the seismometer, since they'd planned it carefully before they'd left Reykjavik.

Once they began travelling west, they could see evidence of the fissure that they'd viewed on the drone footage. There was a wall of steam rising from the fissure, and the magma was visible in places, even from twenty metres away.

'Wow, this is incredible,' said Kári, his face pressed to the window as they drove past.

Aron took a road that forked to the left, diverting them away from the fissure.

'Why are we moving away from it?' Kári asked. 'Isn't this where we want to site the seismometer?'

'We already know what's happening here,' Iris explained. 'We want to see if we can predict what direction the fissure is going to take. If it converges with the fissure that we're monitoring in the town, it might draw magma away from that area.'

'So we're going to monitor further south of here?'

'Exactly.'

Aron pulled off the main road and drove across the rugged terrain until he was as close as he could get them to where they'd planned. They all piled out of the vehicle and dressed in their high-vis outfits before they set off for the exact spot they wanted to monitor, carrying the equipment between them. As they walked, they could feel the odd tremor beneath their feet. They'd probably been too small to feel while they were driving, but they would be across this entire area now.

'Here,' said Bjarkey, who was holding a portable GPS device that showed the location they'd pinned back at the office.

Surveying the area, they could see the steam rising from the fissure they'd driven past and they could see the town in the distance, to the east.

Iris set up the seismometer, recalibrating it to make sure the data it was going to provide was as accurate as possible. She opened her laptop to check that it was collecting data and reporting it.

'It's already showing activity,' she said.

'How will it tell you what's going to happen?' Kári asked, looking over her shoulder.

'If we overlay the data with what the IMO is already monitoring, and look at the other two seismometers that are collecting data, this will show us whether the activity is increasing over here compared to what we are monitoring in town. By the time we get back to the office, we'll have a solid couple of hours of data to work through and we might even be able to predict where the main fissure is going to present.'

'Isn't what we saw the main fissure?' Kári asked.

Iris shook her head. 'That's nothing compared to what we're going to see.'

'I think if you took the job here, you'd have a ready-made assistant,' Bjarkey said to Iris on the way back to the vehicle, once Aron and Kári were ahead of them and out of earshot.

Iris laughed. 'I love how interested he is.'

'We need to capitalise on that. Let him get involved in this monitoring project now he's seen it in the field.'

Iris thought how different that approach was from the way her own career had progressed. How her initial enthusiasm had been tempered by believing there being no prospect of seeing anything out in the field. It wasn't until she'd developed her seismometer through her love for volcanology and her tenacity, wanting recognition for the work she'd been doing, that she had finally overridden Jay's attempts to stifle her. The progress she'd made over the past two years had led to this, and it felt amazing to see all of that come to fruition.

'He can help me look at the data when we get back,' said Iris.

'Have you thought any more about Emil's offer?'

'I'm seriously tempted,' Iris admitted. 'You know that guy who took me to Hraunvik the first time I went, and to Fagradalsfjall?'

Bjarkey nodded.

'The thing is, I've been seeing him. And we're getting on really well. Obviously I'm not basing my decision on that at all, it's too soon, but when I told him about the job he freaked out and now, I don't know whether it'd be a bad idea to stay.'

'Wow, Iris.' Bjarkey grinned at her. 'This is the kind of drama I love, you know that. How have you kept this from me?'

'Because since things got more serious between us, and then he freaked out, I've only seen you yesterday. And I didn't think it would be that professional to bring it up with Aron and Kári when we'd only just met.'

Bjarkey laughed. 'Good point! But don't lose focus because of him,' she said in a more serious tone. 'I know how much this work means to you. Iceland is your best option to hone this new technique. We have eruptions all the time. And if you need to travel to somewhere else, they will support that. There is a lot of investment in this type of thing because it is so important to the country.'

'I know. It's an amazing opportunity. And I would love to continue working with you.'

'You have to think of this without thinking about what this man wants. It is about what you want.'

'I know, and this is what I want. It's been incredible working with you and the team. This is incredible,' she said, stopping and stretching her arms wide. 'We're standing on what might be the most volcanic area on the planet at this very moment. Why would I ever want to leave?

'Is that a decision made?' Bjarkey asked.

Perhaps making the decision before she had any chance of knowing what Siggi thought was the best thing. She needed to make it for herself without reference to what he thought or wanted. She had worked for years for an opportunity like this and it was stupid to throw it away over someone she had known for two weeks.

'Yes, I think it is.'

'That is fantastic!' Bjarkey hugged her, awkwardly, because

the stiff padded jackets they were wearing made it difficult to bend their arms. 'I will talk to Emil this afternoon and we will make a formal offer for you to consider.'

It already felt to Iris as if she'd made the right decision. She had no regrets about leaving British Geology Labs behind. They'd given her a great start, but she'd realised now that to progress in the way she wanted, she needed to leave. Having worked there for so long was holding her back. She was always going to be the girl who kissed Jay at the Christmas party, as much in her own mind as anyone else. And the only way to evolve from that into the accomplished scientist she hoped she was on the way to becoming, was to leave all of that behind.

'Brilliant, thank you Bjarkey. It wouldn't have happened if it weren't for you.'

'Nonsense,' said Bjarkey, linking her arm through Iris's. 'I am just happy that it is working out for both of us. And who knows, when you tell your man that you are staying, it might make him feel differently.'

On the drive back to Reykjavik, Iris's phone pinged with a message from Siggi saying that he would be back later and wanted to see her. She was so happy to hear that. She'd missed him and wanted to clear the air between them, no matter what the outcome was. They'd had an amazing couple of weeks together and she'd never forget that. Even though she'd fallen in love with him, she would accept that if he couldn't give her anything more, that's how it had to be. She couldn't expect him to fall into a relationship with her just because she was planning to stay in Iceland. But what she hoped, more than anything, was that he would tell her that if she stayed, he wanted to be together. That she was still his love.

23

The road that Siggi had taken to circumvent the roadblock was not really a road. It was generous to call it a track, and his jeep was not up to the job at all. The further he drove, the rockier the terrain got. And he was still miles away from the town. What was he doing? It was ridiculous. He couldn't rock up, find Hekla and Arna and insist they leave with him. Arna had no idea who he was. And that was before he'd even thought about how Hekla's husband would fit into the scenario.

He stopped battling with the increasingly large rocks that were scattered across the road in front of him and came to a stop. He dropped his forehead onto the steering wheel.

'*Fokk!*'

He had to turn back before he made a fool of himself, or worse. He was right in the middle of somewhere that was about to erupt. As if to remind him of that, the earth shook briefly. Enough was enough. He had to get back on the road.

A three-point-turn ended up being a five-point-turn as he tried to avoid the worst of the rocks. He only hoped he hadn't shredded his tyres and that they'd get him back to the main road. Once he'd made the one-eighty, he carefully drove back along the way he'd come. He took it steady now that the impulse to race to Hraunvik had left him and common sense had prevailed. His priority wasn't Arna. He had to accept that. And he *had* accepted that a long time ago. It was the stress of the situation that had led to him forgetting that for a moment or two. What he ought to be doing was getting back to Reykjavik to tell Iris he was an idiot. Perhaps he was always an idiot? That's definitely how the last couple of days were looking.

After another ten minutes, he thought that he should have made it back to the road by now, but maybe he had gone further than he thought before he'd turned around. When he came to an enormous boulder with a ditch on one side of it and a steep bank rising to the left, it was clear he wasn't on the road he'd set out on at all.

He reversed the jeep ten metres. Twenty metres. There was no other way he could go. Unless he turned around again and tried to find the way he'd come originally. But because the ground was basically an old lava field, like most of Iceland, his jeep wasn't leaving any tracks, so chances were he'd end up taking the wrong turn again and end up lost. He opened the door of the jeep and stood up in the footwell to get some height and see if he could see the road, or Hraunvik. Anything to help him get his bearings. Grabbing his phone in desperation, he found he still didn't have a signal. He opened the maps. The dot that showed his location was far from anything resembling a road. It looked as if the main road where the roadblock had been was a couple of kilometres away, if he walked on from the other side of the boulder. Maybe he should walk to the road and flag someone down.

But that would mean leaving his jeep, and although he didn't want to do that, his tour guide safety training kicked in and he knew he needed to get out of the area as soon as he could. He grabbed what he could carry, loading only the most essential things into his rucksack. He shoved some spare clothes in there and the small amount of food and water that he had left. It should only take half an hour to get to the road, but he might have to wait to be picked up for a while longer than that.

Keeping his phone in his hand to make sure he was heading in a straight line, he began walking. On foot, it was easy to get past the boulder, and if he had more time, he would have back-tracked and found a way to drive out. But by now, there had been another couple of earth tremors and he didn't want to push his luck.

After a few minutes, his phone came to life, having connected to the network again. Siggi whooped and scrolled through the messages to see if there was anything from Iris. There was. She was ready to talk. He checked that his own message to her had finally sent and, with a big grin on his face, he carried on walking. Rather than type out a message, which would take ages, he sent a voice note to Jonas telling him what had happened, and hoped that it would send before he lost the signal again.

The relief at being in contact with the world again was so immense that he lost concentration for a second and stumbled over a rock. He ran a couple of steps to catch up with himself and stop himself from falling over, but his foot went over and pain shot through his leg.

He called out as he fell, unable to stop himself, landing on rocks that hammered into his ribs despite the layers he was wearing. With his rucksack on his back, he couldn't roll off them, and it took him a minute to gather himself enough to be able to sit up. His breathing was ragged. The shock of the fall disorientating him and the adrenaline coursing through him, meaning it was another minute before he realised he was hurt.

He reached down and pulled his trousers up from his ankle. Even that slight movement was agony for his ribs and his ankle, and he thought he might pass out. But he took a deep breath and tried again while he exhaled, trying to visualise pushing the pain away. What he saw was enough for him to know, if he didn't already, that something was wrong. Something that was going to mean he wouldn't make it to the road without help. His phone had flown out of his hand when he fell and was lying a couple of metres out of his grasp. Reaching it seemed next to impossible. He shrugged the rucksack off his shoulders and propped himself against it.

If he could just get the phone, he might find that there was still a signal and be able to call for help. Sitting here for any length of time wasn't an option. Being sat on the cold, wet ground was sapping the warmth from him.

He put his hands on the ground behind him, and lifted himself and his injured leg up from the ground, then shuffled his hands along behind him while trying to shift his bottom across the ground as gently as he could. A small earth tremor stopped him in his tracks, but at least he was closer to the phone. Another couple of tries and he would be there.

He just needed a minute to gather himself. He pulled the rucksack over to where he was, and laid back against it again, closing his eyes, then forced himself to open them, knowing how important it was to keep himself alert. A couple of deep breaths helped, then he manoeuvred himself further towards his phone. This time, he carried on until he got there, his fingers curling around his phone as he collapsed back to the ground.

He was exhausted. Holding the phone above his face, the screen now cracked but thankfully still working, he tried to call Jonas.

Nothing.

Maybe sending a text would work.

He typed out a brief message, hoping that the information he'd given Jonas in the voice note before would give him something to go on because the words were swimming in front of his eyes and he couldn't be sure that he was making any sense. He had tried to say he'd had an accident and had pressed send, hoping for the best.

After all that, he deserved a rest. He closed his eyes for a minute.

Just a minute.

24

Iris was on cloud nine. Everything was coming together. Less than an hour after she'd been dropped back at her hotel, the HR department at the IMO had sent over a formal job offer. From the speed of that happening, she had a hunch that Bjarkey had set that in motion before she'd even said yes. The job was as good as hers and the offer was amazing. After only a minute's hesitation, she'd sent a resignation email to HR at British Geology Labs, trying not to feel let down that no one had responded yet to her email about Jay threatening to sack her. It would have been nice to feel like anyone there understood her and what she'd been up against with him as a boss.

Now, she was waiting, never more restlessly, for her phone to ring. She was desperate to see Siggi and make things right with him. Since she had decided what she was doing, she could at least tell him what her plans were. Then it was up to him. But she'd missed him so much that she had decided to be clear with him about her feelings. He'd told her she was his love. Whether that meant he was *in* love with her, Iris wasn't sure. But she knew she was in love with him and she needed to tell him. It felt important to seize the chance of a future with everything in that she wanted, rather than have the career but lose the man she loved because she was too scared to tell him how she felt. For now, she was putting out of her mind the thought that she could face rejection. It was a small price to pay for being able to move forward knowing that she'd done everything she could, to be honest with Siggi.

Tucking her phone into her pocket, she ventured downstairs to the bar, something she hadn't done before, but she felt like celebrating. Hopefully, as soon as Siggi called, she could invite him to come and join in. That would be okay. She was sure he'd be happy for her about the job, even if he decided it didn't change anything between them.

Anders was behind the bar. 'What can I get for you?'

'A glass of red wine, please.' She perched on a bar stool. There was no one else there, so it seemed inevitable she would end up chatting to Anders.

'Merlot?' he asked, smiling.

'Merlot's great, thank you.'

He poured the wine and set it on the bar in front of her. 'How have you been enjoying Iceland?' He began chopping some lemons and limes into segments.

'You're the first person I've told, but I've just got a job here.'

'You are moving here? Congratulations,' he said, stopping his chopping. He poured a tiny amount of wine into the bottom of a glass and held it up. '*Skál!*'

'*Skál!*' Iris said, clinking her glass against his.

'Is that why you are here? For the job?'

'No, but I've been working with the team at the Met Office and they offered me a job. It's in my field and will give me opportunities I wouldn't have where I am now.'

'That's great news. I hear from Embla that you and Siggi have been seeing a lot of each other, so I guess that is also a reason to stay.'

Iris could tell by the look on his face that what he'd just

said wasn't the question he actually wanted to ask. If he was good friends with Siggi, presumably he knew all about his ex-girlfriend, or at least would know that Siggi wasn't the settling down type.

'I'm not sure whether we're in that kind of relationship,' she said, smiling. 'We'll see what happens.'

'Siggi's a great guy. Embla says he is different with you.'

'Did she?' Iris couldn't help herself. In the absence of knowing what Siggi's current thoughts about their relationship were, anything anyone else had to say about it was incredibly interesting. Especially Embla.

Anders nodded, downed the last of his wine, and resumed chopping. 'She told me you had a disagreement and that he was devastated. He left you a note that took him a long time to write.'

Devastated? She hadn't expected that after how cold he'd been to her at breakfast yesterday. His note had barely been an apology, but she had hoped from the tone of it, and the text message he'd sent, that he was feeling differently now. And now, the report from Embla helped her think she was right, and he felt as awful about the whole thing as she did.

'We're supposed to be meeting tonight when he gets back from his surfing trip.'

Anders laughed. 'That is so like Siggi to take off. I hope it works out for you. Embla thinks he is actually happy for once.'

'We'll see,' said Iris again, smiling at Anders.

Her phone vibrated in her pocket. 'Message from Siggi,' she said.

'Ah, he is on his way.'

'This is weird. He's messaged me in Icelandic.'

'Want me to look?'

Iris nodded, hoping she wouldn't live to regret it.

Anders frowned. 'It is saying he needs help and that you

know where he is.'

'What? How would he think I know where he is?'

'The message is in Icelandic. Perhaps it is meant for someone else?'

'If he's asking for help, it'll be Olafur or Jonas. They knew where he was going.'

Before Anders could say anything else. Iris had run out of the hotel, heading to the Icelandic Adventures office.

She burst in, finding Jonas at the desk.

'I think Siggi's in trouble,' she said, thrusting her phone at him.

He scanned the message. 'I think he meant to send this to me. I have a message from him saying he'd taken a wrong turn and had to leave his jeep. He was heading for the main road to get a lift back to town, but with everything that is going on in Hraunvik, he wanted me to know where he was.'

'We need to find him,' she said desperately. 'If he's had an accident, he might be hurt.'

Jonas nodded. 'Let me call Olafur. We will go to the location he told me and start from there. I will also let the civil defence know because he was inside the cordon around Hraunvik.'

'Why? I didn't think he had to go that way to the beach?'

'I don't know,' Jonas said calmly. He made a brief call to Olafur. 'Gudrun is coming to the office to cancel the Northern Lights tour for tonight. You should wait here with her.'

'No, I want to come with you.'

Jonas shook his head. 'No. Stay with Gudrun. Please. If he calls or messages you again, there is a better chance for you to receive it here than out with us where there is no signal.'

He said it gently but firmly, and Iris nodded. It made sense.

The few minutes they waited for Olafur and Gudrun to arrive were interminable. Iris was imagining all kinds of things.

'Siggi is smart.' Jonas said. 'Try not to worry.'

But Jonas looked worried, which told Iris everything. At least the fissures weren't due to erupt for another twenty-four hours, according to the data she'd pored over that afternoon with Kári. If she thought that was about to happen, it would be so much worse.

When Olafur and Gudrun arrived, Jonas was ready to leave, crossing Gudrun in the doorway.

'*Takk*, Gudrun. You know what to do. We'll use the sat phone to call if anything happens.'

She nodded. 'You go.'

Olafur and Jonas set off, jogging along the street to wherever the vehicle they were taking was parked.

'They will find him,' Gudrun said, with such certainty it was comforting.

'Jonas knows where he is.' Although whether the place Siggi had told him was where he was now, none of them would know until they looked. Iris needed to believe that he was right where he'd said he was because what else was there to cling to?

'He might be alright. The phone signal is terrible. Maybe he lost contact?'

Iris held out her phone so that Gudrun could read the message.

'An accident could mean anything,' she said, but they exchanged a glance that told Iris they were both thinking the same.

'Can I help you with the Northern Lights cancellations?' she asked.

'We could split it between us,' said Gudrun. They went over the details, knowing who they would offer a rain check to the following night and who would need a refund because tonight was their last chance. 'The forecast is terrible, anyway,' said Gudrun. 'It has been cloudy all day, so no one will be surprised.'

It took them an hour to rearrange all the clients, and by the time they'd finished, there was still no word.

'They must be there by now,' Iris said, looking from her phone to Gudrun's, which was lying on the desk.

'They will call when there is something to tell us. They know we are waiting.'

'Could we —?'

'No,' said Gudrun, interrupting Iris before she could get any further. 'They are searching. We can't bother them.'

Iris knew she was right, but every minute felt like an hour.

'We must wait,' Gudrun said gently. 'But we can do something to help pass the time.'

They locked up the office, and Gudrun led the way to the Snug store.

'This might seem like I am taking advantage of you, but it is the best distraction I know,' she said, unlocking the door.

She led the way inside. The only lights that were on were the ones in the window. They walked to the back of the store, where Gudrun shrugged her coat off and laid it across the counter, and Iris followed.

'It's quite exciting being here when it's closed,' Iris said. 'It feels like we're being naughty.'

Gudrun laughed. 'I still feel like that when I'm here by myself, even though I am in charge.'

'What are we going to do?' Iris asked.

'We are going to decorate for Easter,' Gudrun said. 'But first, we are going to pour ourselves a glass of wine.' She opened a cupboard underneath a kitchen island that sat to one side of the counter, displaying all manner of crockery and other kitchen paraphernalia like wooden chopping boards, and pulled out a bottle of wine and two glasses. 'This always takes the sting out of a late-night job,' she said.

'Would you be doing this tonight anyway?' Iris asked.

Gudrun shrugged. 'It needs to be in the next few days, but now is the perfect time. I will fetch everything we need.' She disappeared down the stairs to the basement.

Iris took her glass of red wine and perched on the edge of a navy blue velvet chair that had several cushions artfully arranged on it.

When she came back upstairs, Gudrun was carrying a large cardboard box and the better part of a tree balanced on the top. She put it all on the counter, then took a sip of wine before she began pulling out various decorations.

'Okay, we will put these pieces of tree in vases and then decorate them,' she announced, pulling a few vases of various types out of the same cupboard the wine had come from.

Iris watched as Gudrun sorted through the branches, choosing the best twigs to stick in the vases. As she waited for the perfect tree to be assembled, she picked through the box of decorations. 'Wow, these are beautiful.'

'The first year we were open at Easter, we commissioned some of our artists to make decorations for us. We did the same at Christmas and it is a great way to celebrate and show off their talents at the same time.'

There were solid wooden eggs, which were intricately carved with Icelandic words and small flowers, hand-blown glass eggs, eggs knitted with the tiniest of stitches, delicate ceramic eggs with beautiful designs painted on them. It was incredible.

'Don't mix different kids of eggs on one tree,' Gudrun advised. 'It will look terrible.'

'That's exactly what the Christmas tree at my parents' house looks like. It's just a mish-mash of all sorts of baubles, stuff we all made when we were kids, naff tinsel, but it always looks amazing.'

'My tree is also like that,' Gudrun grinned. 'But we have to be boring and tasteful here.'

Iris chose the glass eggs to hang on her first tree. 'I love these. What does this person make?'

'Ah, Sigrid's speciality is hand-blown shot glasses that sell out almost the minute they go on the shelves.' Gudrun rummaged in the cupboard again and pulled out a small vase. 'This one is hers, but it is chipped on the rim. We use it sometimes anyway because it is so pretty.'

It was cobalt blue glass with swirls of opaque white that spiralled around it from top to bottom. The bulbous shape appealed to Iris. 'It's gorgeous. Could I buy it from you? I don't mind that it's chipped.'

'It's yours, and it is just sat in the cupboard so if you want to give it a home, there is no charge.'

'Thank you. It'll look great in my new place.'

Gudrun didn't need it spelled out. 'You took the job! Congratulations!' She came round and hugged Iris.

Iris hugged her back, then something inside her broke. Before she knew what was happening, she was sobbing into Gudrun's shoulder. Gudrun didn't say anything, and she didn't pull away. She held Iris until she had cried herself out.

'I'm sorry,' she said, sniffing and wiping her eyes as she pulled away.

'Don't apologise. There is only so much some Easter decorating can do.'

Iris laughed, wiping her cheeks with the palms of her hands. 'I know I've made the right decision, but it's so hard to think about being here without Siggi.'

'Siggi is going to be okay,' said Gudrun.

'Even if he is, he might not want me.'

'You don't know that, and there is nothing to be gained from guessing what is going to happen.'

'I need to talk to him.'

'I know,' Gudrun said gently, pushing Iris's glass towards

her. 'I am sure there will be some news soon.'

Iris took a deep breath. 'I'll do the wooden ones next.'

25

When Siggi woke, it was dark. His phone was in his hand, but when he looked, there were no messages because there was no signal. He lay for a moment, assessing himself. He was cold. That was a problem. Pushing himself up to sitting made him groan at the pain in his side, but he managed to pull the rucksack in front of him. The extra layers he'd packed were going to be vital now. He only hoped he wasn't too cold already. If he could get up and move around, it would be okay, but then if he could do that, he wouldn't be lost in the dark in a cordoned off area of the country. Shrugging off his coat, he pulled a long-sleeved top and a fleece over the top of what he was already wearing, then put his coat back on. There was a head torch in the rucksack's pocket, which was a relief because his phone torch would have drained the battery quickly and he still hoped to find a signal and be able to call for help.

What was he going to do? Waiting here wasn't an option. Surely if Jonas had got his message, he would have been here by now. There was no option but to make his way to the main road. Pulling his good foot as close to him as he could, he took his weight onto it and heaved himself up. Standing on one leg, he bent forward, his hand on the rucksack, and took a minute to ready himself before he picked it up and swung it onto his back. His ankle throbbed, although it wasn't as painful as it had been earlier, but as soon as he tentatively took a step, pain shot through it. It took everything he had not to drop to his knees and give up. He knew he was in a life or death situation; the pain was the worst he'd ever experienced, but he had to move on.

With his phone in a trembling hand, pointing him in the right direction, crying out in pain with every step, Siggi began a very slow journey to the main road. Eventually, his mind seemed to accept the pain as something that had to be dealt with and he felt as if he were having an out-of-body experience; almost looking down at himself from above as he limped along.

He didn't know how long he had been walking, and couldn't remember what time it had been when he set off, but a large rock ahead was begging him to rest against it. For the first time since he'd left the car, he felt thirsty and drank an entire bottle of water. It sharpened his senses, elevating the pain, but giving him the presence of mind to try shouting for help, which hadn't occurred to him before. There could be people from the civil defence nearby, in the vain hope that he wasn't too far now from the road.

'Hjálp!' He shouted into the darkness, hearing nothing but silence, save for the far off creaks of the earth which was continuing to move under the strain of the underground lava. Siggi supposed the time to worry was when those noises became closer.

Pushing himself off the rock, he carried on, wishing he'd never stopped because everything hurt so much worse than it had before. He called out every few steps. There was still no signal on his phone, and he was a depressingly long way from anything resembling a road on his map.

Then he heard a noise. At first, he thought it was the sound of the fissures, and his heart almost stopped because it sounded close. Too close. But then he realised it was a vehicle, the sound getting closer. Around twenty metres to his left, a truck was winding its way along what Siggi assumed must be the track he'd taken originally. The headlights were too far across and pointing in the wrong direction to pick him out. In desperation, he pulled the head torch off and waved it in his hand, while he shouted as loud as he could to get the attention of whoever was in the truck. But it took a turn away from him, and it wasn't long before he couldn't hear the engine anymore.

Trying to concentrate on his goal and not feel defeated, Siggi set his head torch back in place and carried on with his slow progress. It took everything he had not to give up. He thought about Arna, how if he died, he would never have the chance to know her; something he still hoped was possible. He needed to tell Iris how sorry he was to have pushed her away. How he loved her and hoped she might think about being his girlfriend if she was staying in Reykjavik. A vision came to him of her sleeping in his jeep on the way back from the volcano, her curls falling over her eyes, the hint of a smile on her lips. He wanted to see that again. He wanted to love her without being stifled by the thought of what the future might hold. Because maybe he didn't have a future. And he'd wasted the only chance for happiness that had come his way since Hekla. Why hadn't he seen what he had with Iris for the special, rare, once-in-a-lifetime gift that it was, instead of rejecting it as if it were something that happened to him every day?

'Siggi!'

It took him a moment to register that someone was calling his name. He stopped and turned to see two figures coming out of the darkness towards him. It was Jonas and Olafur. Everything would be alright now.

'Hey, Siggi!' They came towards him, catching him as he fell to the ground with relief and exhaustion.

'Well, you were kind of where you said you were,' Jonas said. 'It's good to see you. Tell me where you're hurt.'

'My ankle. And my ribs.'

'Let me take a look?'

'It looks bad,' he said, wiping tears from his cheeks while Jonas gently took his boot off, then using scissors he pulled out of a first aid bag, cut his trousers and took his sock off to take a better look.

'It is not so bad. Let's strap it up and then get out of here,' he said, grinning and patting Siggi on the shoulder.

Olafur crouched on the ground, letting Siggi lean into him. 'Iris is with Gudrun,' he said. 'They are waiting for news.'

'Iris knows?'

'You messaged her. I guess she is in your contacts next to Jonas?'

He hated that he'd sent his SOS message to Iris. The last thing she needed was to be worrying about him when he'd treated her so badly. Because he knew she would be worried. She wasn't the kind of person who could turn her feelings off in the face of rejection. The shame of how he'd spoken to her washed over him like a cold mist.

'I need to talk to her.'

'We'll call them when we get to the jeep,' said Olafur.

'I love her.'

Olafur laughed, a low rumble. 'I think she might feel the same way.'

Jonas finished up his first aid, which had been painful enough to make Siggi think he might pass out, but bizarrely, had helped with the pain. Jonas and Olafur had a brief conversation about what to do next. Siggi didn't get involved, knowing that none of this was up to him now. He was happy to be in the hands of his friends.

'Siggi, we are going to walk to the jeep. It's not far and we cannot risk leaving the track we came in on.'

'That is exactly what I did.'

Jonas and Olafur said nothing. Siggi knew they wanted answers as to what the hell he was doing here in the first place, but appreciated they knew that didn't have to be now.

With Jonas and Olafur on either side of him, they helped him to stand and took his weight as he hopped back to the jeep between them. It wasn't that far away. He collapsed gratefully into the back seat and sat across it, watching as Jonas directed Olafur's three-point-turn from outside the jeep to make sure they turned back exactly the way they'd come.

Once they were underway and back on the main road, Siggi closed his eyes, hearing Jonas make the call to Gudrun. He hadn't the energy to ask to speak to Iris. Now that he wasn't going to die tonight, he could wait.

26

As soon as the phone rang, Iris realised that helping Gudrun in the shop had been the distraction she'd needed because the feeling of dread she'd had since Siggi's text now descended on her again.

'He's okay,' Gudrun said before continuing the conversation in Icelandic.

Iris rubbed at the smooth wooden egg she held in her hands while she waited for the call to finish.

'What happened?' she asked when Gudrun had ended the call.

'Jonas thinks he took the wrong road and his jeep got stuck. They don't know any more yet.'

'But he's okay? Are they taking him home?'

'They are going to the hospital. Jonas thinks he has broken an ankle.'

'Oh my god.' Iris wasn't sure what to do. 'Should we go to the hospital?'

Gudrun shrugged. 'We can. We will have to walk, or get a taxi.'

'I'd like to walk. Are you sure you don't mind coming with me?'

'Of course I don't mind,' she said.

'Do you think it's okay for me to go? I mean, I don't know how things stand between us. He might not want me there.'

'Iris, I do not think you will be able to do anything without seeing for yourself that he is okay.'

That was true. She was desperate to see him, and she didn't think all of the Easter decorating in the world would change that.

She nodded. 'I need to see him.'

The two of them tidied up.

'Can we call in at the hotel on the way? I didn't bring a coat.'

Anders was behind the reception desk. 'Is there any news?'

'He's okay,' Iris said. She left Gudrun to fill him in on the few details they had while she ran up to her room for her coat and hat.

'Anders has offered to drive us,' Gudrun said.

'Thank you, that'd be great.' The idea of walking had seemed like a way to clear her head before seeing Siggi, but the offer of a lift was too good to refuse. She wanted to be there as soon as she could.

'Call the hotel if you need a lift back,' Anders said as they climbed out of his car. 'And give Siggi my best wishes.'

Iris had butterflies as they walked through the doors of the emergency department at the hospital. It wasn't the best time to have this big conversation about everything, when Siggi had just had an accident. Could they gloss over that for now?

'They have said we can wait through here,' Gudrun said, taking Iris's hand.

Jonas and Olafur were both waiting in the same place. Olafur grinned when he saw Gudrun and stood up to embrace her.

'Hey, Iris, he will be pleased to see you.' Jonas gave Iris a hug.

'What happened?'

'We don't know anything more than what Gudrun probably told you. But the main thing is that he is safe and will be okay.'

They sat in silence together in the waiting area. Eventually a nurse came out and spoke to them.

'We can see him for a few minutes,' Jonas said.

Iris was torn between wanting to see him and being scared to death of what she was going to find. She held back, letting the others go into the room before her, almost peeking out from behind Olafur to get her first glimpse of Siggi. He was sat up in bed, leaning back against a lot of pillows, but he looked like himself. A tireder version, but he was smiling as everyone said hello to him. His right leg was on a pillow, sticking out from underneath the sheets that covered the rest of him, and heavily bandaged.

'Iris,' he said, and held his hand out to her.

Olafur stepped aside, and she walked over to the bed and took Siggi's hand. He pulled her to him and kissed her, the fingers of his other hand pushed into her curls, cupping the back of her head. 'I'm sorry,' he whispered. 'I want you to stay.'

Iris smiled and bit her lip. 'We don't have to talk about this now,' she said, but she was happier than she could have imagined to hear him say that.

'But I need you to know that I did not mean what I said. I would love you to take the job and stay here.'

'Okay,' she said, placating him with another kiss so that he would rest. 'I hear you. We can talk about all of this, but not tonight.'

'The nurse said you need to sleep. Our time's up,' said Jonas glancing to the door where the nurse was hovering ready to kick them out. We'll see you tomorrow. Olafur and Jonas fist-bumped Siggi, then Gudrun gave him a quick kiss.

'*Takk fyrir að bjarga lífi mínu,*' Siggi said to them with a nod.

'*Ekkert mál,*' Olafur said, with a similarly sombre nod.

'Siggi's saying thank you for saving him,' Gudrun explained to Iris in a low voice. 'We'll wait outside while you take a minute.'

'Can I see you tomorrow?' Siggi asked once they were alone.

He was still holding onto her hand and Iris didn't want to leave. The couple of minutes they'd had wasn't enough. She didn't want to do all the talking now, but she did want to be with him.

'Yes. I'll come first thing in the morning. How long will you need to stay?'

'I don't know, maybe only until tomorrow. I need to see someone about my ankle tomorrow, then maybe I am good to leave.'

'Bye.' She kissed him again, their lips pressing together as if they might never see each other again. Because they both knew that could have been the case after the last time they'd kissed.

It was on the tip of Iris's tongue to say that she loved him. It was almost overwhelming her but she didn't say it. It wasn't the right time, and however much she wanted to let herself go and take the second chance that they seemed to have been given, she was worried that it was the intensity of the situation that was driving Siggi's turnaround. Perhaps in the cold light of day he would feel differently.

Olafur drove the four of them across town.

'Do you think Siggi is going to manage at his flat?' Iris asked the others.

'I asked Rachel to see if he could stay at Anna and Ned's place while they are in London,' said Jonas. 'He could stay with us, but we have stairs too and our place is out of town. At least he can get around if he is at their house.'

Iris wanted nothing more than to move in to Ned and

Anna's and look after him, but they were a long way from that being a good idea. Hopefully tomorrow, they would have a chance to talk.

Iris was woken by her phone ringing. She reached for it, still half-asleep.

'Iris! It's happening!'

'Bjarkey?'

'The fissure is erupting!'

Iris sat up in an attempt to rouse herself. 'Where are you?'

'At the office. Can you come? I'll come and pick you up?'

Iris checked the time. It was four in the morning. By the time she'd been dropped back at the hotel last night and calmed her mind enough to fall asleep, it had been around one o'clock. Only three hours sleep. She groaned, but climbed out of bed reminding herself that this was what she'd been waiting for.

She washed her face, cleaned her teeth, and pulled her hair into a ponytail to avoid having to think about making it look presentable, dressed in the usual multiple layers that she was now used to, then ran downstairs to wait outside for Bjarkey.

The street was eerily quiet. It was the first time she'd seen it with no one around and it felt like a real adventure to be pulled from her bed, and be out and about in the middle of the night.

'Hey!' Bjarkey said, looking much livelier than Iris felt when she climbed into the car. 'You are not going to believe this.'

They pulled around the corner and Bjarkey turned right, onto the main road that ran along the seafront.

'Oh my god!' Iris's hands flew to her mouth. In the distance, there was a line of red fire running across the far horizon. 'I can't believe we can see it from here!'

'I know. It is completely unprecedented. Stunning.'

Iris nodded. It *was* stunning. To think that the fissures they'd been looking at yesterday morning had all of this waiting underneath, ready to put on this spectacular display.

'Oh god,' she said again. It hit her what a close call Siggi, Jonas and Olafur had had. 'Siggi had an accident yesterday and was stuck out on the Reykjanes peninsula somewhere. His friends went out to find him.'

'Is he okay?' Bjarkey asked, her joy turning to concern.

'He is, but if this had happened a few hours earlier.'

'But it didn't.'

'But —'

'Iris, you will drive yourself mad thinking of things like this. If they are all okay, that is good. There is nothing to be gained from dwelling on it.'

Iris nodded, but she couldn't get the thought out of her head. It had been too close. What had Siggi been doing? He knew it was a dangerous area.

'So is it all back on with you two?'

'I don't know. We still haven't talked properly, and he doesn't know I've decided about the job yet. But I want to be with him.'

'Good for you.'

'Anyway, how is the data looking?'

'Oh, Iris. The data is beautiful. Wait until you see what those seismometers told us.'

The monitoring room at the IMO was buzzing with more people than Iris had ever seen there before. As she and Bjarkey moved through, Bjarkey introduced her to a few people as a new colleague. It felt strange but in the best way. It was just hard to believe that her life had changed so much in the space of two weeks.

Kári was sitting at a desk with extreme bed-head hair and a smile on his face. 'Iris! I have been transposing this data like we did yesterday.'

Iris sat down with him, marvelling at the evidence she'd been hoping for, right on the screen in front of her. 'This is amazing. We can see the activity heighten just after midnight on the fissure outside of the town, and at the same time the activity on the seismometer in town drops. And how did the regular data look then?'

She and Kári spent the next few hours poring over the data, building up a picture of what had happened, with the focus now on the progress of the eruption. She had more than enough information to finish her report, something she was determined to do as soon as possible to put an end to any involvement she needed to have with Jay.

When they came up for air, Iris realised that she had completely lost track of time and had probably missed the first-thing-in-the-morning slot she'd promised Siggi. She pulled out her phone and texted him but there was no response and she could see the message hadn't been read. Why hadn't she got Gudrun's number?

'Bjarkey, could you do me a favour? Would you mind calling the hospital and seeing whether Siggi has been discharged?'

Iris gave Bjarkey all the details she could. It turned out that Siggi had been discharged. Iris felt guilty, but then it wasn't as if she could have picked him up herself. He had good friends, and she wasn't part of his support network. She had to remember that. As much as she hoped he might want her to be, she was in a kind of limbo situation until they'd talked, and that didn't mean she had anything to feel guilty about.

She thanked Bjarkey and called the Icelandic Adventures office. Rachel answered the phone and Iris explained what had happened.

'We thought it would have been the eruption that kept you away,' she said, which made Iris feel better. 'He's fine. Jonas dropped him off at Anna and Ned's.'

'Do you think it would be alright if I went round?'

'I think he'd love that.' Rachel explained where the house was. 'It used to be mine and Jonas's place,' she said wistfully.

The directions didn't fill Iris with confidence that she'd find the house, but she'd noted them down diligently; take the road off Laugevegur as if you are heading to the church, then opposite a particular shop — she'd written the name of that phonetically — go up the cobbled path and it's the red house with the trolls in the garden.

'I'm leaving now if you want a lift,' Bjarkey said.

'That'd be great, thank you. I'll be in tomorrow morning to see how things are going.'

'Hey, Iris.' Bjarkey put a hand on her arm. 'Why don't you take some time out now that the eruption has started? Slow down, get your report finished. All of this is a big change and you need to give yourself time to adjust. Let things settle.'

'There's still data to analyse,' she said, unsure of how she felt about what Bjarkey had suggested.

'There is always data to analyse, but now it is not going to save anyone's life. You have already done that.'

The thought of having some down time was suddenly appealing. She could get stuck into writing the report because she wanted to do the best possible job of that so that she could leave her old employer with dignity and to show Jay the level of professionalism he could never show her. Perhaps she would go home. Maybe finish the last of her days at British Geology Labs actually in the lab itself. Deliver the report in person and say a proper goodbye, because not all of her colleagues were people she'd be happy to leave behind. She wanted to leave with her head held high, not disappear into the night as if she'd done something wrong.

'You're right. I should concentrate on finishing off the job I have before I start my new one.' Iris said as she climbed into the car.

Bjarkey grinned. 'And maybe spend some time with that man of yours.'

'We don't know he's my man.'

'I have my fingers crossed for you.'

'It just isn't possible to be in love with someone so quickly.' Iris didn't phrase it as a question, but she looked at Bjarkey. She valued her opinion and she needed someone who could see things more clearly.

'People fall in love all the time. For some people it is an instant, for others it grows over years. It is different for everyone. If you are in love with him, it's not wrong to feel like that. You are a scientist, Iris. In your professional life you do not jump to conclusions without evidence to back them up. I expect your personal life is no different. You make calculated projections. Is being in love any different?'

'I feel as if I'm listening too hard to my heart instead of my head. It's as if my feelings are drowning out any reason that tries to make itself heard in my head.'

'Oh, Iris. If this man doesn't already know you are in love with him, he is an idiot and he is an even bigger idiot if he is not in love with you too.'

Iris laughed. 'Thanks Bjarkey. That sounded like good advice but I'm none the wiser. Can I jump out here?'

Bjarkey pulled over and Iris got out and thanked her. She beeped the horn as she drove away. It felt like encouragement for what was about to happen next, and Iris loved her for it.

She took a deep breath and began following Rachel's directions through the town to Anna and Ned's house. As she went past Te & Kaffi, she called in for coffee and pastries, buying a selection so that Siggi could pick his favourite.

It only took a few minutes more for her to find the cobbled path to the little house. There were indeed trolls in the garden, similar to gnomes, but less friendly looking. There was a tiny veranda with a couple of chairs on it and there were fairy lights twisted along the railing and along the the tops of the garden fences. It was idyllic. And Siggi was just on the other side of the door.

27

She knocked on the door and heard Siggi call out in Icelandic. It was unlocked when she tried the handle, so she went inside assuming he might have said come in.

'Hi,' she said, poking her head around the door. It opened straight into a spacious lounge which had a mezzanine level over half of it. It was decorated as if it were from the pages of an interior design magazine. In fact, Iris recognised lots of the cushions, throws and lamps as having come from Snug. The high-end look didn't mean it wasn't cosy and lived-in, though. It looked exactly like the home she would love to have one day.

'Iris.' Siggi was lying on the sofa, a book open on his chest and his leg, now sporting one of those surgical boots propped up on the cushions across the back. He began pushing himself to sitting.

'Don't get up,' she said, closing the door behind her and coming inside properly. 'I'm so sorry I wasn't there this morning.' She took her coat off and hung it on a spare hook on the wall by the door. Unlacing her boots, she put them neatly by Siggi's and padded over to the chair.

'You don't need to be sorry. The eruption is why you are here. Of course you were working.'

Iris tried to catch any bitterness in his tone, but there was none. He genuinely didn't mind.

'How are you?'

'This will slow me down for a while,' he said, pointing to his leg. 'I am lucky Ned and Anna are letting me stay here, otherwise I would have to stay at Jonas's and that would be worse than this.'

Iris laughed. 'I bought coffee and pastries.'

'Now that is worth sitting up for.' He slowly pushed himself up, propping himself in the corner of the sofa.

'Do you want a cushion under your leg?'

'Thanks, if you can find one.'

There were about thirty-four cushions within arm's reach. She chose a couple of the bigger ones, gently lifting his boot and stacking them underneath.

'You get first dibs on the pastries,' she said, handing him the bag.

'I should get lost more often.'

She said nothing for a minute. The feeling of dread she'd had while he was missing hadn't been gone long enough for her to joke about it. 'Too soon,' she said softly.

'I'm sorry you were worried. I meant to text Jonas.'

'What were you doing there?'

He sighed and stared into his coffee. 'It is so stupid.'

'Tell me.' She piled a couple of cushions on the floor next to him and sat down, taking his hand.

'I have a daughter. She lives in Hraunvik with her mother.'

'In the house we went to?'

He nodded. 'She does not know me as anyone but a friend of her mother's from a long time ago. She does not know I am her father, and that is because for a long time I did not want her to know.'

Iris thought her heart might break for him when he looked at her with tears in his eyes. 'And now you do?

He nodded. 'I have wanted to for a while.'

'And you thought this was the best time to introduce yourself?'

He choked out a laugh. 'I know. Stupid.'

'Siggi. Don't be so hard on yourself. It's natural to want to know your daughter.'

'But you are right. I cannot turn up at their door and tell her who I am.'

'No, but have you talked to her mother about this?'

'Hekla and I, we do not talk. I left her at the worst time. It was something we should have done together.'

'It's easy to say that now. You're not twenty-odd with your whole life disappearing before your eyes. It's easy to think a different decision would have been simple to make.'

Siggi looked at her with enormous relief in his eyes. 'I couldn't tell you before. I didn't think anyone would understand.'

'When I made you knock on their door in Hraunvik, we'd just met. I'd have thought it was so weird if you'd blurted out your life story to explain why you didn't want to do that.'

He smiled. 'When you put it like that. Can I have another pastry?'

Iris tried to stifle a yawn as she passed the bag to him. Now that she'd stopped, she felt exhausted.

'You look tired,' Siggi said, tucking a stray curl behind her ear. 'Want to nap together?'

'I don't think there's room for me on the sofa. I might go back to the hotel and come back later.'

'Don't go.'

She didn't want to go, but now that she'd noticed she was tired, her bed was calling.

'Are you sleeping on the sofa?' she asked, nodding at the mezzanine where the bed was. There was no chance of Siggi making it up there.

He shook his head. 'There's another bedroom in there,' he said. 'Come on, stay.'

She went through the door he'd gestured to, into a very smart kitchen. A door off to one side led to a small room which was entirely filled with a bed. It was a very inviting-looking bed, almost entirely covered with various throws, blankets, and more pillows.

'Okay,' she said, frowning when she went back into the lounge, where Siggi was standing on one leg, grappling with his crutches. 'How did you even get into the house?'

'Jonas helped. You expect me to be an expert with these already?'

'I'm sorry. Are you alright?'

'Yes,' he said, sounding more confident than he looked.

'Is there anything I can do?'

'Nothing except get into bed.' The glint was back in his eye, just as it had been before.

What was she meant to do? Pretend the breakfast conversation had never happened? Did the fact that he could have died yesterday mean that there was some kind of free pass and everything just went back to how it had been before?

The thing was, she wanted it to be like it had been before and she was too tired to fight that. The bed was beckoning her.

She watched anxiously as he made his way to the doorway of the bedroom. He sat on the edge of the bed and propped the crutches against the doorjamb. Iris pulled off her jeans and top until she was standing in the kitchen in her underwear. Maybe it gave the wrong message, but all she could think about was sleeping. It was getting harder by the minute to keep her eyes open.

Siggi reached for her and she took a step towards him. He put his hands on her waist and pulled her closer, then laid his head against her chest. 'Iris...' he breathed into her.

Now would be the perfect time to launch into the conversation about where they were heading. What did he want? What did she want?

Instead, she kissed the top of his head, then clambered over him onto the bed. She pushed the pillows aside, pulled the covers down, and climbed in, moving over to the wall to make space for him. He lay down beside her, shifting around until he was comfortable, then he took her hand and almost immediately, she fell asleep.

When she woke up, it was dark, and Siggi wasn't there. She didn't know what time it was, but she felt rested, as if she'd slept for hours. Picking up the softest throw in the world from the bottom of the bed, she wrapped it around herself and went to look for him. He was exactly where he had been when she'd arrived; lying on the sofa reading.

'Hey,' he said, grinning. 'Better?'

'Mmm. What time is it?'

'Seven.'

'We need some dinner. I'm starving.'

'There is no food here,' Siggi said. 'I was going to go to the shop.'

'You are not going to the shop,' Iris said, imagining him trying to negotiate the cobbled path when he'd had enough trouble getting from here to the kitchen. 'Not until you're better at the crutches. Let's get a takeaway. I don't mind picking it up.

'Have you seen outside?' he said, nodding to the window.

Big fat flakes of snow were falling. 'Oh my god!' Iris said with glee. 'It's snowing!' Although it had snowed when they'd been camping, being inside and watching the snow fall from the warmth of this cosy little house was on another level. 'Honestly, I'm happy to go.' It was a chance to see the city as she hadn't before; a winter wonderland. She imagined the streets dusted with snowflakes glistening in the glow of the fairy lights and full of people bundled up in their coats and boots.

'I can't believe you are excited about going out in this weather,' Siggi said, laughing. 'Can you pass my phone?'

Iris loved listening to him speak Icelandic. It was sexy. She carried on looking out of the window because otherwise she'd be staring at him. She was almost back to where she'd been two days ago. Before the ill-fated breakfast, before he'd gone missing, before she'd taken the job. But there was a lot for them to talk about before anything more than falling asleep together could happen.

'I have ordered fish and chips for us. They will deliver in half an hour.'

'Oh, okay.'

'Hey, Iris.'

Tearing herself away from the window and the snow, which was getting deeper by the minute, she turned. He was sitting now, patting the seat next to him.

'Keep your ankle up,' she said, putting a pillow on the coffee table and helping him lift his foot. Now that they had broken the ice by seeing each other again, Iris could sense that very little was going to be said about anything until they talked about what had happened between them. One of them had to start the conversation, otherwise they'd be dancing around it forever.

'I took the job at the Met Office.' She sat next to him. It was easier to talk if she didn't have to look at him.

'I am glad about that, Iris. And I am sorry that I was a... *skíthæll.*'

'Hopefully that means an arse.'

'Something like that,' he said.

Iris glanced sideways. His eyes crinkled at the corners as

he gave a rueful smile.

'I know it changes things between us now that I'm staying. Neither of us planned this to be anything more than two people having fun together while they happened to be in the same place for a while. And I heard what you said, and I know you feel bad about it, but that's not the same as not meaning it.' She paused. 'Did you mean it? That me staying doesn't change anything?' It hurt to say it out loud.

'Iris, I am so sorry. It is unforgivable that I said that to you. The moment you left, I knew I had made a mistake. Until I met you, I thought I wanted the rest of my life to be the opposite of what it would have been if I had settled down with Hekla. To come and go as I please without anyone else to think about. When I said those words to you, I had not even realised that I didn't feel like that anymore. It was different with you. I had not imagined being with someone who I would rather be with than be apart from. But that is you, Iris. I know now. Last night, before Jonas and Olafur found me, I thought that might be the end for me and all I could think about was you.'

Although that had gone through her own mind, she hadn't realised it could have been a reality until now.

She snuggled closer to him. 'I'm so sorry, Siggi. I've missed you so much.' It all made sense. 'I know how it can be to feel something for so long that you kind of assume that's how you will always feel.'

'That is it exactly,' he admitted. 'But the moment you left, I realised that wasn't how I wanted to feel. Because everything is different with you, Iris.' He reached for her hand and squeezed it. 'Is it okay if I explain about Hekla?'

'Of course it is.' If they were going to be together, she needed Siggi's version of the story to be the one she knew, not Olafur and Gudrun's.

'When Hekla and I were together, we were so young. We

thought we were in love, but it was never that. We were friends who enjoyed hanging out with each other. The future together was only the trip we planned to take after university, nothing more. When she got pregnant, I thought the only option was to leave. I didn't love her, but I know now that if I'd explained how I felt, we probably could have worked something out.'

'So that you could have been a dad without having to be with Hekla.'

'It's terrible.'

'Siggi.' Iris twisted so that she was perched on the edge of the sofa, looking at him. 'You can't keep beating yourself up about a decision from so long ago. My new colleague, Bjarkey, gave me some great advice when I was deciding whether to take the job. She said that you have to know what you want before you can factor anyone else into a decision.'

He smiled and raised his eyebrows. 'Who were you thinking of factoring in?'

'Don't change the subject.'

He sighed. 'I am not used to talking about things like this.'

'It's important. You have to deal with this. You've been carrying around this regret for years. Last night you could have died because you thought you needed to save her from the eruption. If you want a relationship with her, talk to her mother. If you explain how you feel, she might understand. It was a long time ago.'

He nodded. 'You are right. Arna does not know I am her father. I would like her to know, even if she does not want anything to do with me.'

Iris could understand how after last night, that would be important to him.

'Maybe yesterday is a sign that things can be different.'

'Can things be different with us?' he asked, looking tortured as he waited for her answer.

'I love you, Siggi. That's why it hurt so much when you said if I stayed, it wouldn't matter. I'd fallen in love with you and whether I decided to stay or leave, I was going to end up with a broken heart.'

'I love you, Iris. I want you to stay. You deserve the job of your dreams and I am so glad that you didn't let me stop you from taking it,' he said, taking her hands in his and pulling her towards him. 'Mind my ribs on this side.'

She hugged him gently, trying not to touch him anywhere apart from around his shoulders. 'Is that okay?'

'It is.'

She pulled back and put her palms on his cheeks, then kissed him. He was more stubbly than usual, and it made Iris's lips tingle.

'This is the worst time to be out of action,' he groaned.

'Have we agreed there is going to be any action yet?'

'Haven't we?'

There was a knock at the door. Iris jumped up. 'Fish and chips!'

'Hæ Siggi, hvernig hefurðu það?' The delivery guy said to Siggi.

'Good, thanks,' Siggi said, waving from the sofa. 'Thank you for the delivery. I owe you a favour,' he said in English.

'Enjoy,' the guy said, grinning and waving goodbye as he ventured back into the snow.

'Brrr,' said Iris, shivering at the icy blast that had come into the house. 'I'll plate it up.'

They ate together on the sofa. Iris made mugs of tea for them after finding a carton of long-life milk in the cupboard.

'What do you think, then?' Siggi asked, when they snuggled on the sofa together afterwards.

'About?'

'Us.'

'I'd like to pick up just after the camping trip. Imagine

we've had that amazing weekend, and delete the bit in between then and now.'

'You're happy to forget?'

'We both know what we want and I think that's each other.'

'I cannot believe that I can go from despair to being so lucky in one day.'

'Me neither.'

'So we're together now, officially,' he said.

Iris could hear the smile in his voice. She was feeling the same way.

'Iris and Siggi. Gudrun's going to love it.'

'So what now? Do you want to stay?'

'Desperately.'

'I am not sure I can celebrate our new start in the way I would like to.'

'There's no rush,' Iris said. All that mattered was that they were together. Everything else could wait.

28

Iris woke long before Siggi the next morning. He was sleeping closest to the door, and she didn't want to disturb him by climbing over the top of him, so she lay, alternately watching him sleep and dozing herself.

It was only when they came to move from the sofa last night that Iris realised how fragile Siggi was. It took him a while to stand up and get to the bedroom, then when she had to help him pull his top off because he couldn't lift his arm properly, she saw the extent of the bruising all down his right-hand side. No wonder he'd slept for hours.

She was propped up on one elbow, looking at Siggi and wondering if she should start thinking about getting up, when the doorbell rang. Having no choice, she clambered over Siggi as carefully as she could out into the kitchen, then pulled on her thermal top and leggings and ran for the door.

'Oh! Iris!' Gudrun was wide-eyed and very quickly thrilled to see Iris answer the door. 'We came to check on Siggi.'

'Come in,' she said, holding the door open while they knocked the snow off their boots and came inside. 'It's so pretty out there.'

'Huh,' Gudrun said in disgust. 'It is almost April. It should not be snowing.'

Olafur stepped inside and handed her a large paper bag. 'We brought brunch.'

'Let me wake Siggi,' said Iris.

'How is he?' Gudrun asked in a low voice.

'Battered and bruised, but pretty upbeat, considering.'

'And he is staying off his ankle?' Olafur asked.

'Yes, he's being really careful,' Iris said. 'Although he did suggest going to the shop yesterday.'

'Ha! That is exactly what I was expecting,' said Olafur. 'He needs to be sensible. We are not young men anymore.'

Gudrun looked at Iris and rolled her eyes. 'Come on then, let's make some coffee.' She marched into the kitchen before Iris could suggest that maybe Siggi might want to get up without an audience, but he was sat on the edge of the bed, trying to pull a top on, his modesty covered with the sheet.

'Oh my god, sorry Siggi, I forgot about this tiny bedroom in the kitchen,' Gudrun said, making no moves to leave.

'It's fine,' he said wearily.

Iris helped him dress while Gudrun made coffee for them all. 'I'm sorry,' she whispered.

He smiled and dropped a kiss on her head when she bent down to pull his sweatpants over his boot. She thought her heart might explode.

'Need a hand?' Olafur said, appearing in the doorway.

'*Takk,*' Siggi said, as Olafur helped him up and gave him a hand to the bathroom.

'Tell me everything,' Gudrun said as soon as they were out of earshot. 'You stayed last night?'

'He can't manage by himself.' As if that were the reason.

'He would not let any of us help, so you must have something to offer that we do not,' Gudrun said, laughing.

'We've sorted everything out,' Iris said, putting Gudrun out of her misery.

'You're together? I knew it! A near death experience was all it took.'

'Gudrun!'

'Sorry,' she said, looking genuinely regretful. 'I am sure it would have happened anyway.'

Iris gave her a hug. 'It probably speeded things up.'

'He is okay and you are together. That is all that matters.'

'We're in the lounge whenever the coffee is ready,' called Olafur.

'What's in the bag?' Iris asked.

'Boring cinnamon buns,' said Gudrun. 'Olafur did not want to walk further than the bakery.'

'Cinnamon buns are never boring, especially when there's nothing else to eat.'

They carried the buns and coffee into the lounge and put everything on the coffee table. Siggi was sitting in the corner of the sofa with his leg on a tower of cushions and Olafur had squeezed into the remaining space in the other corner.

'Gudrun says you are staying, Iris,' Olafur said, passing a mug of coffee to Siggi. It was touching how he fell into the role of looking after his friend.

'How could I resist when there's an eruption on the doorstep?'

'And the man of your dreams,' said Gudrun.

Siggi spluttered over his mouthful of coffee and started laughing, as did Olafur. Gudrun and Iris looked on in amusement, waiting for them to gather themselves.

'*Þú ert draumamaðurinn hennar!*' Olafur said, collapsing into laughter.

Siggi was trying to stifle his laugher, and was holding his ribs, saying, '*Nei! Nei!*'

'Well, obviously he is not the man of her dreams in this state,' Gudrun said indignantly.

'Gudrun!'

'Iris took the job before we were back together,' said Siggi, still holding his side.

Back together, as if them being together before went without saying. Something everyone knew about. Something solid. But she loved him for letting it be known that the decision to stay was hers, not because of their relationship, even if that would be the reason now.

'Congratulations, Iris,' Olafur said, toasting her with his coffee mug. '*Skál!*'

'*Skál!*'

'We should go to the bar tonight and celebrate,' Gudrun suggested.

Iris and Olafur looked at Siggi.

'What?' he said. 'I can go to the bar.'

'I don't think tonight would be great.' Iris was thinking about how Siggi looked about half an hour ago. He needed a bit of peace and quiet to heal, and thankfully, Olafur agreed.

'Next week will do just as well,' he said.

'Exactly,' said Iris.

'And we will leave you to rest now,' he said, standing up.

'If you need anything, let us know,' Gudrun said, collecting the coffee mugs up and taking them into the kitchen.

Iris saw them out and watched them make their way along the snowy path back to the road, wondering what was going to happen now. Was she staying here with Siggi? She ought to stay until he could get around well enough that she'd feel confident he wouldn't topple over every time he stood up.

After Gudrun and Olafur had left, Siggi lay down on the sofa, his leg up on the back again. Iris made a pillow stack and sat next to him on the floor.

'I feel like we're suddenly living together,' she said.

'We are suddenly living together.'

'But just until you're okay.'

'Okay,' he said easily.

'Because I don't think I'm ready to actually do that.'

'That's okay.'

Him agreeing with everything she said wasn't telling her what he thought. But she was also aware that she was probably over-thinking it. It was as simple as being here to help him out. If he didn't have a broken ankle and a flat on the third-floor, there would be no need.

'So I'll stay until you're up and about and then I'll find somewhere to live.'

'Okay,' he said. 'You know I am happy whatever you want to do. I don't want to take things slowly. I love you and I want to be with you, but that does not mean I think we should move in together today either.'

'That's good,' she said, grinning as a wave of relief swept over her. 'So we won't count this. I mean, I could be anyone. I could be Olafur. That's what I'm here for, just to help.'

'Iris,' he said, pulling her closer. 'I do not want you to be Olafur. I hope that while you are here, we will be together like we were on the camping trip. This can be like a holiday, maybe like the honeymoon of us getting back together.'

'I love that,' she said, kissing him.

He pulled her towards him for a deeper kiss, with a gentle hand on the back of her head. His kisses were melting her insides.

'I can help you look for somewhere to live,' he said, a little later, by which time Iris was lying by his side on the sofa.

'That would be great. I don't want to end up in a dodgy area.'

He laughed. 'There are no dodgy areas in Reykjavik, but I want you to have a nice place. Not too far from me.'

'As soon as you're okay, I'll have to go home to England,' she said, allowing a flicker of reality into their bubble. 'Just to finish up at work.'

'Could I come? I cannot do tours for a while and Jonas has given me a couple of weeks off before I start working in the office instead.'

'I'd love that,' Iris said. 'We can get an Airbnb. You won't be bored while I'm at work?'

'I'm never bored.'

'I'll need to go to my mum and dad's to pack up some stuff to send over here.' Her parents didn't even know about Siggi. They'd only just got back from their holiday and she hadn't had a chance to speak to them. Finn was the only one who knew, and probably Felix by now. 'I'd better warn them I'm bringing my boyfriend home with me.' It sounded wonderful to say out loud.

'I am meeting the parents.' He shuddered.

'Is it the same when you're thirty-four?'

'It's always the same, I think. They will want to know I am a good guy for you, however old you are. That is what I would think.'

She paused, knowing what he was thinking. 'Do you think you might call Hekla?'

'I will call today before I forget how I felt.'

Iris wasn't sure that the memories of that night would fade so quickly, but she was glad for his own peace of mind that he wanted to see if there was a way to have a relationship of some kind with his daughter.

'I may as well check out of the hotel. I can write my report here before we go back to England.'

'You don't need to go to the IMO?'

'Bjarkey said not to. She thinks I need a break between finishing in the UK and starting here.'

'Bjarkey talks sense. I'll do some reading while you are out.'

Iris kissed him, reluctantly peeled herself off the sofa, and handed him his book. By the time she'd got dressed, he'd fallen asleep with the book splayed open on his chest. She crept out of the house and headed for the hotel to pack up her room. It was a beautiful day. The snow glinted in the sunlight and she could swear there was some warmth in the sun when it hit her face.

'Good morning, Iris,' Embla said, greeting her with what looked like a genuine smile. 'We haven't seen you for a couple of days.'

'I'm staying with a friend for a few days until I go back to the UK. Can I check out, please?'

'You're staying with Siggi.' It wasn't a question.

Iris nodded. Embla didn't look like she wanted to kill her, but the change in her was unnerving.

'I am happy for you both,' she said, sounding like she meant it. 'He is happy, and he never looked like that when he was with me.'

'Thank you.'

Iris went up to her room, marvelling that Embla had a heart after all. And a big one at that, if she was ready to admit that Siggi wasn't the man for her. But it was like living in a tiny village where everyone knew everything about everyone. That was going to take some getting used to.

She packed up her things. It seemed like she'd been here forever. So much had happened in just a couple of weeks. Her bag of goodies from Snug didn't quite fit into her case, but she didn't need to take everything back to England with her now. She could leave some of her things at Siggi's until she found her own place. The first thing she was going to do when she found somewhere was make it into a cosy home like Anna and Ned's. Hopefully, with the help of Snug and Gudrun's staff discount.

When she got back to the house, Siggi was awake and reading again. His face lit up when he saw her, and he started to get up.

'No! Stay where you are. I can manage,' she said, not sure that she could. The suitcase wheels jammed as she hauled it over the doorstep while the enormous holdall on her shoulder stuck in the doorway and the bottom of the paper bag from Snug disintegrated where it had grazed the snow on her way up the path.

Siggi started laughing and holding his ribs, which made Iris laugh, making her go all weak. She shoved the bag off her shoulder, leaving it on the veranda while she brought the suitcase inside, then rescued the shopping out of the paper bag. She laid her purchases on the floor near the door.

'You've been shopping? How long was I asleep?'

'It was the other day.' She headed back outside to fetch the empty paper bag and the holdall, then closed the door. 'It's not all for me, some of it is presents.'

'For your family? Can I pretend I bought them?'

'If you like,' she said with a grin. 'If you think the only in is to buy their affection.'

'Could be a useful back up.'

Iris made them both a drink, then climbed up the ladder to the mezzanine, where there was a huge double bed that looked just as inviting as the one downstairs, and a desk that looked down over the lounge. Helpfully, it had a monitor that would plug into Iris's laptop.

'You don't think they'd mind if I worked up here?'

'Of course not. I would sleep up there if I could get up the ladder,' Siggi said. 'It is much nicer than that tiny room.'

'The tiny room is cosy,' Iris said, climbing back down.

'And I don't mind where I sleep as long as it is with you,' Siggi said, catching her hand as she went past.

'I have work to do,' she said, pretending to be serious but sitting down next to him and leaning in for a kiss.

'This is more important.' He put his arm around her back, encouraging her to lie next to him again.

'You're standing in the way of a volcanologist who has a report to write that will change the world.'

'Did you know endorphins are the best pain killers?'

'I'm meant to lie here and kiss you periodically when you could just take some pills?'

He grinned. 'Only if you want to.'

'I do want to.' Because it was important to make time for what mattered the most. The report could wait. Today, she was grateful that this man, who she loved, was still here.

'Thank you for saying we should not go to the bar tonight.'

'You're welcome. I didn't really want to share you with anyone else.'

'If we can stay here for a few days, just us, I think that would be perfect,' he said. 'And I need a lot more kisses before you can leave this couch.'

'Kisses because you love me, or just for the endorphins?'

'Always because I love you.'

The End

Other titles in the Icelandic Romance series
Snug in Iceland
Hideaway in Iceland
Stranded in Iceland

Also by Victoria Walker

Croftwood Series
Summer at Croftwood Cinema
Twilight at Croftwood Library
Festival in Croftwood Park

The Island in Bramble Bay

Sign up to Victoria's mailing list at
www.victoriaauthor.co.uk
to receive a monthly newsletter, with
information about new releases, special offers
and exclusive content.

Author's Note

The idea for this book, and Iris especially, was as a result of the real life volcanic eruption early in 2024 in Grindavik, Iceland. The situation there is still ongoing, although as I write, things have stabilised. Hraunvik in the story is based very much on Grindavik, but as I used some artistic licence in a lot of my volcanology references, I thought it best to make a fictional place since this is not an exact account of what happened in Grindavik.

I read *Introducing Volcanology* by Dougal Jerram which informed my geological references but any mistakes are mine. The monitoring technique that Iris invented is, as far as I know, completely made up.

Thank you for choosing to read this book! Three years after Snug in Iceland was published, readers are still discovering this series and I am so happy to continue writing stories set in this wonderful country. If it weren't for the support of fabulous readers like you, there would never have been a sequel, let alone three more books! Reviews mean such a lot to writers, so if you have time to leave a review for this book, or any book you've enjoyed, it make's all the difference.

Thank you as ever to Berni Stevens for another beautiful cover. I was keen to get the red tones of the Northern Lights in there this time, since we've been lucky enough to see those from the UK in the past few months! Thanks to Catrin for editing and to James and Claudia for proofreading. Thanks to Jake for the IT support at all times of the day and night.

The best way to keep in touch is to sign up to my exclusive mailing list at victoriaauthor.co.uk. I send a newsletter every month or so to keep you up to date with what I'm up to, as well as any special offers, new releases and exclusive content. You can also find me in all of these places:

Instagram @victoriawalker_author
Facebook Victoria Walker - Author
Twitter @4victoriawalker

Printed in Great Britain
by Amazon

52459318R00146